Always BASKETBALL

Always BASKETBALL

Ashley R. Lang

Edited by: Holly Althof

Always Basketball
Copyright © 2026 by Ashley R. Lang

Published by Local. Pub. Co.
103 East Main Street
Denver, Iowa 50622
www.localpubco.com

1st Edition
Paperback ISBN: 979-8-9948373-0-6
Library of Congress Catalog Number:

For information about speaking engagements, bulk purchases, book signings, or media appearances, please contact
Local. Pub. Co. at: speakers@localpubco.com
Phone: (319) 303-1017

Credits
Cover design by *Tony Lang*
Interior layout by *Ruth Kokila*

For the dreamers, the defenders, and the ones who play to win.
This book is for those who know that even when the game is hard,
there is usually something or someone that makes it all worth it.

And now for the introduction of your Hills University Basketball starting line ups:

For the **Hills University Lady Big Horns...**

Starting at *Power Forward* and your *Captain*, a 6'2 senior from Port, Connecticut, number 51, **Jessa Blakely**.

Starting at *Center*, a 6'5 senior from Gales, Texas, number 55, **Lexi Wright**.

Starting at *Guard*, a 5'10 super senior from Chicago, Illinois, number 11, **Bexley "Bex" Collins**.

Starting at *Guard*, a 5'11 junior from Forest, Pennsylvania, number 34, **Hazel Nova**.

Starting at *Point Guard*, a 5'9 senior from Chester, Washington, number 23, **Char Jones**.

Head coach for the Lady Big Horns is **Hayden Morris**.

For the Hills University Big Horns...

Starting at *Point Guard* and your *Captain*, a 6' super senior from Turtle, Oklahoma, number 3, **Monroe "Monty" Oakes**.

Starting at *Guard*, a 6'6 senior from Hills, Oklahoma, number 25, **Greyson "Grey" Hastings**.

Starting at *Guard*, a 6'4 sophomore from Petri, South Carolina, number 12, **Bryce Anders**.

Starting at *Forward*, a 6'7 freshman from Hills, Oklahoma, number 54, **Corden Hastings**.

Starting at *Center*, a 6'7 junior from Boston, Massachusetts, number 33, **Sky Butler**.

Head coach for the Big Horns is **Benjamin Hayes**.

1

Jessa

Greyson looks hot without a shirt on. His tanned and toned body glistens with sweat as he carries the heavy black couch into our new condo. I catch myself staring, lips parting before I can stop them. He looks good enough to lick.

"Jessa... earth to Jessa..." Greyson's voice snaps me out of my thoughts.

I turn to face my best friend and now roommate, who's looking at me with a puzzled expression. It takes a moment for my eyes to refocus, and I realize I'm standing in the living room of our condo. Monty stands beside Greyson, a shit-eating grin on his face.

"What?" I ask, trying to sound casual.

"Where's your head at?" Greyson asks. "We said your name like thirty times, and your face is all flushed."

"Uh, nothing. I'm just warm from carrying boxes. What's up?" I ask, trying to focus on the conversation and not the masculine curve of Greyson's still tense arm muscles.

"The couch—where do you want it?" Greyson asks. He's still

holding up an end of the couch, and his eyes tell me he's about to lose his patience with me.

"Oh, right! Sorry, yeah, the couch...Right over there." I point to a random corner of the living room, hoping he'll stop questioning me.

What am I doing? I shouldn't be having thoughts like this about my best friend and roommate. Plus, he's a player on the men's team, and the coaches have strict rules against dating within the two teams. The heat and exhaustion from moving must be getting to me. I smile, convinced that's it. But then I notice Greyson's cocky grin, and it's directed right at me.

"Shit," I mutter, annoyed Greyson knows me so well. He would notice me checking him out.

As I'm leaving the condo to grab more boxes off the truck, I hear Monty say, "What was that all about?"

I pause, waiting to hear Greyson's response. "I'm not really sure," he says, with uncertainty, clearly trying to analyze my behavior.

Greyson knows I rarely get flustered. But today, I'm really distracted and out of sorts, much in part to his shirtless body. I keep sneaking looks at him, and each time, I'm more frustrated with myself. What is my deal? I'm with Dillon. And Greyson is my roommate now.

It had been my idea for Monty, Bex, Greyson, and me to live together during our senior year. We're all basketball players at Hills University (HU) and share similar lifestyles. Not only do we spend a ton of time together anyway, but our practice and training schedules often line up, too. It just makes sense.

I met all of them my freshman year through basketball. Bexley "Bex" Collins transferred her sophomore year to play basketball for HU, which makes her a fifth-year senior. Monroe, known as Monty Oakes, is also a fifth-year senior because an injury sidelined him for a full season. He and Greyson met through junior high travel ball and have been best bros ever since. Greyson, my 6'6" icy-blue-eyed best friend, is one of the most generous souls I've ever met. You'd never know he was from a wealthy family and an affluent Oklahoma city because he doesn't flaunt it. Freshies together, Greyson and I met in such a unique way that it was impossible not to become friends.

The four of us clicked right away, and I couldn't have asked for a better group of friends. Lately, I've been picking up on some weird vibes between Bex and Monty. I keep wondering if there's something going on there. But it's possible I'm imaging it to make myself feel better about my own wandering eyeballs.

2
Greyson

"I'm exhausted," Jessa says, flopping down on the black leather couch in the shared living room. "I can't believe we're finally living here! And that our coaches actually approved us all living together."

"I think it helped that my dad is letting us live here for free. No jobs to pay bills means more time on the court or in the weightroom." I say, plopping myself next to Jessa on the heavy ass couch Oakes and I muscled in earlier today.

"I, for one, am excited to only share a bathroom with Jessa instead of the entire team," sighs Collins—how I've referred to Bex since I met her my freshman year. She perches on the kitchen counter, her black curls still stuck to her neck from the day's sweaty events.

Oakes, gray sweatpants hanging low on his hips, strolls in, droplets still clinging to his bare chest from the shower.

"Well, don't you smell mountain fresh? Couldn't be bothered to use a towel though?" I joke, watching Collins out of the corner of my eye. I swear she looks Oakes up and down before her eyes fall to the *Semper ad Meliora* tattooed across his shoulder blades. It means

"Always towards better things." Oakes got it on a trip we took last year.

Collins notices me watching her watch Oakes and sticks her tongue out before looking away.

"Yeah, yeah," Oakes says, dismissing my riff with a wave. "But on to more important things. We eating pizza or Chinese?"

Jessa's head perks up at the mention of food. "Would it be inappropriate to have both? I'm starving."

"Neither are good for you," Collins reminds us. She jumps from her spot on the counter and pulls a container of raw vegetables from the fridge. She nibbles on a carrot while the rest of us consider how gluttonous we feel. Somehow I get hungrier for greasy junk watching her munch on rabbit food. I hope she isn't planning to act like our nutritionist all the time. That'll be a buzzkill.

"Of course you packed *vegetables* to eat on moving day, Bex," Jessa whines. "But I'll have you know, calories don't count when you move a million boxes and furniture into a condo in ninety-degree heat. We've earned it."

"Hastings?" Oakes asks. "Pizza, Chinese, or both?"

"Both work for me. Besides, we aren't in season yet. Let's feast!" I raise my fist in the air in solidarity with my other two gluttonous roommates.

While Oakes orders the food, I consider what Jessa said. This really is an ideal living situation. Not only will I get to hang more with my best friends, but our schedules and lifestyles align well. Misalignment of those things is sometimes the worst part about having roommates. Once official workouts start in October, our lives will be hectic. It'll be nice to share meals, snacks, and support with a group that gets what I'm balancing. In the meantime, we've got six weeks of our senior year to live it up before our coaches control us.

We all have goals outside of the sport. During the season, those goals get pushed aside. We're swamped with practice and schoolwork, leaving us little time for even sleep. And relationships? Well, those are pretty much nonexistent.

I glance at Jessa and smile, thinking about my future and how much I hope she's a part of it. We met three years ago when she literally ran into me when I was watching her play in a pre-season scrimmage. I was hit from behind and then mixed up in her legs, arms and chestnut hair. I remember fondly how I sat there stunned by her intense green eyes and aggressive play.

I wonder what life holds for us after this year. I want what my parents have. Someday I want to marry the love of my life and have little ballers of my own.

For now, I just want to focus on the present. I don't believe in regrets, and I have a feeling this year will be my best yet.

It's started off great so far. I'm feeling fresh after an amazing summer internship with ESPN Headquarters in Bristol, Connecticut. Bristol is near Jessa's hometown, so we spent long weekends hanging out on her family's yacht. I got the feeling this was much to the dismay of her boyfriend, Dillon, who was busy being a tennis pro in North Carolina. But who cares, right? His loss.

I abruptly return to the present at the sound of snickers and question whether someone just said my name. "What?" I ask, hoping no one noticed I was lost in thought.

No such luck.

"You look creepy with that clown smile, staring off into space." I can hardly understand Jessa through her fit of giggles.

"Yeah, man, total creeper status right there," echoes Oakes, looking up from his phone. "But while you were zoned out like a weirdo, I got dinner ordered."

I shrug and let the clown smile spread further across my face.

I won't let them ruin my good mood. Not when I'm sure this year holds so many possibilities. I stand up and stretch, the soreness in my muscles settling in. A hot shower to wash away the aches and stink from the day is what I need while I wait for food to be delivered.

Fifteen minutes later, I return to the aromatic scent of orange chicken and pizza, combined with a soft hint of ocean breeze. Jessa's smell. She's in her typical bedtime attire–booty shorts and a tank that's so tiny it leaves little to the imagination. Her wet hair is piled in a messy bun, and she looks relaxed and happy, shoveling a Crab Rangoon in her mouth. A soft laugh escapes as I watch Jessa unsuccessfully trying not to get crumbs and sweet and sour sauce everywhere. Collins sits beside her, wearing her baggiest sweats and temporarily withholding judgement about our food choices.

Oakes nudges me hard in the side. "Man, get it together. And stop staring. Boundaries..."

Damn, he's right. I force my eyes away from Jessa and grab a plate to partake in the feast laid out on the coffee table.

"What are we watching tonight? One of our faves or something new?" I ask. As a group, we tend to fall back on our favorites when we're stressed and tired.

No one responds. Collins gets up and carries her veggies to the fridge before mumbling something about doing bedtime yoga and meditation. Oakes answers a video call from his three older, busybody sisters. Thankfully, he spares us the drama by heading to his room. Then it's just me and Jessa.

"Guess that means it's on us to clean up and decide what to watch."

Jessa groans and snuggles further beneath her favorite gray Minky blanket.

"Or you could call Dillon? Let him know you got settled?" I suggest.

I'm proud of myself for keeping my opinions about Dillon to myself. I mean, the guy thinks he's God's gift to women. Dillon's been a part of Jessa's life since before she came to HU. They met in high school at a country club their families were both a part of and I think it was more a relationship of convenience and societal status. Dillon likes to be in the public eye, while it's Jessa's mom that likes to keep up appearances. I'm not sure how involved I'd really consider Dillon in Jessa's life. It's more like she's expected to fit into *his* life, never the other way around. Which, understandably, makes Jessa feel crappy whenever she realizes that's what's happening. They've broken up a few times over the last couple of years, often for months at a time. But he always manages to charm his way back to her heart.

I dislike Dillon for more than just how he treats Jessa. He considers himself part of the "New Ivy," whatever that even means. If you're picturing a pink button-up with khakis, you're close. Dillon's the clean-cut, overly-groomed, stylish in a preppy kind of way type. Not my kind of style. Every time I see him, his brown hair is swept across his forehead with a side part, the bangs covering one eye like he's getting ready for a photo shoot. The guy plays *tennis*, for crying out loud–mostly singles, but he's been dabbling in doubles since last year. His idea of fun is country-clubbing. He actually says that. Is that even a thing? *Country clubbing?*

Jessa shrugs. "He's hosting a mixed doubles tournament at the club to wrap up his duties for the summer. I'm sure he's busy."

I stay quiet, unsure what to say in response to that. When Jessa's mom —*the* Lauren Blakely, former NCAA star—forced her to go back to Connecticut for one-on-one coaching all summer (Lauren's obsessed with Jessa breaking the NCAA records), Dillon hardly had time for Jessa. Unless, of course, she was with me. He seemed to have a sixth sense for when we were hanging out. Then he'd video call, interrupting whatever we were doing. It was annoying. Only because he didn't seem to have time for her calls any other time. Jessa and I are just friends. There's only been one time we crossed into more-than-friends territory. It happened on a trip to Turks and Caicos where she and Pretty Boy were broken up. And the things that happened there are probably the reason I'm still a little hung up on my best friend. I don't admit it to myself often. But it's hard not to when I'm struggling to look at anything but her right now, even as she nods off on the couch beside me.

Turks and Caicos is beautiful. Picturesque blue skies, turquoise waters, and white sand so soft, it's like baby powder. The luxury beach resort we stayed at was equally as beautiful, and full of exclusive parties, days lounging by the water, and adventure-filled excursions. It was exactly what Jessa and I needed after a tough semester. When we'd first mentioned a beach vacation, our parents were quick to gift us the trip. They feared we'd choose value over safety, hence "risking our lives," and ending up like the college students who've been reported abducted or mugged in Mexico. Maybe we should have been offended by their assumptions that we lack so much judgement, but it's hard to be mad when you're privileged enough to get a free trip to Turks and Caicos! Please, dear parents, ensure our safety every spring break. We looked forward to the sunrises, sunsets, and even sunburns. Our days were spent swimming, playing sand volleyball, and drinking the endless fruity cocktails delivered by the top-notch service included with our private cabanas. We were with mostly couples, so Jessa and I roomed together. We knew we'd want a break from all the lovey-dovey drunkenness after a day in the sun. Plus, after a crazy basketball season, we looked forward to some stress-free quality time together. The guys lived in swim trunks and ball caps the entire week. We had it easy. The girls, however, seemed to be competing for skimpiest swimsuits. All accessorized with sheer skirts, large floppy hats, and oversized sunglasses. It was its own kind of heavenly hell.

The beach bar was loud in that loose, sunburned way—too many laughs, too much rum, sand everywhere it shouldn't be. Someone's playlist kept jumping between throwback pop and reggaeton, and no one bothered to fix it.

Jessa was perched on the arm of a chair, sunglasses still on even though the sun's half gone. I tossed her a napkin.

"You're dripping," I said.

"Hydrated," she corrected, wiping condensation off her wrist and flicking it at him. "Unlike you. You've had, what—two waters all day?"

"I had coconut water."

"That does not count."

Around us, friends were sprawled in mismatched chairs, talking over each other—inside jokes, plans for the night, exaggerated retellings of an excursion earlier.

I leaned back, stretching, my knee knocking into Jessa's thigh. She glanced down at the contact, then up at me.

"Careful," she said. "You're getting bold."

I smirked. "Or you're just more aware."

She snorted, but she didn't move away. Instead, she tilted her head and studied me.

"You always like this on vacation?" she asked. "Or is this a Turks thing?"

"Only when I'm surrounded by bad influences."

Across the table, someone wolf whistled. "Are you two flirting or arguing? Because the energy is confusing."

Jessa raised her glass in a mock toast. "Multitasking."

Laughter rippled through the group, and the moment should have dissolved with it—but it didn't. I caught myself watching the way her fingers toyed with the rim of her glass, slow and absentminded.

She caught me looking and arched a brow.

"What?" she asked.

"Nothing," I said too fast.

Damn, a man can only take so much torture from an attractive woman. Jessa paraded around the resort in an array of barely-there bikinis, and she couldn't ever get sunscreen on all her parts without help. Between lathering her back with lotion and watching her toned body run in and out of the water, I was in agony.

The next day, Jessa wore a red string bikini that covered little more than her nipples. To get a better tan, she'd said, which naturally drew my eyes to the pale skin contrasted by the tanned curve of her breast. Her bottoms were cut high, exposing perky cheeks and tan lines. She's evil, I'd thought more than once.

"Um, what's going on there?" Jessa asked, pointing down at my trunks.

I hadn't even realized I'd been fixated on her body until then. When she was three feet away from me in our cabana, ringing out her dark hair and staring at my *very* visible dick. And it wasn't even trying to hide its reaction to watching her walk out of the water. I'm not sure who was blushing more, me or her.

"Sorry. I only came back because it felt awkward being the only single person around all the couples riding each other in the ocean. But apparently, it turned *you* on." Jessa joked, but she didn't look away from the bulge I was attempting to cover with my hand.

I felt exposed under her gaze. My face was hot—hell, my whole body was hot—and I could tell by Jessa's amused expression that I looked as flushed as I felt. Did I just own up to the fact that it was her causing my erection? Because honestly, I hadn't even noticed the others.

I didn't even have to settle on my story because Jessa sighed and said, "It did make me a little horny, especially since I haven't come in a while."

What the fuck is happening right now, I'd thought? So many thoughts rushed through my head at once. Did Jessa really just say that? And did she mean it? We're friends but it feels like our friendship crossed into a different kind of territory in the last five minutes.

I couldn't explain it but somehow her comment made me brave. Brave enough to choke out, "What if we help each other out a bit? You know, some dirty talk while we take care of ourselves? Just to release some tension, of course. It doesn't mean anything, just two friends being friendly."

But Jessa nodded slowly, as if she was not against the idea. I waited a minute, giving her ample time to come to her senses before she threw a pillow at me or something. But she didn't. She didn't look mad or weirded out. She actually looked more turned on. And that made my head spin even more. I'd always found Jessa incredibly attractive. But since we're friends—best friends—it kept me from doing anything foolish. But at that moment? My brain worked in overdrive and tried to understand the situation. It searched for reasons to justify acting on our urges. It felt like fast forwarding a movie to the end, to make sure that if we crossed a line, nothing would be ruined. We'd still be friends afterwards.

The logical side of me screamed it was a terrible idea. But my mind and body weren't in sync and refused to get in sync. Instead, my hand found the cord holding the curtains of the cabana back and pulled. In seconds, the bright cabana darkened, with only a sliver of sun shining in from the remaining open panel. Jessa loosened the cord on that side, and the cabana went almost completely dark. The only light came from slits at the base of the curtains where they didn't quite meet the sandy floor.

I'd told myself it wasn't a big deal. No one even had to know. We were two friends scratching an itch, per se.

We hadn't talked about it anymore. The unspoken words were enough for both of us to lose all sexual shyness. Maybe it was day drinking in the sun that made us lose inhibition. Or being over a thousand miles from home and all sense of reality. Whatever the reason, it was happening and we were both all in.

I rubbed my erection over the fabric of my orange and yellow board shorts. There was just enough soft friction that it felt like silk between my palm and dick. I bit my lip and willed myself to keep my eyes open, even as the heat and pleasure expanded throughout my body. Jessa pushed aside a red triangle and pinched a hard nipple between her thumb and index finger. Her heavy-lidded eyes locked in on me, and her breathing deepened. My watching her touch her body seemed to stir something primal in her. Her other hand moved between her legs and her long fingers dipped beneath the fabric of her bikini bottoms. I watched, fascinated, as her fingers moved in slow circles. Her eyes closed, and her hips swayed in a matching rhythm until a low moan escaped her mouth.

I couldn't take my eyes off of her and my dick stiffened, pressing hard against the seam of my shorts. It took all my effort not to groan out incoherently. Watching her was almost too much to handle.

Jessa noticed my shaft fighting to escape. "Pull it out," she breathed, her voice a lower, sexy octave I'd never heard before.

I obliged, exposing only the tip, already glistening with precum. Jessa groaned and fingered herself faster, so fast I could hear the wetness of her pussy. I was losing control. The more noises she made, the more her breasts jiggled, the more I thought I was going to die from pleasure. My sweet friend Jessa was a page out of my wildest dreams. A seductress in a way I hadn't expected.

If I didn't gain some power in this little game, I was going to blow my load too fast, and I wasn't ready for it to end. Not yet. I pressed the tip of my thumb against my head, spreading the precum in circles across the tip. Competitive even while masturbating it seemed, Jessa narrowed her eyes at me and spread her legs wider. Now, I had a courtside view of her pussy. It was mesmerizing, watching how deftly her fingers moved between the folds before moving down to her slick entrance, pushing her two fingers in, then out, over and over again until once again I thought I'd explode. Jessa was definitely not going to let me win. "I want to see you come," she begged.

As if her words alone weren't enough to make me come undone, she added another finger and thrusted. Harder and faster until my cock jerked. I gripped it and squeezed, groaning from the pressure of my palm circling the shaft. My hand pumped, matching Jessa's pace until my eyes closed and I surrendered to the pleasure.

I was so focused on my pleasure, I didn't realize Jessa had moved closer until I felt her hand slide over my fist.

"Fuck," I growled and forced my eyes open. Jessa, hand still wrapped around mine, straddled my thigh with her swimsuit bottoms pushed to the side, her bare breasts brushing against my arm. Her warmth and the wetness from her pussy against my leg unleashed a frenzy deep inside of me and I yelled out incoherently, letting my head fall back as pleasure consumed me.

"Is this okay?" she asked.

"More than okay," I rasped, watching as Jessa put her hand that wasn't helping me jerk off between her legs.

"Taste me," she said and pushed her pussy-soaked fingers between my lips. I sucked using my tongue to lick every drop from her fingers.

Her pussy dripped on my thigh as she continued to tug and squeeze my cock, my hand still beneath hers. My dick had never been so hard. Jessa rode my leg and pressed her breasts against my chest. The feeling of her on me caused me to lose all control, the liquid heat rising up my shaft. I let out a low growl. The warm stream splattered on my flat stomach between us and Jessa grinded harder, pressing down in small wet circles on my leg, close to her own release. To further surprise me, she leaned close and licked her tongue along the trail of white liquid displayed on my stomach and chest.

"Mmm," she moaned until her own climax came and she collapsed on me in a puddle of hot breaths and whimpers.

As I lay there with her still on top of me, I couldn't help but wonder what this meant. We're just friends still, right?

3
Jessa

The next morning, I'm sweaty and disoriented. What's worse is I can't seem to move my body, no matter how much I wiggle to free myself. For a split second, I panic, stuck in that weird limbo between sleep and alertness. But then a soft snore jolts me awake, and I'm face to face with sandy-blonde hair. Well, that explains it. I can't move because I'm pinned down by 200 pounds of muscle.

Shit. We must have fallen asleep on the couch last night. Our legs are *intertwined*, and half my body is numb where Greyson's weight has cut off blood flow. I use the hand that isn't a worthless tingling mess to push against his shoulder, but he doesn't budge. He doesn't even stir.

"Grey," I hiss, pushing harder. "Wake up. You have me trapped."

Greyson moans but doesn't move. Instead, he buries his face in my neck and goes back to snoring.

"Greyson," I say, louder this time. There's no sign of him waking up, so I pinch the sensitive skin in the crook of his arm.

"Ouch! What the—Jessa?" Greyson mumbles and rubs his palms against his eyes. It takes a couple of long, agonizing minutes before he wakes up enough to angle his body to a half sitting position. He squints around the room before focusing his blue eyes on me. "Jessa? We fall asleep out here?"

"Looks like it," I say, rubbing my stinging limbs to get the blood moving again. Not being able to feel my fingers and toes sucks, but this part might be worse.

Greyson is still shirtless from his shower last night. With every movement, his masculine scent seems to get stronger. God, he smells so damn good. His off-season workouts and the summer sun have defined his athletic build. I can't help but stare at his broad shoulders and muscular arms. Without thinking, I glance down at his basketball shorts. His morning wood shows through the thin fabric. *Well, hello...* I think, but try to ignore the sensation in my lower regions.

"Hey!" Greyson exclaims, jumping up and using a throw pillow to cover himself. "Avert your eyes, young lady."

He steps back toward the kitchen but stumbles over a pile of pillows and blankets that fell on the floor last night. Righting himself, he walks into the kitchen as if nothing happened. I consider making a smartass comment about his clumsiness. I've mortified him enough this morning, so I keep my mouth shut.

"Breakfast?" Greyson asks, and I nod in agreement. Somehow I'm famished, even after gorging on pizza and Chinese last night.

Bex's bedroom door creaks open. Greyson and I watch as Monty strolls into the living room, staring at this phone. A yawning Bex follows. Well that's weird. Did Monty come out of Bex's room? Greyson and I share a look, but neither of us says anything.

In the kitchen, the three of them start talking about how they still hurt from yesterday, but I tune out. I'm too busy thinking about what happened the last time I noticed Greyson's morning wood. Turks and Caicos sure was a trip to remember. Damn. Why did I even let my mind go there? I focus on seeing Dillon's face instead of Greyson's erection, but I can't seem to picture it. Fine, I won't think of either of them, I tell myself. I shake my head, willing myself to think of anything other than Greyson's dick. *Definitely do not think about your roommate's dick,* I scold myself.

I join the rest of them in the kitchen, where Grey is pulling pots and pans out of a cardboard box.

"Chef Hastings at your service. What'll it be ladies? Omelets? French toast? Cereal? I'll make whatever your hearts...er, bellies desire," Greyson quips. I get the feeling he's trying to avoid the elephant in the room. Which elephant? Who knows? We've got a couple of elephants taking up space in the room right now.

"Hey, what about me?" complains Monty "Am I invisible when the lovely ladies are present?"

"Basically," Bex retorts, as she pulls an assortment of ingredients from the fridge. "Since you're offering, I'll take an omelet."

"Same for me. Throw one in there for Monty, too," I say, giving him a playful wink.

Greyson responds with an exaggerated bow. "Coming right up, madams."

"We need our strength to unpack this place and get organized before school starts," I say, heading to my bedroom, ignoring their grumpy replies.

Rather than watching Greyson cook, I may as well get ready for the day. I dig through boxes until I find a sports bra, shorts, a hair tie, and a headband. As I'm trying to wrangle my hair into a ponytail, my phone rings. I cringe at the name on the caller ID. It's too early for this.

"Hi mom," I say, rolling my eyes. Can she *not* go an entire day without micromanaging me?

"Jessa," she says. Her terse voice comes through too loud, and I switch the mode to speaker. Has the woman ever heard of beginning a phone conversation with a simple hello? It's not that hard.

"Have you gotten your workout in this morning yet? You can't let the day get away from you. The season is approaching, and you have work to do."

Ugh, this woman. "Mom, it's nine o'clock in the morning. We spent *all* day yesterday moving in." I make sure to really emphasize the *all*, hoping she'll realize she sounds like a drill sergeant. But that would take some kind of self-awareness now, wouldn't it.

"But anyway, Greyson's cooking breakfast now, and the plan is to unpack today. We all want to get settled before school starts. I'll get some shots in later though."

How doesn't she see the pressure she puts on me? Not a day goes by that I'm not reminded that my mother is Lauren Blakely, former college basketball star. She'd been over the top with her not-so-subtle dream of me following in her footsteps all summer. I have similar goals, so it would be easier to accept this *if* she hadn't treated me like a child all summer. I'm grateful she wants the best for me. She put a lot of time into training with me over the summer, but it was more for her than for me. Man, things would be easier if I had a sibling for her to focus on, too.

I love basketball and have the competitive drive to want to be the best player. But I also need time before graduation to be a normal college student. If only she'd given me the summer to let loose a little. Maybe then I wouldn't feel so overwhelmed by my responsibilities— basketball, school, and living up to others' expectations. It's exhausting.

Will she be proud of me if I don't have a good season? All signs point to no.

"Jessa, are you listening to me?" My mother's voice is impatient.

"You need to stay focused. Put in the work. These records will not break themselves, you know."

My eyes close. *Inhale, exhale. Inhale, exhale.*

"Okay, Mom. I gotta go. Breakfast is ready. Talk soon," I say, disconnecting the call before she objects.

"What's with the face?" Bex asks when I enter the kitchen a few minutes later. "Never mind. I gather you talked to your mom? Nothing and no one else flips your mood that fast. You okay?"

I shake my head. "You got it. She acts like I don't have any goals, as if I don't want to win. It's so annoying."

Greyson holds out a plate with a steaming omelet. "At least she's several states away and can't just pop in on you every day."

"Thank goodness for that," I say. "And thanks for making breakfast. This smells amazing!"

I'm quiet as I eat, thinking about my mother and all the ways she adds to my stress. I wish I could figure out a way to tell her to back off without hurting her feelings. Always trying to be the nice, respectful daughter makes me want to scream.

4

Greyson

We've fallen into a comfortable routine after the first few weeks of classes. Every day, we get up with the sun and head to the Hastings Center as a group. It's always weird to see my last name on the building but the embarrassment of it mostly wore off after freshman year. It makes me proud to know my family's donation made it possible for HU to have a state-of-the-art facility for the students and fans. It's such a nice building that none of us mind spending so much of our days here lifting, running, and playing ball.

My favorite part of the day is coming home from class in the late afternoons to find Jessa, Collins, and Oakes milling about the condo. It makes me smile to know the evening routines of my favorite people so well—there's a comfort to it I didn't know I needed.

Collins is usually starting on dinner, using us as her nutrition plan guinea pigs. I can't complain because it keeps the rest of us balanced with protein and vegetables. She's even gotten creative about making healthy desserts, knowing how much we'll whine if we don't get something sweet after dinner. While Collins is cooking, Oakes is usually sprawled across the couch being lectured by his sisters about something or other on video calls, and Jessa is often cross-legged on the floor in front of the coffee table surrounded by her laptop, textbooks, and stacks of papers. She's nearly always chewing on a highlighter, with intense concentration on whatever task is at hand. It's weird, for sure, but Jessa's a creature of habit. And I find it endearing as hell.

Thursday nights are dedicated yoga nights. Collins teaches a yoga class at the Hastings Center, and while the rest of us originally started going in support of her, it's become a much-needed recovery activity. I sleep like a baby afterwards. Oakes is into it, too, but I think it's because of his crush on Collins.

It took a bit of prodding but Oakes finally owned up to his crush on Collins. As if it hasn't been obvious for awhile now. Oakes is an expressive guy, but Collins is skittish about relationships. She's never been in one before. Her parents are solid people but Collins had a strict upbringing. They didn't allow her to date. Between that and the coaches repetitive lectures about dating and staying focused, it seems like Collins is almost afraid to even open up to the idea. Oakes and I discussed a lowkey plan to help him win her over. It's subtle and will test the waters on where Collins is at with dating. The plan goes into effect tonight.

During dinner, I notice Jessa ignore a call while we're working on a sheet pan of roasted chicken and veggies. It's obvious she's frustrated with whoever it is but I don't know if that means it was her mom or Dillon. She seems to be avoiding calls from both lately. I'm not sure what's going on, but something's been a little off since her stay at the Lauren Blakely Summer Camp. She's made a few comments here and there but we haven't gotten into it on a deeper level yet. If I had to speculate, though, I'd say her mom's extreme training and nutrition plan strained their relationship more. Dillon's also been MIA lately, but I'm okay with that. I'm sure Jessa has feelings about it, especially since they spent most of the summer apart. He told her over and over again that he'd visit her, but something always came up. She looks upset right now and I try to make eye contact with her from across the table, but it's like she's intentionally avoiding my eyes.

Once the dinner mess is cleared away and the dishwasher is humming in the kitchen, we head out for yoga. The weather is beautiful, and we agree that walking will be a good way to warm up for the class. Jessa seems to have cheered up a little, and the four of us banter back and forth until we reach the Hastings Center. Collins leaves us at the front door to set the studio up, and Jessa follows with our mats to save spots.

"Okay, man, it's time," I say, nudging Oakes as soon as the girls are out of earshot. I'm trying to be a good friend, but my excitement feels forced. Part of my mind is still worried about Jessa. "Are you ready for your first act as a secret admirer?"

"I was born ready. I don't want to come on too strong though. I'd hate for the plan to have the opposite effect. What if she's freaked out by it?" Oakes laughs this last part off, but I can tell he's nervous.

"Nah, this is the perfect way to win Collins over. No one has ever done something like this for her. It'll make her feel special. You ready to get Operation Bex underway?" I offer him my fist, which he bumps with his own. "You got this, man."

In the darkened studio, I take the mat next to Jessa. Collins's soothing voice floats above the ambient music. She encourages us to take a moment settling in our mats, taking deep breaths, clearing our minds.

Clearing my mind isn't easy to do when the person I'm worried about lays on the mat beside me. I glance over at Jessa. Her eyes are squeezed shut but her face isn't relaxed. It's apparent she's struggling with the mind clearing, too.

She must feel my gaze because her eyes open and she peers at me with an irritated expression. "What?" she hisses. "Stop looking at me."

"Sorry. I didn't mean to. I'm just trying to get settled," I lie. Now is not the time to bring up her mother or Dillon.

On my other side, Oakes is in an easy seated pose—Sukhasana, I've learned it's called—breathing in and out audibly with his eyes closed. At least one of us is figuring it out, I think. I close my own eyes and try to emulate Oakes.

Collins is an attentive and personable instructor, and I find that it isn't as difficult to get into the Zen mindset as I'd thought. When the class is over, I stretch out in an extended Savasana, feeling more relaxed than I have all week.

I'm still stretched out on my mat when the door opens and a beam of light brightens the dark room. An employee from the snack shop on the first floor walks in and hands Collins a smoothie and a straw. Collins looks confused. She has a smoothie after every yoga class but it isn't standard practice for an employee to deliver it before class has even ended. For a second, it looks like Collins wants to reprimand the employee for interrupting Savasana. But then she notices the note taped to the bottom of the plastic cup.

She reads it aloud. "'Call me a yogi because I've been meditating on how beautiful you are.'"

"Oh my gosh! How cheesy. But adorable, too," Jessa says, standing behind Collins to reread the note over her shoulder.

Collins giggles in a way I've never heard from her before. "It isn't signed. I wonder who sent it," she says to Jessa.

"Looks like you have a secret admirer," Jessa teases. I'm grateful this has turned out to be a fun thing for Jessa, too. She looks genuinely happy for Collins.

Collins slurps on the smoothie as we head back to the condo. Her stride is bouncier and she's more animated than normal as she talks Oakes's ear off. The two of them don't notice when they outpace Jessa and me. They're too far ahead for us to catch any words, but every thirty seconds or so, their laughter echoes off the buildings back toward us. I assume act one was a success. I use the distance as an opportunity to talk to Jessa.

"How are you doing?" I ask, hoping she'll open up so I don't have to pry. Sometimes pushing Jessa to talk makes her shut down more.

She peers over at me, but I can't read her expression. "I'm okay. Why do you ask?"

"You've been quieter than usual. And I've noticed you keep avoiding phone calls, like at dinner tonight. Earlier you seemed so far away."

Jessa's silent, her eyes cast downward on the concrete. She pulls her hands into the sleeves of her sweatshirt and sighs. "It's nothing new. My mom won't leave me alone. It's like she doesn't think I know the season is coming up. Like she thinks I don't work hard, but even when I work my ass off, it's as if she doesn't notice or it's not good enough."

She pauses, as if gathering her thoughts. When she continues, her voice quivers and her eyes shine. "I guess I just thought by my senior year, she'd see that I'm doing my best. Maybe cut me some slack."

I'm a little taken aback when she stops midstep and puts her hands over her face. But it's too late. I see the tears streaming down her cheeks and falling from her chin to the ground.

"God, I fucking hate crying! How does she do this to me when she's miles away?"

It kills me to see her like this. My hands grip her shoulders and turn her towards me, pulling her hands from her face. I brush a few stray strands that have escaped her headband and hug her as tightly as I can. Her body shakes as she buries her head into my shoulder.

"I've got you," I say. My hand rubs her back in circles in an attempt to soothe her, but the irritation builds in me. Her mother is a frustrating woman. I saw it firsthand over the summer with every tiny remark coming out as a slight against Jessa's resilience, abilities, and dedication to basketball. Lauren Blakely acts like basketball is the only thing in the world that matters. It never seems to occur to her to spend time with Jessa off the court, doing other things mothers and daughters should do together. We'd had similar discussions while in Connecticut, but Jessa hadn't let her mother get to her this bad. I guess distance doesn't remove the pressures of another person; maybe it actually emphasizes it somehow.

"I'm sorry," I say, "It sucks, but you can't keep it all inside like this. I get that she's your mother but maybe it's time to focus on your own life, your own future, and the things you really want on your own. Without her say. At some point, you'll need to talk to her. But for now, let's try to focus on what you can control now and over the next few weeks your birthday, hanging out with our friends, having as much fun as possible, *and* getting the shit done we need to before the season officially starts. Got it?"

Jessa pulls back and wipes her eyes with her sweatshirt sleeves but angles her shoulder so she's using me as a leaning post. "You're right. I have way more important things to focus on. Thanks, Grey. I don't think I realized how much I'd been bottling all that up. On another note, did you see how excited Bex was about that secret smoothie delivery? Let's get home so I can talk to her about it."

We continue down the sidewalk, my arm draped around Jessa and she leans her head against my shoulder. Up ahead, Oakes and

Collins have moved closer, their arms nearly touching, and the scene looks intimate from where Jessa and I follow. Oakes extends a pinky toward Collins, who links hers around his. Was that a pinky promise? Do people our age even do that anymore? Jessa looks as confused as I feel but I want to talk to Oakes before I discuss it with Jessa. Maybe our plan worked so well that Oakes already told Collins how he feels.

Both Collins and Oakes are in their rooms when Jessa and I get home. I go directly to the side of the condo Oakes and I share. Oakes stands in front of the bathroom mirror. Since the door is wide open, I don't bother to knock before entering. "What the hell did I just witness?"

He smirks at me in the mirror. "What are you talking about?"

I stare at his reflection with my arms crossed. "Dude. Don't play games with me. I'm your partner in crime. I deserve an update, no? You two were awfully chummy on the walk home. And did I witness an old school pinky swear? Or were my eyes playing tricks on me?"

His cocky smirk is replaced by a full-faced grin. "You saw that, huh?"

"Sure did. You going to tell me about it?" I ask, leaning against the wall. I'm not sure why we're still standing in the bathroom but since Oakes hasn't made a move, I figure I may as well get more comfortable.

"Okay, but you're going to think it's crazy," Oakes says, rubbing shaving cream on his face.

"Try me." It can't be that weird, I think. But I'm wrong. I definitely do not expect the next thing to come out of Oakes's mouth.

"I'm going to be a practice boyfriend of sorts." Oakes shrugs at me, like it's a totally normal thing to do with someone you have an *actual* crush on. Oakes is a nice guy and a hopeless romantic, despite what most people know about him. But this seems a little over the top, even for him.

"You're what?" I ask. "I don't really know what that means."

"So, you know how she doesn't have a lot of experience with dudes? Well, I guess it's an insecurity she has, which makes her avoid dating even more. But since she actually wants the experience and knows she's holding herself back, I might have offered to, like, help her learn how relationships work."

Clear as mud, I think. But I'm not quite ready to express all the sirens going off in my head, so I shake my head at him. "How exactly are you going to do that?"

Oakes rolls his eyes at me. "Seriously? I need to spell it out for you? We'll go on fake dates to give her a feel for what a real one would be like. Maybe practice some of the more... uh... intimate things involved. That kind of stuff. We didn't make an agenda to follow or anything. It'll all be no strings attached."

"You're shittin' me, right? This is not even remotely a good idea." I don't like it. How can Oakes have two different plans with Collins— be a secret admirer *and* a practice boyfriend? Doesn't he see how this could go terribly wrong. He could do all this work and drive her into a relationship with someone else, when he has feelings for her. It's insanity by definition.

Oakes finishes shaving beneath his nose before responding. "Listen, this is what Collins needs right now. So, just trust me."

"Okay," I concede, backing out of the bathroom to let him finish shaving in peace. "Good luck."

But my gut tells me some shit will go down, and I'm not sure how to save the guy from himself.

I knock on Bex's door, hoping she hasn't already hopped into bed for her nightly meditation. She calls for me to come in, and I find her staring at the note that arrived with her smoothie after yoga.

"Who do you think it is?" she asks.

"It could literally be anyone. But it must be someone you already know. Otherwise it's creepy that they know your yoga schedule *and* favorite smoothie. Though you are fairly predictable." I smirk knowing there's no way Bex can argue that. With our training, we're all predictable. I shriek as I dodge the pillow she throws at my head.

"So...," I say. "What did you and Monty talk about on the way home. There was a lot of laughing. Maybe even flirting?"

I don't bring up the pinky hook, hoping she'll tell me about it so I don't have to ask.

"It was nothing," she says.

I wait to see if she'll say anything more, but when she doesn't, I raise my eyebrows and stare at her with mock sternness. "Oh? Then why can't you look me in the eyes right now?"

Bex takes a shirt out of a laundry basket of folded clothes, refolds it, then puts it in a dresser drawer. She does this three more times before I prod her again. "Bex?"

"Somehow Monty got me talking about how excited I am to have someone interested in me. Like, enough to send me a surprise smoothie. Stuff like that doesn't happen to me. That turned into me blurting out my whole stupid story about how inexperienced I am with guys. And I mentioned that even though I'm flattered, I'm simultaneously anxious about it because I have no idea how to talk to guys, let alone how to make anything evolve into a real relationship. If I ever get to that point." Bex laughs in a way that makes me a little sad.

How does this girl not know how special she is? She's gorgeous and has no idea. But all I say is, "Oh, Bex." I think about our late night talks about this very thing. How basketball is so intense that it leaves no time for relationships.

"No, it's okay. Monty was really great. He even offered to coach me, and as embarrassing as that is, I think it could help."

"What exactly does this coaching look like?" I ask, trying to keep the concern from my tone.

"Well, we'll go on some pretend dates, have some conversations you'd have..." she trails off, but she can't hide the blush from creeping up her neck. When Bex blushes, she's splotchy all over. Her voice lowers so much that her next statement is almost a whisper. "And... we might even practice the stuff beyond flirting. Like kissing... and anything else that could come next."

I can't help it. My eyes narrow and I tilt my head in the way Greyson says I do whenever I'm about to analyze the hell out of something. "Wait, so, you are going to do this with Monty? *Our* Monty? The one who lives across the condo? That guy?"

Bex laughs and hurls the pillow at my head again. This time in lands, and I pretend to fall back in defeat.

"Yes," she says. "The one and the same, Monty Oakes. I know it sounds crazy but he's actually perfect for the job."

She says it like this is a position she's been actively seeking candidates for, unbeknownst to me. I'm only her best friend. It sounds like a bad move, though. I've definitely noticed the lingering looks between the two of them, but I thought it was just flirting for fun. Monty flirts with everyone.

"Think about it, Jessa. Monty can get any girl and has tons of practice. I get insight on men and relationships. It's win-win. Nobody gets hurt," she assures me. "But anyway, let's talk about something else. What do you want to do for your birthday?"

"Well, what a subtle subject change." I roll my eyes. "I need to survive a special dinner with my mother and Dillon before I can focus on my party."

Bex looks surprised. "How did I not know your mother was flying in?"

"I've been pretending it's not happening, so I didn't mention it," I say. "I was hoping it was going to be just me and Dill since we've barely had time alone since school started, but she's insisting on taking me to The Tiny Spoon."

The Tiny Spoon is an upscale restaurant I wouldn't treat myself to, but my mother is more than willing to pay for. Had I suggested any place less classy for my birthday dinner she would have overrode me. It's all about appearances for her, so it's easier to let her choose.

I'm sure some people would think I'm bratty with a mother willing to spend so much one-on-one time with me on the court and to fly in on my birthday. But if only they knew. It's always too self-serving to truly be about me. And I was hoping for a longer break from my mother. I'm in a weird headspace lately. There are so many

Last Times happening this year, and I don't feel like I'm able to be truly present for any of them. And things with me and Dillon have been off, so that's constantly in the back of my mind. Not to mention all the freakin' Greyson ogling I keep catching myself doing. It's all sending me into a spiral. Or was. Greyson really helped by letting me vent about my mom earlier. I wonder what he'd think about me checking him out all the time.

I manage to survive the days leading up to my mother's visit. It helps that I'm too busy to think much about anything other than school and workouts. But with each day of successful practices and keeping my head above water with schoolwork, I feel like I'm getting my groove back. The closer it gets to my birthday, the more my body hums with a strange vibration. It's like it knows that with my birthday comes a party. A chance to let loose with my friends, some I've only seen in passing at the gym. It's a good thing I live with Bex, Monty, and Greyson. If I didn't, my social life would be nonexistent.

Seeing my friends isn't the only thing I'm looking forward to about my party. Greyson's brother, Corden, is a freshman at HU this year, so he, along with their little sister, Soren, are coming, too. I adore Greyson's siblings. They make up for the lack of my own siblings. And for Greyson's sake, I'm thrilled he has his brother close now. Since we first met, it's been obvious how much he misses his family. So yes, I'm pumped for the party. *If* I survive dinner with my mother first.

The night of the dinner, I make plans with Dillon to pick me up at five-thirty. My mother has been obnoxious with her text reminders that our reservations at The Tiny Spoon are at six o'clock. If we're late, birthday or not, I'll never hear the end of it.

I'm putting the finishing touches on my hair and makeup—I've both blown dry and curled my hair, something that happens maybe twice a year—when I hear the front door open, then Greyson's amicable voice followed by Dillon's slightly irritated response. I'm sure he's annoyed it wasn't me inviting him in.

Well, shit. I'm not dressed and leaving those two alone does not seem like a great idea, especially since I've been so into Greyson lately. They always make it so awkward, so I scurry out of the bathroom and into the living room, body wrapped in a towel and wrangle Dillon into my room before Grey can say much. I close the door to my bedroom and turn to see Dillon, his expression one of disbelief.

"What?" I ask.

"Do you often flaunt around the apartment half naked in front of Greyson and Monty?" he demands, now glaring.

I know I can handle this one of two ways. I can get defensive, which will just increase the tension between us. Or I can try to be lighthearted.

"You jealous?" I tease, deciding on the latter. I lean into him, still wrapped in nothing but a towel, hoping it'll distract him enough to stop being mad. It's been awhile since I've seen Dillon in the easygoing way that was his norm when we first started dating. We met at the country club at home. Dillon and I had both just finished grueling workouts and reached for the last towel on the shelf. I remember his genuine smile when he made some kind of tennis joke, accusing me of breaking the imaginary rules of the towel area, claiming I was being too aggressive. We shared a laugh and then he offered to buy me a drink to make up for trying to steal the last towel.

"Jessa, I'm serious. People already talk, so why are you giving them more to talk about?"

"What the hell, Dillon? It's a *towel*. It covers more than a bathing suit or the sports bra and shorts I wear during practice. You never seem to have a problem with that." I challenge, as the rage soars through me. *Who the hell does he think he is?*

"I'm just saying, it's bad enough you live with two dudes. You don't have to flaunt your shit around them, too."

"Flaunt my shit? That's what you think I do? Interesting. Well, you and I haven't seen each other in weeks. You have no idea if I walk around in a towel all the time nor have you considered that the only reason I did today was because I heard your voice. And when we should be making up for all the time we don't see each other, you want to talk about me flaunting my shit in front of Greyson." I air quote 'flaunting', knowing damn well my exaggerated use of his word will push his buttons. I'm ranting but can't seem to make myself stop. "Do you hear yourself? It's Greyson and Monty, for God's sake. Two of the nicest, most protective guys you'll ever meet. They're practically my brothers. They aren't interested in ogling my goods."

I step back from him, shaking my head. "You know what? I'm not doing this right now. Give me a couple minutes to get dressed, then we can go."

"Jessa–" he begins, but my expression stops him. Instead, he nods and exits my room, leaving me to get dressed in peace. Which is good. I need a second to cool down. I don't want the night to be ruined over this.

By the time I finish getting dressed, my anger has dissipated and I'm determined for things to be good with Dillon. When he knocks on my door to see if I'm ready, I'm pleased with his wide-eyed reaction to my navy cocktail dress and know he's forgotten our argument. I'd picked the dress out specifically for the occasion. It hits my curves in all the right places with a low V between my breasts and an open back. I know I look hot. Which is exactly how I want—need—to feel tonight.

"Damn, babe. I'm not sure I should let you go out in this either," Dillon says, pulling me in close. He strokes the upper part of my arms before pushing my hair aside to kiss along my collar bone.

The affection should send chills down my body. But somehow, his comment makes my blood boil and I pull away. "Let me? I do not *need* your permission to go out looking sexy."

"Geez, what's your deal tonight?" Dillon says, his hands lifting my chin to force me to look at him.

There's so much I want to say, but I also know I need Dillon on my side tonight. Going to dinner with my mother while also in a fight with Dillon sounds like my own personal night in hell. I'd rather get my wisdom teeth pulled out without anesthesia.

"I'm sorry," I say. "You know my mother puts me on edge. I think I'm just anxious. Let's just go." I grab my clutch off the dresser with one hand and Dillon's hand with my other before leading him from my bedroom. As we step into the living room, Monty cat calls from the chair and Bex's once over with her eyebrows raised lets me know she approves.

Greyson looks like someone splashed him in the face with a glass of water. His posture is rigid, his mouth is hanging slack, and his eyes are round as he takes in my dress before dragging his eyes up to meet my gaze.

"Damn," he whispers, then looks startled by the sound of his own voice as if he didn't mean to say that out loud.

I'm not sure how long my eyes stay locked on Greyson's, but the sound of Dillon's not-so-subtle cough makes me stammer, "Okay, ready, Dill?" He nods, his mouth pressed in a thin line. My face is on fire, made worse by the way his hand possessively grabs my waist before nearly pushing me out the door.

"Have fun, kids!" I hear Bex yell before the door slams shut behind us.

6

Jessa

Dillon and I are silent on the short drive to The Tiny Spoon in his beloved Aston Martin. I've never told him this, but I think his car is obnoxious, especially in the custom magnetic silver finish he picked.

I can tell from the way he chews the inside of his cheek that he's holding back saying something, but I don't ask what. I have a fairly good idea what it is. And I really don't want to talk about it.

My mother is already seated at a table near the entrance and stands to greet us as we enter the dimly lit restaurant.

"Happy Birthday, Jessa. You look beautiful," my mother says. She pulls me in for an awkward embrace before pulling Dillon into one that looks much more natural. It stings a bit watching the two of them so comfortable with one another while I can't seem to feel comfortable with either of them. It's always been this way, them bonding over the high-status lifestyle from the moment my mother learned we met at the country club all those years ago. They both thrive in the exclusive and cliquey environment that ultimately alienates others.

"Don't you look dapper, Dillon?" my mother says, smoothing out the collar of his jacket. *Barf*, I think, do not feed the ego.

We sit at the candlelit table where my mother has already ordered a high-end bottle of Moscato and three glasses. Good to know she can remember at least one non-basketball related thing about me, I think, getting saltier by the minute. Why is she always so much nicer to Dillon than she is to me? It's my birthday, isn't it? After a few sips, the wine takes the edge off, and I try to be an active participant in the conversation. However, it's mostly centered around Dillon and his job as a tennis pro. Neither of them say much to me, but I keep my smile bright and nod or laugh at all the appropriate times. I find myself watching the other restaurant patrons instead of focusing on the small talk until Dillon mentions that he's searching for a mixed doubles partner. Then I snap my attention back to their conversation.

"...I figured it was a good time to add mixed doubles instead of only focusing on singles. I think I've found the perfect candidate, too," he's saying.

Well, this is news to me. I guess this explains why Dillon's basically been MIA lately. But how could he not have mentioned this to me? Not only has he decided to find a female partner, but he's already been spending time with potential candidates. And he thinks he's found one? I have so many questions—and frankly, a few nasty comments since he made me feel bad about walking around in a freaking towel earlier but never mentioned this!—but it's not the right time. That is one conversation I do not want to have in the presence of my mother. She'll side with him and both of them will act like I'm a jealous lunatic without recognizing the hypocrisy.

We're on the first course when the discussion turns to my roommates. Of course, the first time my mother includes me in the conversation, this is the topic. Even though we're not touching, I feel

Dillon stiffen beside me.

My mother is not an idiot and picks up on the tension. "Everything okay with your living situation?" my mother asks, eyes narrowing slightly.

"Yeah—uh—fine," I say, stabbing at my food. "It's fine."

She glances at Dillon. He shifts in his chair. She notices. Of course she does. Fortunately, she changes the subject...to basketball.

"You know," my mother starts, turning fully toward Dillon, "I've watched every one of her games since middle school."

Here we go.

"And I'll be honest," she continues, "she doesn't train nearly enough."

I look up. "Mom—"

"She doesn't," my mother says firmly. "And when she does train, it's too short. Thirty minutes here and there isn't going to cut it."

Dillon nods. "Consistency really matters."

I stare at him.

"And variety," my mother adds. "She does the same drills over and over. No creativity. No adaptation."

"I adapt," I mutter.

"You don't," she says without missing a beat. "And that's why your handles haven't improved the way they should have by now."

Dillon swallows, then nods again. "I mean... she's not wrong."

I drop my spoon. "Wow."

My mother smiles, satisfied. "I'm just saying—if she trained smarter and longer, we'd be having a very different conversation."

Basketball used to be my favorite topic. With my mother, it always ends the same way—me sitting there, half-eaten dinner in front of me, wondering why I ever opened my mouth in the first place. And, cool. Glad I can count on Dillon to back me up. What an asshat, I think, making dagger eyes at him. Which, he seems to take as a look of endearment because he only smiles sweetly at me in response.

I direct my attention to my mother. "Yes, mother, I hear you. But I'm training nearly every day because I'm well aware the season starts soon. We have been going to the Hastings Center every day, mixing up cardio, weights, and shooting. We do it all. So, despite what you believe, we actually have a solid routine and are putting in the hard work." So back off, I resist the urge to add.

My mother makes a tutting sound like I'm a contrary child. "Alright. I'm just checking. I'd hate for all that hard work we put in this summer to go to waste."

Again, I bite my tongue. She wouldn't want to hear the report on how the summer went in my mind.

Then she says, "Did I tell you I'll be in town the week leading up to the opener? I've been asked by the Athletic Director to speak to the Student Athletic Council, and we're working on plans for some kind of skills camp for team practices that week."

Wow. This evening just keeps getting better and better. My mom, in town for a whole week. A week where she'll be celebrated and I'll be on edge. Sounds fantastic.

"Wow, that's great mom," I say, forcing my tone to come out more positive than I feel.

"Yes. I'm excited for it. Dillon, what are your plans for the season opener? Perhaps we can attend together?" My mother says this last part pointedly. Dillon isn't used to being on the receiving end of Lauren Blakely's direct questions.

"Um... Sure. Definitely... If I can make it," he responds, shifting in his seat like he's trying to teleport out of The Tiny Spoon. "I'll have to double-check my schedule."

While I would normally love watching someone else squirm

under the eyes of my mother, I'm too shocked by his response. What in the hell did he say? He's going to check his schedule to see if he can fit my season opener in? I stare at him, knowing my eyes probably look crazy, but I'm having trouble wrapping my mind around the fact that his girlfriend's first game of her one and only senior year isn't already on his calendar.

Dillon avoids eye contact with me, but his lucky ass is saved. A server places a slice of the most decadent chocolate layer cake I've ever seen in front of me, a single candle burning in its center. My mother and Dillon join in as the server and a few nearby diners sing Happy Birthday to me.

"Thank you. This looks delicious." I say and blow out the candle as Greyson's face comes to mind and I wish he was the one here. I'm stuffed from dinner, but the cake is one of the best desserts I've ever had. If Dillon and my mom hadn't shared it with me, I'd have eaten the entire piece.

Once the server has cleared away the plates, my mother hands me a box. It's beautifully wrapped in the almost-too perfect way that tells me she had it professionally wrapped. I'm not sure why that bothers me so much but it does. I slide my finger under the paper, careful not to rip the paper—the Lauren Blakely way—and open the box to find a gift certificate.

"Thanks, Mom," I say, wondering why she bothered with the box when an envelope would have sufficed.

"Enjoy, darling, it's for a spa weekend for unlimited services for you and a guest. I thought it would be nice to take time for yourself before the season begins. You need to take care of yourself." My mother smiles, proud of her thoughtful gift.

Time for myself. It's laughable. When does my mother think I'll find this time for myself? In between her constant reminders to train?

Even over my summer vacation, she tried to kill me with intense training, never once telling me to relax and enjoy my break. She wants me immersed in basketball morning, noon, and night. Every day of the year. The same woman who has never let me fully be who I am unless it fits the basketball star she wants me to be.

"Thanks, Mom. I'm sure it will be lovely." I lean over and kiss her on the cheek and bite my tongue from sharing the reality that I never intend to use it. She beams at me and, for a second, my negative feelings are replaced by something else. Something warmer. Like a moment where I actually feel my mother's love.

"My turn." Dillon says and pulls out a tiny Tiffany blue box from his jacket pocket. He hands it to me. "Happy Birthday, Jessa."

My heart skips. I'm suddenly very nauseous and wonder how embarrassed my mother would be if I vomited right here in the dining room of this upscale restaurant. There are only a few things small enough to fit in this blue ring-sized box. And Dillon knows—at least should know—that I'm not one for flashy jewelry. Not to mention, we've never broached the subject of marriage in all our nearly four years together. I'm not ready for that. Not now. Maybe not ever. But would Dillon really propose in front of my mother? Yes, I answer, because Dillon loves an audience, he loves flashy things, and he loves the ego trip that would come with a proposal that includes both. My hands shake as I open the box at the pace of someone who knows that an angry rattle snake is inside. "Oh, thank God," I say, letting out the breath I'd been holding. There's no ring, only a pair of diamond earrings that gleam as they catch the light of the chandelier above us.

I realize at that moment that I haven't said anything else and lean in to give Dillon a peck on the lips. "Thank you. They're beautiful."

Dillon doesn't lean into me, but he doesn't pull away either. After the rocky start to the evening, I pray I didn't offend him. I just want to wrap this dinner up and spend time catching up on our time apart. It bothers me that I knew nothing about his doubles plan and that we seem to be so disconnected from one another.

On the off chance Dillon didn't notice my minor freak out over his gift, my mother won't let the moment fade without making it a thing.

"Jessa, are you all right? You look as though you've seen a ghost," she says, her voice dripping with concern.

Nope, no ghost. Only a flash of a future that I've never envisioned. And, apparently, don't want.

"I'm good, Mom. I think it's just all the wine and food. Everything's great. Aren't these earrings beautiful?" I plaster the too-bright smile back on my face and hold the box out to show my mother.

"Well, yes, they're simply gorgeous. You have fine taste, Dillon." My mother holds the box this way and that, examining the earrings from all angles before passing it back to me. She smiles at Dillon and coos like she's talking to a baby. "It's been a lovely evening. Thank you for being great company."

Eye roll. Guess my company was mediocre in comparison, I think, unable to control the bitterness taking over.

"Yes, thank you for inviting me. It's been a pleasure seeing you again." Dillon's smile is warm as he stands, offering me his outstretched hand.

I take it, hoping this means he isn't upset with me. I turn to my mother, offering her a small hug. "Thanks for dinner and the spa gift, Mom. I'll see you in a few weeks."

The three of us are walking through the lobby when my mother says, "Oh, and Dillon, do let me know if you will be joining me for the season opener. I'll secure the tickets."

"Sure thing," Dillon nods another goodbye in her direction before guiding me by the small of my back to the car. He makes a show of opening the door from me, my mom watching in approval from the curb before sending us off with a wave. Dillon maneuvers his 'baby' out of the lot at a painful slowness that makes me want to scream. But I know better than to comment. It'll end in a lecture about loose rocks in parking lots and the cost of paint chips. No. Thank. You. The Aston Martin's engine is silent, the only sound—inside and outside of the car—a steady hum of rubber on pavement. I search for something to say that won't start an argument, but Dillon beats me to it.

"Well, that was only slightly awkward," he says. His tone is thick with sarcasm, and after he puts the car in park in front of my condo, he turns accusatory eyes on me.

"What?" I ask, annoyed by the blame I see in his eyes and his interruption of my replay of the events at dinner. As if I'm the only one who acted weird tonight.

"First, the pressure from your mother to come to your season opener... Did you put her up to that? And then—God, your reaction to my gift was... I don't know. What was that, Jessa? You panicked. I saw it." Dillon tilts his head against the headrest. He appears drained and defeated, like he just came from a long, grueling ordeal. Which maybe, in his mind, he did.

The thought of him feeling that way makes the storm brewing inside me swirl faster, pressing against the walls of constraint I've been holding up.

"Pressure to come to my season opener? No, I didn't ask her to pressure you at all. But doesn't it seem like the kind of thing you'd want to come to? You know, to support your girlfriend? And no, I did not panic. I was surprised, that's all."

The look Dillon gives me makes it clear he doesn't believe me. Which I guess I can't blame him for. I did panic a little, but I'm sure as hell not admitting it.

"You clearly thought it was a ring, that much was obvious. But the thought seemed to make you sick. How should I take that?"

Guilt replaces some of my rage, and I reach for him, determined to make up for it. But Dillon intercepts my hands, placing them both in his. "Look, tomorrow's your birthday. I don't want to end tonight fighting, so I'm going to go."

We hadn't make specific plans to stay together tonight but I'd assumed we would. Especially after it being so long since we've slept in the same bed. I open my mouth to protest, but he cups my face in his hands and gives me a light kiss. It feels like a consolation prize, lacking in any passion.

"I have to work in the morning but I'll come by for your party. If you want to talk after that, we can," he says and lets go of me, putting the Aston Martin in drive. I'm dismissed, it appears.

"Guess that means I'm spending the night alone," I say, unable to keep the annoyance out of my tone. I open the door—no audience, no need for him to act chivalrous now—and step out, leaning my head in to give him one last look.

The next morning, I'm woken by a tapping on my bedroom door. Bex enters with a tray holding two of my favorite fall treats—a steaming pumpkin spice latte and a still-warm pumpkin cream cheese muffin.

"Happy Birthday, Jessa!" she says, hugging me with her free arm before handing me the goods.

I breathe in the spiced pumpkin scent and smile at my best friend. "Thanks, Bex. And thanks for the pick me up, I needed this."

"Don't thank me," she says with a wide smile "I'm just the delivery girl."

"Greyson?" This makes sense, considering how worried he looked when I'd come home without Dillon last night and escaped to my room to wallow.

"Yep. He ran to the coffee shop the second they opened, saying he wanted your big day to start off right."

"Well, that's sweet," I say between bites of the muffin. "Where is he now?"

"Picking Soren up from the airport."

I sip on the latte, unsure if the warmth running through me is from that or Greyson's thoughtfulness. He never lets a birthday go by without making me feel special.

"He may have mentioned you seemed a little down when you got home last night. Everything go okay at dinner?" Bex asks, her eyes wary. She knows how Dillon and my mom together can sometimes lead to me feeling ganged up on.

I groan, my mind replaying bits of the evening on fast forward. "That's an understatement."

"Wanna talk about it?" Bex asks.

"Not particularly. Dinner was how I expected it to be. And things with Dillon are just..." I stop, worried I'll cry if I tell Bex about how things ended with Dillon last night.

She seems to get the point though and stands. "Well, I'm here if you want to. But you'd better get out of bed and get ready. Our nail appointments are at ten."

I'd forgotten Bex had scheduled appointments for me, her, and Soren for my birthday. The idea of a little pampering to start my day perks me up. "Right! I can't wait. Is Grey bringing Soren here first or dropping her off to meet us at the salon?"

Greyson's little sister is a younger, female version of him. Soren has the same icy blue eyes and sandy blonde hair but their similarities don't stop at the physical. Like Greyson, Soren is sweet, thoughtful, and always up for an adventure with me. Greyson is fiercely protective of her, which I know sometimes drives her crazy, but I think it's adorable. With her being the only girl in their family, I try to include her when Bex and I do girlier things when she visits. It's nice to pretend I have a sister sometimes. Today, Soren's tagging along for manis and pedis in preparation for the party later.

"Soren," I say an hour later as she, Bex, and I sit in a row of massage chairs, soaking our feet in bubbling spa tubs. "How's school? Anything new going on? It feels like forever since I've seen you!"

"Meh, high school is high school," she responds, scowling. "My brothers made sure that even though they're no longer physically present in town, they have a looming presence that surrounds me all day."

"What do you mean?" I ask.

"Well, they've basically threatened all the guys at my school. So now, none of them will really talk to me, let alone date me." Soren sighs and relaxes deeper into the vibrating chair. "I know they mean well, but seriously."

One of the nail technicians lifts one of my feet out of the tub, dries it with a towel, and uses her thumbs to massage tiny circles into my arch. It's heavenly. I've forgotten how relaxing it is to take time for myself and hang out with girlfriends. If my mother had done something like this with me instead of giving me a gift card, maybe we'd have a different kind of mother/daughter relationship.

Before I fall too far into a pit of irritation with my mother again,

I redirect my attention back to Soren. She's still telling Bex about the boys at school being afraid of Greyson and Corden.

"I get it," I empathize. "But it's nice to have someone looking out for you, too. Even if those someones happen to be older brothers who use intimidation from afar."

"It's not just that," Soren whines. "Greyson and Corden chatted with the entire boys' basketball team, *including* their coach."

"Oh no..." Bex says, grimacing.

"Yep," Soren grumbles. "Said I'm off limits. Which is embarrassing enough, but now the whole team acts like my personal bodyguards. It's so annoying! I have like twenty overbearing big brothers, deterring anyone brave enough to approach me with their crazy threats."

"Yikes," Bex and I say at the same time. The look on Bex's face says maybe she didn't have it so bad with her parents, even if she is now relying on Monty for dating practice.

As if knowing I was reading her mind, Bex says, "I thought it was bad with a twin brother. But you win. Your situation is much, much worse."

"I'll talk to Grey," I assure Soren. "Maybe between me and Bex, we can talk some sense into him. And Corden."

"Really?" Soren's face lights up and she kicks her feet in a little celebratory dance. "That would be amazing. Thanks, Jessa."

"No promises," I say. I don't want her to get her hopes up. Greyson is very protective and I may have sounded more confident than I am. "He's a tough nut to crack when it comes to you."

"And you, too." Soren blurts, then clamps her palm over her mouth. Her face has turned a drastic shade of pink, too.

"Huh?" I say, unsure what I missed. Bex looks smug on the other side of Soren. I feel giddy once I process what Soren is implying.

"Oh, it's nothing," Soren says, but she shifts her attention to the massage chair's remote control. After a few seconds, she decides on a setting and leans back with her eyes closed.

How convenient, I think. What does she mean? Of course Greyson is protective of me, too. We tell each other everything. Or almost everything. I definitely don't tell him how often I admire his muscular physique. But he's close to his sister, too, and that's what Greyson does when he's close to people. He's protective of them.

We sit through the rest of our pedicures in silence, each of us enjoying the pampering. I try to wipe my mind blank and relax, but my mind starts to drift to the weirdness with Dillon last night. He hasn't even texted to wish me a happy birthday yet.

On top of that, I find myself replaying the look on Greyson's face when I walked out in my navy dress. The way he'd muttered, *damn*, sends shivers up my spine every time I think about it. I puff my cheeks out, trying to expel all my crazy thoughts about him. I'm just feeling this way because Dillon disappointed me. That's all.

"Jessa," I hear as I blink my eyes open and stretch. I must have dozed off in the massage chair. "You must have had a rough night. You never nap. Come on, time to get you excited to celebrate another year of you." Bex exclaims as I see her give a look of concern to Soren before she pulls me from the chair and to the door.

Back at the condo, we're greeted by Corden, Greyson, and Monty.

"Happy Birthday, Jessa!" They shout in unison, each taking their turn to hug me.

"Thanks for the coffee and muffin this morning," I whisper in Greyson's ear when it's his turn. He winks and goes back to blowing up more balloons for the arch he is working on.

The guys have been in full out party prep mode while we've been gone. The kitchen counters are wiped down, the pillows are fluffed and distributed evenly across the couch, and both bathrooms are clean. Monty and Greyson are rearranging the already overly stocked fridge—charcuterie and bite-size desserts—to make room for the rest of the food they prepared. Rose gold, gold, and white balloons are blown up in different sizes and arranged in an arch on one wall with a birthday banner scripted in gold. String lights are draped deliberately along the windows and walls, casting a soft glow instead of harsh overhead light. Candles—battery-powered—sit in clusters on tables and shelves. All the borrowed coolers are already stocked with ice and overflowing with all of my favorite beverages. Solo cups are stacked next to the glassware that lines the countertop with a signature cocktail named after me:

The Blakely Breakaway

Smooth. Sharp. Unstoppable.

A clean finish with just enough edge to remind you who runs the floor.

"Thanks for doing all this, guys! The place looks great." I'm touched that they're working so hard to make the party successful and stress-free for me.

"All for you—our lady of the hour." Grey smirks, pretending to bow at my feet. I laugh at the ridiculousness of it, when he looks up, our eyes lock and neither of us seem to be able to look away.

A flicker of awareness I didn't invite. There's a half-second where the room drops out, where the joke dissolves and I become conscious of how steady his gaze is, how long this pause is stretching past normal. *This is nothing,* I tell myself immediately. But my pulse has already betrayed me, ticking faster, louder.

I break first, keenly aware staying like that too long is inviting speculation.

"Come on, ladies," I say to Bex and Soren, beckoning them to follow me to my bedroom. It's time to decide what we're wearing.

"Hey!" Greyson yells after us. "Remember, we have gifts for you before everyone gets here!"

"Got it!" I shout back before pushing the door closed. We spend the next couple of hours trying on outfits, dancing to a birthday playlist Bex made, and experimenting with different shades of makeup. Soren tries a contouring trick she learned on YouTube, and I'm shocked at the results. She looks older—at least twenty years old—and very, very chic. Greyson will flip his lid when he sees her. He's already worried about a college guy hitting on his little sister, and this look pretty much guarantees it.

"Ladies, you about ready?" Greyson calls from outside the door.

"Almost!" We all say at once, giggling as we dab the final touches of lip gloss to our mouths.

When I open the door a few minutes later, Greyson almost falls in, catches himself, then leans nonchalantly against the doorframe. He scans the room, his eyes settling on his sister first.

"Absolutely not," he says, glowering. His hand swings up and down the length of her, gaping at me and Bex like we'd let her wear a see-through bodysuit instead of her very tasteful skirt and cropped tee. "You are *not* setting foot in this party looking like *that*."

"Why? She looks hot!" Bex exclaims, looking Soren up and down with approval.

"Precisely my point. My sister is not allowed to look hot at a college party where there will be college boys. Especially our teammates. She is only sixteen and I haven't adequately warned them off yet."

"Greyson, cut her some slack. She looks gorgeous. Wouldn't you rather her look hot right here in *our* condo at *our* party where you can keep an eye on her? It's not like we're setting her free at a club. Just chill out. She'll be fine." I end with and cross my arms, daring him to challenge me.

Bex snorts. Soren smirks and cocks her head at Greyson as if to say, *Well, what are you going to do now?*

Greyson raises his arms in defeat and directs a huff at me. "Fine."

"Oh," I say, as I move toward the door, hoping Greyson will finally stop analyzing his sister's appearance, so we can all leave this room. But a promise is a promise, and I've only half-fulfilled my duty to Soren. "Make sure you tell Corden to back down, too. Soren doesn't need you fools hovering all night."

Greyson finally looks at me for the first time since entering my room. It looks like he's about to give me a smart ass remark but stops once his eyes land on my breasts. There's only an inch of cleavage peeking out from the top of my fitted top, but it's enough to distract him. He pauses there long enough for Soren to snicker beside me. Then, Greyson lets his eyes travel down the remaining length of my body before he lifts them to meet my gaze. With raised eyebrows, he clears his throat and croaks out, "Well, you ladies clean up nice."

Then he turns and stalks out of my room, finally letting the three of us roam into the living room. Soren barks a laugh. "OMG, Grey. You are *such* a dude. Be more obvious, why don't you?"

Greyson ignores her and sits on the couch next to a stack of wrapped gifts. When I sit next to him, my skirt hikes up, and I see Greyson's eyes graze along my thigh. My skin feels scorched every place he looks, and I scan the room, hoping someone has opened a bottle of white wine or something. I obviously need to calm my nerves.

Bex saves the day by plopping down on the other side of me, and hands me a package wrapped in bright pink paper. "Here, open this one first."

I tear the gift open and bust out laughing. It's a pink pajama set covered with Bex, Monty, and Greyson's faces. "These are amazing. It'll be like I'm sleeping with all of you every night."

Monty hands me his gift next. Most people don't know this about Monty, but he's a very thoughtful gift giver. This time is no different. I have a lump in my throat as I stare down at the framed print of the four of us in our basketball uniforms at the end of last season. "Monty, thank you. This is perfect for that one blank wall in the living room. Is there time to hang it before everyone gets here?"

"We'll make time," Monty says, already up and moving toward the closet where we keep the toolbox.

Soren's hands are clasped together and she's beaming. "You are the cutest friend group. All beautiful, all basketball players, all living in this one place. It would be the best reality show. I want to be you all someday." Corden huffs from across the room and Soren rolls her eyes. "Yeah, I mean you, too, Corden."

"Damn right," Corden says. "I'd make that reality show."

Soren and Corden start to bicker over who would be the best person on their pretend TV show, but Greyson's quiet voice pulls my attention from them. "All right, mine next, Jessa."

He hands me a small package with an oversized bow. I can feel everyone watching as I remove the bow and open the box. Maybe all the attention is why I feel so much emotion when I see the elegant gold chain with a basketball charm encrusted in small diamonds. I hold it up from the chain, watching the charm spin and see that it's engraved on the back. *Always.*

My vision blurs and it's hard to force words out, but I manage to whisper, "Grey, this is too much. But I love it."

"I knew you'd love it!" Soren says. "Grey had it custom-made months ago."

"Soren," Greyson hisses.

"It's perfect," I say, knowing that while it's from Greyson, both Soren and Corden look like they were every bit as excited for me to open his gift. It wouldn't shock me to know they'd both gone with him when he'd bought it. I hand Greyson the chain and turn my back to him. "Help me put it on?"

Greyson steps behind me and brushes my hair back, then loops the necklace around my neck. The charm hangs at the perfect length, and I clutch it in my palm, only releasing it when Monty and Bex come closer to check it out.

"You did good, man," Monty says, smacking Greyson on the back.

"Damn, Greyson. Don't forget about me on my birthday," Bex says with a wink.

Saving me from my emotions, our first guests arrive. It's mostly friends I've made in classes and some teammates, but I'm quickly swept up into the vibe. The music is blasting, drinks are flowing, and the air is a medley of alcohol, sweat, and probably every perfume and cologne you could ever name. Tomorrow, it might be enough to make me vomit, but tonight, it smells like sweet, sweet freedom.

There's still no sign of Dillon. I'm texting him when the front door swings open and in stumbles Dillon.

"Where have you been?" I ask, sidestepping a few guests to greet him.

He doesn't answer my question but kisses my cheek and pins my arms in a hug. "Happy Birthday, babe!"

"I was getting worried," I say once he releases me. I can smell a hint of booze on his breath, and the way it coalesces with his woodsy cologne gives it a putrid quality.

He waves a hand as if to say *no big deal*. "Got hung up at the club with a tennis lesson, that's all. But I'm here now and ready to party."

Knowing a tennis lesson took priority puts an instant damper on my mood. Dillon doesn't notice as he guides me toward the drink table. He pops a cap off a beer. It's only after he's taken a long swig that he finally looks me up and down. Then, he sees the gold charm around my neck.

He jabs a finger at it. "Hmm... that's nice. Where'd you get it?"

"Greyson got it for me as a gift. It's a basketball charm." I don't offer to give him a closer look. Instead, I grasp it in my palm again, as if protecting it from the sardonic remarks I know will come next.

"Where are the earrings I got you?" Dillon asks, his eyes scanning the room. I know he's looking for Greyson the way his nostrils are flared. "What kind of guy buys someone else's girlfriend jewelry for her birthday?"

"The earrings are in my room. They seemed too fancy for this kind of party, but I'll put them on. Come on," I say, tugging on Dillon's arm. Maybe if I get him into my room, I can rationalize with him before he finds Greyson.

When Dillon doesn't budge, I glance around the room for another distraction. "Hey, let's go talk to Bex."

On our way over to Bex, someone from HU stops Dillon to ask about his recent tennis games. Like anytime someone brings up tennis, Dillon dives deep into the conversation to the point that I quickly lose interest. I'm stifling a yawn when Soren waves me over to where she stands with Corden near the food, and I realize I haven't eaten hardly anything today. A sense of relief overwhelms me as I step between the two younger Hastings and Corden hands me a fresh drink. I hadn't even noticed how tense my body had been. It was like I was just waiting for Dillon to explode. Which had seemed inevitable until tennis was brought up. I'm so grateful to the guy who intercepted what could have been a huge buzz kill. But now that the crisis has been averted, I try to relax and focus on the conversation with Corden and Soren. These two are a dream, I think. Just like their brother.

On cue, as if beckoned by my thought, Greyson is at my elbow. "I see Dillon finally made it," he says, nodding his head across the room where Dillon is still talking the same guy's ear off. The dude looks bored as hell, I note, glad to have escaped when I did.

"Yep, finally," I respond, wondering if I should tell him that Dillon isn't happy about the necklace. It's not worth it, I decide. No point in creating drama for no reason.

"Good, I'm glad." Greyson says, but his expression doesn't tell me he means it. "Are you having fun?"

"Evidently a tennis lesson ran late. But yes, I'm having a great time. Your siblings are excellent company," I say, smiling up at Greyson.

"Yeah, they're all right," Greyson agrees, tossing an arm across my shoulder and giving me a side hug. "And I'm happy you're having fun. That's all that matters."

"I'm going to make out with Monty tonight," a slightly intoxicated, but very confident Bex says, appearing at my other side.

Greyson snickers. I nudge him in the side. "Well, alright. Have you told him about this honor yet?"

"I'm sure he heard her. Everyone else did," Greyson says under his breath. I poke my elbow into him again, harder.

"Nope, but I'm gonna go tell him right now." Bex says, slurring a bit. She grins at me, winks at Greyson, then stomps away in search of Monty.

Grey and I shrug at one another. I hope Bex and Monty know what they're getting themselves into.

"Alright birthday girl, time to dance," Grey says, and pulls me onto the makeshift dance floor. Soren trails after us.

I notice the exact moment when Dillon sees us dancing. He zeros in on Greyson, his face beet red, as he beelines it across the room. His eyes are bloodshot and glassy, which means that since he's gotten here, the alcohol has soaked deeper into his bloodstream.

"Hey, Dillon," Greyson says, but he doesn't stop moving to the music, even when Dillon is standing close to us. Too close. He must not notice the intense look on Dillon's face. Or the fact that Dillon is drunk.

"Don't *hey* me," Dillon says, shoving Greyson hard in the chest. The drink—he's moved on to liquor, it seems—in his other hand sloshes over the rim of the plastic Solo cup and onto the carpet. "First, you buy *my* girlfriend jewelry. And now, you're handsy with her right in front of me. You're ballsy as hell, Hastings. Who the fuck do you think you are?"

Dillon is inches from Greyson's face, and panic surges through me as I realize Dillon is drunker than I'd thought. Add in his temper and sense of entitlement, and it doesn't take a genius to know that he's looking to fight. *Fuck, fuck, fuck!*

"Hey, man," Grey says, stepping back with his hands up. "I'm well aware that Jessa is your girl. She and I are just friends. We were dancing as just friends." He draws out the words 'just friends' with emphasis.

With anyone else, Greyson's neutral, non-aggressive tone would be enough to deescalate the situation, but Dillon's rage is too far gone. He steps closer to me, his eyes wild and his fists clenching and unclenching at his sides. Before I can react, Greyson steps in front of me just before Dillon lunges forward. Monty and Corden pull Dillon away as he attempts to throw a punch.

"Alright, Dillon," Monty shouts, holding a struggling Dillon by one arm with Corden still hanging onto the other. "I think it's time for you to settle down or leave."

"Or go sleep it off in my room," I say, my voice choked from holding back tears.

"Fuck that. I'm outta here," Dillon snaps, yanking his arms out of Monty and Corden's grips. He's patting his pockets for the keys to his precious Aston Martin, but Monty holds them up with a victorious expression.

"Looking for these?" Monty asks. "Too bad. You're not driving."

Dillon says nothing. He doesn't even look at me before he stomps to the door, opens it, and slams it with all his power. There's silence in the condo as all of our guests look on, stunned. I stare at the closed front door, unsure of what I should do next. I settle on nothing. Because what can I do? The damage is done.

Happy Birthday to me.

7
Greyson

Whoa. Jessa's boyfriend was just kicked out of our party. I did not see that coming. Dillon's a dick, but this seems extreme, even for his entitled ass. I look at Jessa, her face contorted like she's trying hard not to cry. For a moment, I consider taking her to my room to make sure she's okay. But I don't have to because Jessa smiles and shakes her head at our friends, making a joke about her and Dillon having differing ideas about birthday surprises. Everyone laughs, not because what she said is particularly funny but more out of a collective relief that the situation didn't escalate. After a few minutes, Jessa's acting like none of it ever happened. I knew it, I think. I know Jessa and I've been able to tell for a long time that she isn't happy with Dillon. How could she be now?

"Thank God for you guys," I say to my brother and Oakes as I pass them on my way to get a drink. "Or I might have a broken nose right now, thanks to that asshole. How could he be like that at Jessa's birthday party?"

This was supposed to be about celebrating Jessa. I should have known, considering how unhappy she was when she got back from dinner with her mom and Dillon. I always hate seeing her upset, but especially on her birthday. She's a trooper though, so I have no doubt she'll act like nothing's wrong until the end of the party. Hopefully she'll talk to me later.

I make my way over to Jessa, who's showing her teammates her new basketball charm. My eyes migrate to the ocean wave tattoo on her forearm. I hide a smile, knowing it matches the one on the inside of my left bicep. We got them in Turks and Caicos at a shop called Tats & Tings. It was a spur of the moment decision, but I think we both wanted to bottle up the memories from that trip. For me, it's a constant reminder of the moment I really fell for my best friend. Dillon wasn't around and there were no pressures from school and basketball, so things felt a lot less complicated. We could just be us.

I inhale until my lungs can't hold anymore air, watching Jessa's genuine delight with talking to friends she hasn't hung out with in forever. She's been put through the ringer tonight but somehow she still radiates this light that everyone is drawn to. To say she looks beautiful is an understatement. Her dark hair flows loosely down her back in waves until she scoops it over one shoulder, revealing an open-backed top. There's no way she's wearing a bra, I think, swallowing hard. Somehow that knowledge, combined with the skirt that hugs all her curves and enhances her muscular legs feels like a lot to process right now. I've thought about it so many times, but Jessa is a dream. Why is she with someone like Dillon? She can do so much better. Yet, for whatever reason, they always end up back together. This time will probably be no different.

The thought of them reconciling creates a pit in my stomach, and I move closer to Jessa, instinctively putting my arm around her. She leans against my chest, tips her head up and gives me a weary smile before mouthing "thank you."

It makes my heart ache.

Fifteen minutes later, Jessa has hugged the last of her guests. The only two left in the once crowded condo are my brother and sister. They're helping us clean up the discarded plates, napkins, bottles, and cups. The silence allows me to think without distraction, and I want to use this opportunity to talk to Jessa. I catch Corden's eye and mouth, "scram." He nods, drops the garbage bag, and heads for the front door. Soren understands and goes the opposite direction to my bedroom. She'll stay on our couch tonight, but I appreciate her giving us some space for now.

As soon as Corden and Soren are gone, Jessa starts talking, her voice thick with disbelief and frustration. "I still can't believe Dillon tried to pick a fucking fight with you at the party. Last night he wasn't concerned about anything related to me. He wouldn't even commit to coming to the season opener! He's hardly been around lately and is distant more often than he's not. Do you think there's something going on with him and his new doubles partner? The first I even heard of her was last night. It makes me wonder if he was hiding it on purpose. Plus, he lied about a lesson making him late tonight. It was obvious he'd been drinking because he smelled like fucking booze when he got here."

Jessa finally takes a breath, followed by a giant sigh. Her body is shaking and unshed tears rim her eyes. Because I'd been watching her so closely all night, I know she's had quite a bit to drink. I'm sure it's causing heightened emotions.

I'm not sure what to say, so I pull her into my arms and hold her. I can't stand seeing this girl cry. Especially when it's obvious how hard she's been trying to keep it together. Jessa isn't the kind of girl to mention things that are bothering her unless asked, so she's been keeping the Dillon stuff pent up for awhile. It's understandable that his behavior tonight has her feeling this way. She needed to let all that out.

My hands have found their way to her hair, and I stroke the soft strands. It's meant to soothe her, but I can't help thinking how good she feels in my arms. It feels natural to be this close to her.

I'm startled when Jessa's head jerks back and she's suddenly staring into my eyes. She holds them there for a minute, and I worry she can see everything I'm thinking. Then she closes her eyes, relaxes into me, and says, "Why do you put up with me?"

Well, that's an easy one to answer. Without missing a beat, I respond, "Because it's always you and me."

Jessa brings her arms around my waist and presses her body into me. Then, without warning, her lips touch mine.

"Is this okay?" she whispers. When I look down at her, there's so much feeling in her eyes—desperation, hesitation, and maybe even fear.

I don't have time to respond before her lips are on mine again, this time with more intensity. Her tongue sweeps across mine, and a groan escapes me. There's no thinking. Only my hands acting on their own accord, pulling her closer, roaming selfishly over her body. We're breathing in rhythm as we explore each other, and it feels right. So right. I want this. Hell, at the moment I feel like I might die without it. But I also know that this isn't how I want it to happen.

"Jessa," I say, stepping back and forcing myself to breathe.

It's enough to snap us out of the trance we'd been in. We're both panting with need, but our hands fall away from each other. Jessa looks at me with an expectation of something written across her beautiful features. But when I say nothing, she spins on her heel and leaves. A second later, her door slams.

I fall back on the couch and put my head in my hands. Should I go after her? Explain that even though I want it so much, we're friends. She has a boyfriend. He's a dick, yes, but a boyfriend nonetheless. But I can't bring myself to go to her room. Not when I'm still so worked up. No, I need to chill the fuck out before I try to talk to Jessa.

Soren's sitting on my bed when I sulk into my bedroom, mentally kicking my own ass for allowing anything to happen at all. She looks up in surprise and I shake my head at her.

I'm about to close my bedroom door when I hear a clunk from Oakes's room, followed by heavy breathing and a high-pitched giggle. Well, I guess Collins made good on her promise. At least someone is having a good night, I'm thinking, just as Oakes's door opens. Collins stumbles out, her hair a frizzy mess, mascara smudged on her cheek. She's giggling but keeps saying "*shhhh*," which makes her giggle harder. I stare at her, amused, wondering how long it'll take her to notice me and Soren. She loses her balance while trying to pull Oakes's door closed and almost falls down. I grab her by the elbow to steady her and she looks up in surprise, her smile wide but sheepish. "Oh, hi," she says, like weren't witnessing her in-house walk of shame. "I just had to tell Monty something quick."

"Sure," I say, grinning. "Whatever you say."

Collins gives me a two-fingered salute and tiptoes her way down the hall. Soren and I look at each other and break into matching grins. When Collins is out of sight, I wait to make sure she doesn't run into more walls or furniture. When I hear her door close, I close my own, then throw myself down on the bed. Soren barely escapes being flattened and relocates to take a seat at my desk chair.

"Fuck." I mutter, more to myself than Soren.

"What happened? Is Jessa okay?" she asks, her brows furrowed with worry. I don't reply directly. How do I even explain this to my sister? I stare up at the ceiling and say, "Why's he gotta be such an asshole? Maybe it's *me* who's the asshole?"

"Wait, what? Why are you the asshole?" Soren sounds confused. "What did *you* do?"

"We *kissed*. Not just a peck on the lips kind of kiss. But a hot, out-of-your-mind, needy kiss," I say. Then I feel my face warm as the realization that I said that to my little sister sets in. I'm really not on my A-game tonight.

Soren doesn't seem to think it's weird at all though. She looks both shocked and excited, and like it's taking everything in her to not jump up and down. "You finally went for it?"

"Listen, I didn't go for anything. It just happened. A heat of the moment thing." I push my hair off my forehead, knowing it's probably standing up like crazy, and rub a hand down my face. "This probably ruins everything. If Jessa even remembers it."

Soren's eyes are wide, but she doesn't ask more questions. My sister is good at taking hints when I'm done sharing. She's always been a Jessa fan and has long believed we should get together, but the timing has never been right. Why would this time be any different? Dillon will ensure that.

"I'm going to bed," Soren says, grabbing extra blankets and a pillow from my closet for the couch. "Will you be okay?"

I nod. "Thanks. Night."

When Soren's gone, I lay there, unable to get the kiss out of my head. I know I didn't imagine the mutual passion and need. I close my eyes and beg for sleep to come, but no luck. All night, I toss and turn. I can't stop replaying that fucking kiss. Who am I kidding? It was so much more than a kiss. For so long I've been able to keep my feelings at bay, and now this, just a little glimmer of hope. Thinking about Jessa in those tight and revealing clothes makes me hard. I make peace with the idea that if I plan to get any sleep tonight,—or have any hopes in keeping myself away from Jessa—I'm going to have to take the edge off. I let my mind drift again to the only time Jessa and I were really together. To the point where everything changed for me. Turks and Caicos...

Jessa was in the bathroom of our shared room at the resort, showering off the sun and sand from the day at the beach. I was on the bed, unable to stop thinking about how she'd came on my leg in the cabana just an hour ago. This girl was always on my mind, but something had changed. A switch had been flipped and I could no longer hold back how I felt. I heard the water turn off and I sat up, glancing around the hotel room. Jessa was everywhere. Her clothes tossed all over her bed, shoes scattered around the room, and her favorite ocean mist body spray lingered in the air. *Get a grip man. The cabana was just a heated moment of two friends helping each other out. Stop overthinking!*

As I was giving myself a pep talk, Jessa strolled out of the bathroom in a tiny towel, her hair dripping down her back. Her face was scrubbed clean, and the tantalizing scent that followed her was a combination of something fruity and floral. I couldn't look away.

"Damn, you smell good, Jessa," I said, stifling a moan.

She giggled in response and pulled down the blankets on her bed. She shimmied herself under them until she was comfortable. I laughed at the sight of her wrapped up like a burrito, still in her towel beneath the comforter.

"I'm going to shower now. You'd better not have stolen all the hot water." I glared at her, attempting to look threatening though my tone was playful.

"No promises," she said, as she closed her eyes.

A cold shower was the only option, regardless of there being hot water. I needed to get myself under control and out of my head. The trip wasn't over, and I couldn't risk ruining what Jessa and I had, even if she was finally single at the same time as me.

I walked out of the bathroom with a towel wrapped around my waist, beads of water still clinging to my chest. My nipples were rock hard from the icy water. While rooting around for clothes, I felt Jessa's eyes on me. She wasn't even hiding the fact she was checking me out.

I flopped onto the bed next to her and shook my head, splattering her with water. She shrieked and sat up, forgetting all that covered her was a towel. Her towel slipped and she grappled for it, trying to cover herself, but it was too late. Her perfect, perky breasts were exposed. But Jessa didn't seem the least bit embarrassed, even as I stared unblinking. Her nipples were hard, giving away her arousal.

"You like what you see?" she asked, smirking at the sight of the obvious bulge growing under my towel.

"Fuck. I even took a cold shower. But damn, Jessa, you are too much for me to control myself."

In an almost involuntary movement, I pushed stray wet strands of hair from her face. As I was pulling my hand back, she grabbed hold of it and pressed it to her cheek. "A cold shower, huh?" Jessa asked, eyebrows raised. "You smell like me."

"Guilty on both counts." I affirmed.

"Kiss me, Greyson." She sounded breathless.

I hesitated, reminding myself that this was a bad idea. I'd taken a twenty-minute long cold shower to avoid anything further from happening. Those eyes, though. Those gorgeous green eyes were teasing as Jessa stared at me. She was taunting me.

I gave her a curious look but leaned closer until my lips brushed against hers. It was gentle at first but as soon as her tongue swept into my mouth, there was no going back. Our kisses were rough, our tongues moving together in desperate anticipation. I sucked on her bottom lip until she moaned, and leaned back into the pillows, taking me with her. We were separated only by our towels, and when her legs circled my waist, I growled and pressed my erection against her. There was no use hiding it anymore.

"Grey, I want to feel you."

"Shit, Jessa," I breathed out. I moved from her mouth to her neck, finding a sensitive spot and nipping at it until she moaned again. "I want you so bad."

My hands cupped one of her breasts, lowering my mouth to the peaked bud on the other. I swirled my tongue over it, stopping only to give her a gentle bite. Jessa swore under her breath and bucked her hips under me. I switched to the other side and did the same thing to that nipple, but kept the first nipple stimulated, rolling it between my thumb and forefinger. "Oh, God," she groaned. "Don't stop. It feels so fucking amazing."

My other hand slid down her stomach, going as slow as possible to appreciate every inch of her body as I went. When I felt the warmth of her freshly waxed pussy, I slid a finger inside.

"You're so wet. What have you been thinking about?" I teased.

"I may have taken a cold shower, too." she admitted between moans. "Earlier was not enough. I need to feel you inside me."

"Mmm... Patience. Let me work your pussy. I don't think it's ready for me yet."

I trailed my lips from her breasts down and across her belly, until

I reached her clit. Her body tensed as I alternated between licking, flicking, and circling my tongue over the sensitive center.

"Greyson, you don't have to."

"Fuck, Jessa. I need to. I want to," I said, as my tongue moved from her clit to her opening. She was soaked with need. I used my tongue to lap up her wetness and thought of how much time we'd wasted. She tasted so good. Why didn't we do this sooner? I alternated between pushing my tongue in and out of her opening to nipping at her clit. Jessa was making so much noise as she gripped my hair that I thought I'd explode before she even touched me.

"Do not hold back," I demand. "I want to hear you and feel you come on my face."

I whispered praises as I continued to feast on her. At the first signs of her opening contracting, I doubled down, increasing the pressure and speed as I sucked on her most sensitive spot. Jessa's body tensed up as she spiraled out of control, whimpering and panting as she held onto my shoulders. Through it all, I continued to eat her pussy, slowing down bit by bit every time it contracted.

"Grey," Jessa said, relaxing as she regained control of her body. "Come here. I need to feel you."

I moved up her body, laying on my side. She pushed me all the way on to my back. Her roughness was so hot that my dick shot straight up with no shame as I got comfortable on my back. Jessa reached for it greedily with a strong grip. Precum glistened on the tip, and Jessa rubbed her thumb over the head.

"Jessa," I groaned in surprise, arching my back when she fisted my cock with one hand and used her other to cup my balls.

"Good?" she teased.

"So good," I managed to say through gritted teeth, squeezing my eyes closed. If I didn't focus, it was going to be over in no time.

Jessa found a rhythm with her hand moving up and down my shaft, applying pressure to the top ridge. I was about to tell her I was ready to be inside her when the heat of her mouth surrounded my manhood. I forced my eyes open, watching her push my cock back as far as she could, until it touched the back of her throat. The pleasure made me yell out, and she chuckled before gliding her teeth gently across the tip. She pulled my dick out of her mouth and I thought that meant she was ready for me to be inside her, but no. Instead, she used her lips to apply pressure before forming a tight O with her mouth, sucking my dick in and out while circling her tongue over the head. I yanked Jessa off of my erection before I exploded and brought her mouth to mine. It was so hot tasting the combination of her and me in our joined mouths. I couldn't take it anymore. I needed to be closer to her.

"I need to be inside of you," I said, so turned on I felt reckless. She nodded and pulled me towards her, my dick slapping against her pussy. We were both breathing heavily, watching each other through lidded eyes. Jessa hovered over me with a hand grasped around my pulsing cock. She guided, inch by inch, until it touched her wet opening. Once the tip was in, Jessa stopped, teasing me, before pounding her body down. She squeezed my dick as it filled her.

"You keep doing that and this will be over quickly," I said, eyes rolling to the back of my head from the insane pleasure.

"I don't care. I need this. I need you. Come inside me, Grey," Jessa pleaded.

To emphasize her point, she bounced up and down, rocking her hips in circles, her pussy contracting around my cock. She managed to hold on until I couldn't hold back anymore, and my warm release sent her over the edge. She milked my dick, her pace slowing but continuing to squeeze and circle, moving up and down, in perfect sequence. It was fucking magical.

"I think... Oh, fuck, Jessa. I think I'm going to come again," I said, surprised by the second wave. Jessa was there for it all, using her strong leg muscles to spring up and down until she felt the second shot of warmth ooze inside of her.

We collapsed, our sweaty bodies clinging to one another. After a minute, Jessa rolled off of me, onto her back. Her chest rose and fell with each rapid breath.

"I just need to stay here like this for a minute," Jessa said as she relaxed her head back into the pillows. "It still feels good. It's so sensitive."

I wasn't about to argue with her because I wasn't ready to take my hands off of her beautiful naked body. She rolled to her side, facing away from me, and I let myself become the big to her little spoon. It felt like second nature, being that way with her. Our bodies relaxed into each other, our breathing in sync until we dozed off into a blissful, satisfied sleep.

Reliving that moment in Turks and Caicos is a double-edged sword. It helped push me over the edge, so that my erection is finally calming down. But it magnified that nagging feeling I've had since we made out tonight. I can't go on pretending I want to be just friends with Jessa anymore. I'm not sure suppressing my feelings is an option now, especially after tonight. Somehow, I feel like it's my chance.

But there is still Dillon. They always manage to work things out. Could this time be different?

8

Jessa

My mood is rank when I wake up the next morning. For a second, I can't remember why, but then, it hits me like a freight train. Dillon was a drunken asshole at my party last night. Not only was he super late, smelling of alcohol, but he tried to fight Greyson. So now, I know exactly why my mood is shit. I'm embarrassed as hell that my boyfriend—is that what he still is?—had to get kicked out of our condo by Monty.

Maybe my old ass just needs a shower. I smell of stale booze and body odor. I haul myself out of bed, praying the hot water changes my mood. Bex pops into the bathroom as I'm massaging shampoo into my hair.

"Hey, girl," she chirps.

I'm surprised she sounds so cheery, considering how much she drank last night.

"So, I may have been caught coming out of Monty's room last night. But nothing happened. And by nothing, I mean we had a hardcore make out session and may or may not have felt each other up."

I rip open the curtain and poke my head out, my hair still covered in suds. "Sounds like you had a much better night than me. Who caught you?"

"Well, I thought it was just Greyson at first, but Soren was in his room. They looked serious."

My stomach lurches at the sound of Greyson's name. How could I have forgotten that the two of us made out in the living room?

"Shit," I say, then immediately wish I hadn't.

Bex raises her eyebrows at me.

"I just remembered that I may have just killed my friendship with Greyson last night."

Bex blinks at me. "Uh, what are you talking about?"

I pull the shower curtain closed and begin to rinse my hair. "Well, after everyone left, we were alone in the living room. I was talking about how upset I was with Dillon and Greyson hugged me. And because I'm an idiot, I took that as an invitation to kiss him."

Bex gasps, then she rips the shower curtain open until she's staring at me through the plastic liner.

"Tell me everything!" she exclaims. She's practically vibrating with excitement. "You two haven't hooked up since sophomore year."

"Well, it was amazing." I pause, searching for the right words. "After I kissed him, it was like we couldn't stop. We were both so into it. His hands were everywhere. But then, he stopped it. Or, at least, I think he did. I felt so stupid, I didn't even give him a chance to explain. I just stormed off."

"Well, damn." Bex says, giving me back my privacy. I hear her sit down on the toilet seat. "You just walked away and haven't talked to him since?"

"Nope," I say. "We haven't even texted."

Someone knocks on the door and Bex opens it a crack.

I step out of the shower and wrap towels around my body and hair. "Sorry to intrude," comes Soren's voice through the crack, followed by a single red rose. "But this was just delivered."

Bex takes it and opens the door wider to let Soren in the bathroom. "Oh, Jessa, it must be from Dillon as an apology for being such an ass last night."

"Um, no," Soren interjects. "It's for you, Bex."

"What? For me?" Bex sounds skeptical, as if Soren would make that up. But her mouth widens into the brightest smile and she lifts rose to her nose, breathing in the scent.

"Well, open the note," I push, noticing the tiny envelope attached to the cellophane.

Bex rips open the envelope and reads the note out loud. *"Just because... You are beautiful."*

"That's so romantic," sighs Soren.

A pang of jealousy hits me like a wave—and just as quickly, guilt. I'm happy for Bex and she deserves to have someone make her feel special like this. As disgusted as I am with myself, I *want* that. I want someone who loves me enough to do little things like this to make me smile or because they're thinking about me. But this isn't about me, I remind myself. I force myself to focus on Bex.

"I'm so happy for you Bex. Who do you think it's from?"

She doesn't answer because our conversation is interrupted by an aggressive series of knocks on the front door. All three of us jump, startled by the noise.

"I'll get it," says Bex. She's nearly floating with happiness as she exits the bathroom.

Soren and I are too curious, so we follow Bex into the living room. Right when Bex gets to the door, the person on the other side starts pounding again.

"Wait," I say. "Do you think we should get the guys before we answer it? Because who the hell pounds on the door this early?"

"Speak of the devils," Soren says, and we turn to see Monty and Greyson amble into the living room. Both of them are rubbing their faces. Both of them are grumbling.

Satisfied by our safety in numbers, Bex swings open the door. There stands Dillon in the same outfit from last night, looking disheveled and annoyed. I back into the kitchen, not wanting him to see me.

"I need my fucking car keys," Dillon says flatly, barging into the condo. He scans the room for his keys and avoids eye contact with all of us.

"Well, good morning to you, too," Bex says cheerfully.

"Cut the crap, Bex. Where's Jessa?"

"I'm right here. Calm down." I leave the safety of the kitchen, realizing too late that it doesn't look great that I'm once again wearing nothing but a towel.

I feel everyone's eyes on me but after I give Bex a look, everyone scrambles in different directions. From the living room, multiple doors slam shut,—one louder than the others—and then it's just me and Dillon. The front door has been wide open since Dillon's arrival, so I close it before facing him with my arms crossed.

"My keys?" Dillon says, moving farther into the living room. He's making it very clear that he's annoyed, which sets my blood boiling again.

"Kind of demanding for someone who was an ass at his girlfriend's birthday party and then tried to pick a fight with her roommate in his own house." I'd wanted to be the reasonable one, but I'm so worked up that my tone comes out loud and aggressive.

"I'm *not* in the mood, Jessa. Just give me my keys. We can talk later," He grumbles, rubbing his temples.

"No! It's always later with you. We talk now!" I'm shouting but I don't care.

"What do you want me to say? Sorry I caught you and Greyson sneaking around?" He asks, glaring at me like he already knows the answer.

"What? How could you even think that? We're friends!"

"Well, that doesn't explain the diamond necklace he got for you. Or how he was dancing with you," Dillon argues.

"Again, it's because we're friends. We've been through this so many times. Let me ask you this—why were you late last night? And do not give me the same bull about having a tennis lesson. I could smell the liquor on you." I poke his chest with my index finger, punctuating each of the last seven words.

"I didn't lie," Dillon says. "I was at the club because I did have a lesson earlier. But I ran into my new doubles partner and we had a couple of drinks."

"Let me get this straight. Instead of showing up to your own girlfriend's birthday party on time, you chose to hang out with another girl. Then let me guess. You lost track of time?"

"Jessa," Dillon says, rolling his eyes. "She's just my new partner. It's important we get to know each other."

"Get to know each other? There's always an excuse with you, isn't there? You always find some way to justify why what you're doing is fine and what I'm doing is wrong. The whole jealousy act towards Greyson is getting old, especially when you pull things like having drinks with your doubles partner. Greyson has been in my life almost as long as you. He actually cares about me and what's going on in my life. You and I barely talk anymore, and when we do, you rarely ask about my classes or practice. You never even visited over the summer.

Even though you said you would multiple times. You don't give two shits about coming to my games, even when pointedly asked to attend. So, it's ridiculous, and frankly, pretty damn entitled, that you think you get to question every move I make with my *friend*," I say, spitting out the word friend so he understands that he hardly acts like a friend, let alone a boyfriend.

I can't stop. Now that I'm on a roll, I'm feeling braver. And honestly, more exhausted by the same old fights over and over again. There's no end in sight. Dillon will never be cool with Greyson. "You know what? I can't do this anymore, Dillon. It's over. You and I, we're done." I say with a finality I've never felt before with him. I really am done with this relationship. I think I've been done with it.

"Fine, whatever. Don't think I can't replace you. Now, give me the keys to my baby, so I can get the hell out of here."

I grab his keys from the coffee table and throw them at him.

"Now, take your *baby* and get your pretentious ass the fuck out of here." As if the air quotes I made with two fingers when I said 'baby' aren't enough to make Dillon angry, I can't resist adding, "And for the record, it's weird as hell that you think of your stupid, overrated car as your baby, but even weirder that you say it out loud! It's embarrassing."

He flips me the bird on his way out, which I return, then slam the door as soon as he's over the threshold. "What a fucking waste," I mutter and plop onto the couch.

"J?" Bex calls from our side of the condo. I hear her shuffle down the carpeted hallway and then she's sitting next to me, brushing my hair back from my face. "Are you okay?"

"I'm fine," I reply. "Dillon and I are over, which I'm sure you all heard. And to be totally honest, I feel surprisingly good about it. Maybe a bit embarrassed I let this drag on so long." Greyson and Monty join Bex and me in the living room, and I repeat what I'd shared with Bex. As I suspected, my shouting gave them a pretty good idea of what was happening, so I don't have to go into details.

"Can't say I'm surprised or upset about it," says Bex.

"Is it bad I feel relieved?" I say as I let out a deep sigh.

"Nope," Monty says. "It was time. Either you got rid of him, or I was going to be having a chat with you about it after the shit he pulled last night."

Greyson chimes in, "You're too good for him, Jessa."

"For what it's worth," Soren says, giving her brother a wink. "I agree. Never liked the guy."

I give a soft laugh. "Thanks, guys. Though I'm not gonna lie—I thought you all liked him. Now I wonder if I even know how you really feel about me."

"You're different. You know we love you," Soren pipes up. "But why were you with him for so long? Just out of curiosity."

"I don't know. I think probably because it was comfortable. Dillon was from home and then was just down the road at Wellington University (WU). Our relationship didn't take a lot of effort, which worked for me because I've always been so busy with basketball. He was just a constant, I guess." I shrug, unsure what else to say that can defend staying in this so-called relationship for so long. It was dumb to hang on to something deep down I knew wasn't right, but my world is full of unknowns. Staying with Dillon made me feel like one less thing fell into the unknown camp. But now, when I feel so relieved, I wish I'd done it sooner."

The conversation takes a big turn when Monty notices the rose Bex is still holding. Even I'd have thought she'd put it in water by now. It must have meant a lot more to her than I'd thought in the moment.

"Where'd that come from?" Monty asks.

There's a hint of jealousy in his tone, but he's trying to sound nonchalant. I'm not buying it. I smirk at him. "Bex got another gift from her secret admirer."

Monty gives a *"hmm"* in response, but says nothing else. I raise my eyebrows at Greyson but he only shrugs. He looks pale and has circles under his eyes, like he didn't sleep well. I hope it wasn't because of my drunk ass.

"Well, what do you say we do something to take care of these hangovers? And Jessa, maybe put some clothes on first" Greyson says, giving me a wink.

I look down and, sure enough, I'm still only wearing a towel. Which means... I lift my hand to my head and find the hair turban still in place. I'm sure it's dry by now. I'm going to look like a Troll when I remove it.

"Uh, be right back." I say, walking towards my room. I hear Greyson tell Soren she should pack up so he can take her to the airport after we eat. I'd forgotten she was leaving so soon. Probably a good thing, considering what a shit show the weekend was.

As I'm getting dressed and trying to force my hair back into shape, I can't help but wonder what Greyson thinks about me being suddenly single. It isn't lost on me that in every way Dillon really hasn't been a constant in my life, Greyson has been. I think that's why I kissed him last night. Why I felt so compelled to out of nowhere like that. Have I just been blocking out my true feelings for him? Like maybe, just maybe, I think of him as more than a friend? That would explain why I look at him so much. Monty's my friend but I don't stare at *his* muscular chest all the time. And Lord knows that Monty wears less clothes than I do around here.

I need to get my thoughts under control. And I definitely shouldn't act on anything until I'm sure about what I'm thinking and feeling. Plus, the season starts soon, and that means no boys, especially from the men's team. We do live together though, so that *would* make things a bit easier. Oh my God, I think. Look at me trying to rationalize things in my head already. I literally had a boyfriend until five minutes ago. *Pull it together, Jessa!* But as I leave my room to join the crew, I realize my hand has found its way to the necklace from Greyson again. I'm gripping it like a lifeline. Which, ironically, is how I sometimes think of Greyson. I let the necklace go, letting it drop into place just below my collarbone.

"So, what are we having to cure these hangovers?" I ask, my eyes searching for and finding Greyson, not seeing anyone else.

9
Greyson

"Jessa, we should talk," I say.

It's been nearly a week since her break up with Dillon. Since her jam-packed birthday weekend, it seems like we've been passing ships. Or has she been avoiding me? Either way, I can't stop thinking about our kiss and if it contributed to their breakup.

"Sure, Grey. What's up?" Jessa asks, grabbing a drink from the fridge before joining me in the living room.

"How are you doing? We've barely spoken since you and Dillon broke up. And we never really talked about dinner with your mom."

"I've been busy, that's all." Jessa sat on the opposite side of the room than me and is now fidgeting with the lid of her drink. She's not even looking at me.

"Sure," I say. Busy and acting strange."

"Nope, all good," she says, then changes the subject. "Plans for one of the last weekends of freedom?"

Basketball starts soon and with that comes the end to the freedom we've been enjoying. It also means there will likely be some killer parties this weekend.

"I'm hanging out with Julia Knox tonight," I say. I'm trying to be nonchalant but I'm silently kicking myself for blurting this news out so bluntly, but also for even accepting the invitation to begin with. It's only been a week since we made out, but Jessa hasn't acknowledged it once. With everything that's happened since, Jessa would have brought it up if it had meant anything. I'm sure of it. She's never shied away from talking to me before.

"Julia Knox, the tall blonde from the volleyball team?" Jessa asks, disbelief flickering across her face before she resumes the neutral expression she's had with me all week.

"Yeah, she's in my media class. We were talking the other day and learned we share a strong affinity for burgers," I say, laughing because it sounds so ridiculous out loud. "So we decided to check out that new burger place in town."

"You bonded over burgers," Jessa repeats. "And that is where you are taking her on a date?"

"It's not a date," I say evenly. I think back to my conversation with Julia, trying to remember her reaction to my suggestion. Does she think it's a date? "At least I don't think it is."

"Oh, well, it sounds like it's a date. Grey, seriously? You are so clueless sometimes," Jessa huffs.

"Well, what are you doing tonight?" I ask her, wanting to redirect the conversation to anything other than going out with Julia.

"Probably staying in. Still recovering from all of last weekend's excitement," she says. "Sounds like Monty and Bex are headed to the Hockey House party though."

"Yeah, a bunch of the guys are going, too. Which means that half the women's team will end up there."

Jessa shrugs. "Gotta get it out of their systems before practices start. They'll be either too exhausted or afraid of Coach to go to any parties after that."

She rises to her feet and is halfway across the living room when she says, "Don't do anything I wouldn't do tonight, Greyson."

The wink she gives me before leaving the room sends my mind spiraling. What the fuck did she mean by that? How did a conversation intended to be about her, and maybe end on us, turn to me? And why the hell did I even mention Julia? I'm used to telling Jessa this kind of thing, but this was not the normal Jessa response. She seemed confused by me going to eat with Julia, even a little mad. I continue to analyze our conversation, but I should probably get ready if I'm going to meet Julia on time. While I'm changing, I get a text from Julia.

Volleyball Julia: *Greyson, I'll swing by your place so we can ride to dinner together. I've got an errand to run your way before anyway.*

Me: *Sounds great. See you soon!*

Volleyball Julia: *Can't wait.* 😉

Well, the winky-smiley face might mean Julia thinks it's a date, I think. But before I can dissect the message behind it, there's a knock on my door.

"It's open," I say, spritzing cologne on my blue button-up.

"Oh, cologne and a nice shirt?" Oakes says, swinging the door open. "Who you trying to impress?"

"I'm not trying to impress anyone. Can't a guy look nice for himself?" I ask, a half-assed attempt at a joke, but for some reason the question puts me on the defense.

"Woah, dude. Take it easy," Oakes chides, his hands up in mock surrender. "I was kidding. But seriously, where are you off to? I was seeing if you were coming with us to the hockey party. But a button-up doesn't really fit the vibe."

"Nah, Julia Knox is on her way here. We're going to the new

burger joint."

"You're going on a date? Does Blakely know? What happened? You do remember she's available, right?" Oakes is genuinely confused and I feel bad for getting defensive. It's understandable, since I'd told him about what happened after Jessa's birthday party. Hell, I'm confused.

"It is *not* a date," I insist. "We're just hanging out, and yes, Jessa knows. She hasn't said a word about kissing me last weekend, so I assume she was too drunk to remember or too embarrassed to bring it up."

I'm not sure if I'm defending myself or Jessa. Every conversation feels like a trap today.

Oakes narrows his eyes at me but doesn't push the issue. "Have fun *hanging out* with Julia," he says, using air quotes on 'hanging out.' Then he backsteps his way out of my room and into his own, his eyes never leaving mine.

What a weirdo, I think, uncertain if I should laugh or be annoyed.

When the doorbell rings, I assume it's Julia and do my usual run-through, making sure I have my phone, wallet, and keys. By the time I get to the living room, Jessa has invited Julia in. My eyes fall on Jessa first, and damn, what a sight. Her hair is swept up in a messy bun, strands of silky hair framing her make-up free face. I want to reach out and tuck the loose hairs behind her ears for a clearer view of her eyes. Beside her, Julia is wearing shorts so short they barely cover her ass cheeks and a cropped tee. Her long blonde hair flows down her back and the subtle makeup enhances her high cheekbones and plump lips.

I snap out of it when Julia says my name, her voice low and airy. She steps closer to me and tosses her platinum hair over her shoulder. "Hey, Greyson. Ready to go? My mouth has been watering for a burger since we set this up!"

Jessa spins on her heel and gives me a wide-eyed look before turning away. "I should help Bex finish getting ready."

The Burger Shack is only a short drive away, but the parking lot is packed when Julia and I pull in. The mouthwatering scent of grilled meat hits us before we even make it inside. There's a short wait, so we make small talk until our table is ready, but once we're seated and have ordered, Julia says, "Greyson, can I ask you something?"

"Of course," I say, studying her face. Julia really is beautiful in a surfer girl kind of way. Any guy would kill to be in my seat right now, staring across the table into her ocean blue eyes.

"Do you have a thing for Jessa?" she asks, cutting to the point.

I hadn't expected that, so I stumble over my words in a way I know makes me sound like I'm avoiding answering the question directly. "What? Why would you think that? I mean, she's my best friend and a roommate... But we're not dating or anything."

"That doesn't exactly answer my question," Julia says, giving me a crooked smile. "You seemed distracted by her when I came over. It's okay if you have a thing for her but I just want to be sure about what this is." She waves her hand between us.

Julia barely knows me and felt the need to question me after seeing me with Jessa. It seems like honesty is best here.

"Geez, am I that obvious? I'm sorry, Julia. You're amazing and so many guys would kill to be in my seat tonight." I scrub my hand over my face, annoyed with myself. "Jessa and I have history, and she literally broke up with her boyfriend last weekend. Our timing has never been great. I think I'm still trying to figure out what all this means."

"Like I said, it's okay, Greyson. You're a great guy," Julia says, reaching across the table for my hand. "I was thrilled to try this place as an excuse to get together, but I understand. I'd rather know upfront, which is why I felt it best to just ask. Does Jessa know?"

"I mean, she should. But no, it isn't like I've been direct about it. I've never wanted to risk our friendship, even when she and Dillon were apart. Plus, our season is starting up, which makes things complicated." I'm oversharing, but Julia is easy to talk to and doesn't seem to mind.

Our food arrives and after the server refills our drinks, Julia looks at me sternly across the table.

"Greyson, you need to tell Jessa. It's not fair to either of you, especially if there's any chance she feels the same way." Julia squeezes ketchup on her plate and waits for me to speak.

I reach for the ketchup bottle, giving myself time to think before I respond. I'm not sure how Jessa doesn't see how I feel when other people clearly do. Julia had to be in a room with me and Jessa for two minutes to pick up on it. I pick up my burger and take a giant bite. Damn, this is delicious. Wiping my mouth with a napkin, I watch Julia try hers. She chews and makes a satisfying hum.

"It's good, huh?" I laugh.

"Don't think this changes the subject," Julia scolds, gesturing at me, using her burger like a pointer. "But yes, this burger is amazing."

"Alright," I say. "I know I need to do or say something but I'm not sure what yet. I think I need to think on it more. But thanks, Julia. I really appreciate talking about it with you."

"I think I'd make a pretty good wingman," Julia says with a laugh.

"Don't get carried away now," I joke, grinning at her.

After we've finished eating, Julia and I decide to call it a night. I drop her at her car and head into the condo.

"Hello? Jessa? Are you here?"

There's no sign of her in the living room or kitchen, but her bedroom door is open a crack. I knock and the door pushes open further. No Jessa, but her room looks like it was hit by a tornado. Clothes cover the bed and shoes are thrown all over the floor. I've lived with her and Collins long enough to know they have fashion shows to figure out what to wear for a night out. But Jessa had said she was staying in.

When we first moved into the condo, we'd shared our locations with one another. I'd kind of forgotten about it until now, but peek at the app to see Jessa, Collins, and Oakes are at the Hockey House party. I might as well head over there rather than feeling sorry for myself and overthinking things at home. Before I leave, I text all three of them, letting them know I'm on my way.

I'm in my Jeep when I check my messages. No response from any of my roommates, so I head to the party anyway and somehow find a spot to park on the already packed street.

As soon as I walk into the Hockey House. I'm met with deafening music, loud cheers from a game of beer pong, and the Hockey House's trademark smell of stale beer and body odor. Even if I hadn't checked her location, I'd know Jessa was here the second I walked in. I can feel her supercharged energy. And I instantly sense something isn't right.

As I move through the main room of the house, I spot her. Jessa wears a pink crop top, showing off her toned abs, and denim shorts that ride high on her strong legs.

Almost everyone is watching her, and it's not just because she's gorgeous. It's because everyone knows Jessa Blakely is focused and *always* in control. This girl is wild. She's throwing her arms up to the music, her sad excuse of a shirt doing nothing to cover her midriff. She's whipping her hair back and forth. No, this girl is acting nothing at all like Jessa Blakely. And I don't like it. Jessa is always fun but she never lets her guard down like this. I move closer to where she's dancing and see her eyes are glassy and unfocused. My first thought is, *Wow, Jessa is druuuunnnkkk.* My second is, *Where the hell are Collins and Oakes?* My third thought as I glance around at the other people crammed into the Hockey House is, *Three-quarters of the collective HU basketball teams are here. Why is* no one *looking out for her? She's always looking out for them, and they* know *this is not how she acts.* I glare at several of Jessa's teammates as I approach her.

"*Heeeey,* Greyson!" Jessa's slurring her words and waving her hand like an excited toddler. "See? I know how to relax and let loose."

I have no idea what she means by that, but I know better than to try to get clarity from a drunk person. "Hey, Jessa. Where's Collins?" I ask, and refrain from adding, *because I need to have words with her.*

Jessa shrugs and almost falls down from the movement. "Probably sneaking around somewhere with Monty," she says through giggles, then smacks her hand over her mouth until a loud hiccup escapes. Then she drops her hand and resumes her giggling and dancing. Holy shit. This is not going to be easy. I'm going to kill Collins and Oakes.

"Jessa," I say, using a soothing tone in hopes it'll coax her down from the pool table she's now standing on. "How about you come down and tell me about your night?"

She scowls at me. "Where's blondie-long-legs you left the house with?"

If I didn't know better, I'd think she was jealous. But that doesn't track with her behavior this week. I furrow my brows and extend my hand up to her again, silently beckoning her to come down off the pool table before she causes a scene.

"You're mad at me, aren't you, Greyson?" Jessa pouts, crossing her arms. "Nope, not mad."

Her pout pulls into a snarl. "Well, go babysit someone else. I'm sure blondie-long-legs is looking for you. And Sky and I are having fun." Jessa wraps her arm around the waist of Sky Butler, a junior on the men's team.

Butler drapes his arm around Jessa, giving her a sleazy smile and his full attention. Butler's known for being a player and I hate that he's touching her. Even more that she's touching him back.

"Not a good idea, Jessa." I say, glaring at Butler. "Remember our coaches' rules? The season is coming up."

Butler doesn't seem concerned about rule-breaking and leans closer toward Jessa, giving me a fuck-off nod. "I've got her, bro. Coach isn't coming after me. I'm just taking care of everyone's favorite basketball star."

I'm beyond seething.

"Butler, it's not Coach you should be worried about," I say, keeping my voice low and calm. I reach for Jessa's hand and pull her away from Butler. "Jessa, it's time to come down from there."

Jessa yanks her hand away from me. "Stop telling me what to do."

The end of her sentence comes out sloppily because she's lost her balance, catching her heel in the pocket of the pool table. My arms come up instinctively to catch her, watching her mouth open in surprise as she falls, in slow motion, into my arms. I look down at her, flooded with relief. She feels good in my arms and is now one step closer to leaving with me, one step further from becoming another notch in Butler's headboard.

Jessa fights against my hold for a second until she realizes she needs me for balance. When her hand hooks my bicep, the spark from her skin against mine makes us both pause and stare at each other. We hold eye contact until Jessa seems to catch herself. She looks away and calls for Butler to help her back up on the table. He grins and moves toward us.

I'm angry. At Jessa. At myself. But most of all, at Butler for being so willing to help Jessa act like someone she isn't. When he reaches for Jessa, I shove him hard. "Fuck off," I bark at him.

Before he can grab Jessa again, I scoop her up and throw her over my shoulder in a fireman's carry. Jessa flails her limbs, nearly elbowing me in the face before I grab the offending arm and hold it still. She's yelling unintelligible words as I haul her out of the house with everyone watching. Man, Jessa is going to be embarrassed when she hears about this later. I deposit her on the backseat of my Jeep and slam the door shut before getting in the driver's seat.

"For fuck's sake!" she yells, glaring at me in the rearview mirror, "What are you doing? How could you embarrass me like that? I don't need a knight in shining armor, you know."

I can't help but smirk at her reflection. "A knight in shining armor, I don't know—Sir Hastings of Hills has a nice ring to it, don't you think?"

Jessa gives me a death stare. But all I can think as she tries to shoot daggers at me with her green eyes is how beautiful she is. She mumbles things under her breath until she eventually passes out, soft snores audible from the backseat as I drive across town. When I pull into the driveway and kill the engine, I turn in my seat to look at her. She looks so peaceful and serene as she lays there. Now that I'm not battling a strong-willed drunken Jessa, the worry creeps back in. I rest my head against the steering wheel and let the questions scroll through my head again. Why did she get so drunk at the party? This is not the confident, high-strung girl who's become my best friend over the last four years. She has so much on the line—why would she risk it like this? And where the hell was Collins? They are usually inseparable.

After a few minutes, I sigh and begin the process of getting her inside. Jessa's deadweight but I wrap her arms around my neck and make my way inside, not hating the way she feels against me. As I struggle to unlock our door she opens an eye and directs it at me before closing it again. "Why don't you want to kiss me?" she mumbles.

"Jessa," I say, finally turning the lock and walking inside. But before I can finish my sentence, I hear her soft snores and feel that she's gone limp again in my arms.

"I want to kiss you more than anything," I whisper, setting her on her bed.

I'd feel like a snoop going through Jessa's drawers, so instead of digging for pajamas, I jog to my room and grab a clean t-shirt. When I return to her room, she's sprawled out on top of her comforter but hasn't woken. Careful not to disturb her, I pull the crop top over her head to find she's wearing her go-to lucky sports bra. It makes me smile. Jessa is one of the only girls I know who would go to a party with athletic undergarments. I pull the oversized t-shirt over her head before pulling down her denim cut-offs, careful not to look at her body, and then tuck her under the covers. Her sweet face looks peaceful, nothing at all like the girl who'd had nothing but anger for me when I'd been carrying her out of the Hockey House.

"Love you, Jessa," I whisper and kiss the top of her head.

I'm closing the door to her bedroom when I hear her muffled, "Love you, Grey." I let the door click shut.

As I walk back to the living room, I hear the front door open. Collins sprints inside followed by Oakes. "Is she here?" Collins asks, her voice breathless and her words tumbling out unevenly. "I can't find Jessa. She's not answering her phone. I shouldn't have left her, but she seemed fine with the guys she was with. What if something happened to her?"

"Collins!" I say, my voice rising to talk over her. I brace her by the shoulders and force her to look at me. "Get a grip! She's in bed, passed out."

"Oh, thank God" she says. "I'm so relieved. Wait, what are you doing home? I thought you had a date?"

"It ended early. I tracked your phones to the Hockey House, but when I got there, I only saw Jessa. She and Butler had their hands all over each other."

Collins's eyes widen. "You can't be serious? Butler? Jessa would never!"

"Maybe Jessa we know wouldn't but the 'relaxed-let loose-say yes to trying new things-Jessa' apparently does," I say, my tone accusing. "I caught her just as she was falling off the pool table."

"Oh my God! I'm such a bad friend. I can't believe I left her, but she was so sure it was fine," Collins says through hiccups as tears pool in her eyes.

"Where were you?" I ask, anger boiling up, seeing a drunken Jessa wobbling on the pool table with Butler. *I'm gonna kill him*, I vow to myself.

"Come on, man. It's not her fault," Oakes says. "I'm the one who assured her Jessa would be fine."

Oakes turns to Collins, putting his hand on her shoulder and wiping tears from her face. "You are not Jessa's babysitter."

I watch the two of them, noting how Oakes's thumb strokes Collins's over their clasped hands. This seems more serious than what they've both claimed. I wonder if Oakes told her he was her secret admirer.

"Collins, I'm sorry," I say and sit on the couch, dropping my face into my hands. "I shouldn't be blaming you. Something snapped in me when I saw Jessa on that pool table with Butler. It was easier blaming you than it was to believe Jessa has shut me out." I take a deep breath and look up at my roommates staring at me.

"What's going on with you two? Before she fell, Jessa was going on about how you were probably sneaking around somewhere with each other," I say, pointing at their joined hands. "I thought she was just spouting off crap, but there's something to that, isn't there?"

Oakes and Collins pull apart but neither answer. Or look at me.

"I'm going to go check on Jessa," Collins says, walking towards her and Jessa's side of the condo.

Jessa

I wake up with a pounding head and a dry mouth. Thank goodness for the blackout curtains blocking the sunlight from entering my bedroom. I reach for my water bottle on my nightstand and gulp the cool water. Why don't I remember anything? I look down and see I'm wearing one of Greyson's well-worn high school basketball t-shirts. God, it smells like him, I think, holding a fistful of the soft fabric to my nose. How did I get into this shirt and into my own bed anyway? The last thing I remember is dancing with Butler at the Hockey House party. I put my head in my palm. Shit. I was all over Butler at the party and I'm pretty sure I almost fell off the pool table.

"Oh, God," I mutter, as the memories piece themselves together. Greyson hauled me out tossed over his shoulder. I vaguely remember seeing a blur of faces as we were leaving. My stomach clenches. I think I'm gonna be sick.

"Jessa?" I hear Bex outside of my door.

"Come in here," I demand. "And close the door."

Bex flips on the light and crawls into my bed with me. She looks worried.

"You look like shit," she says.

I grunt in response. I feel like shit. So I can only imagine what I look like.

"What happened last night? I was freaking out, thinking we lost you. When Oakes and I got home, you were already asleep and Greyson was ready to murder me and Monty," Bex says, staring hard at me.

I squirm under her scrutiny. "Well, if he was ready to murder you two, he's for sure pissed at me. Fairly sure Grey had to pry me off Butler." I groan and fall back onto my pillow, holding the blankets over my face.

"Sky Butler? Greyson mentioned him last night, but I refused to believe it."

"Well, believe it. I'm an embarrassment. How pissed was Greyson?" I ask, not sure I want to know.

"Pretty mad. Though I'm not sure who he was mad at exactly. I mean, he was pissed at me for leaving you and then he apologized for being pissed at me. But he saw me and Monty holding hands when we got home. Then Monty defended me to Greyson, which made Greyson question what we were doing."

"Wait, wait, wait! What? Are you and Monty...?" I ask, flabbergasted.

"I don't know. I mean, we've had some moments. I've learned from his help that he's just so sweet." Bex's cheeks are pink, like she's the one who should be embarrassed right now. But at least she wasn't hanging all over a player for the men's team in front of everyone.

This all makes so much sense. How could I not have seen it was more than the 'practice' for Bex to get comfortable with romantic experiences. "Do you have feelings for him?" I ask her, keeping my tone gentle and nonjudgmental.

"I don't know. Maybe? This is fun, whatever it is." Bex shrugs.

"Just be careful," I caution, worries about Bex's feelings getting hurt in the long run. "Monty is a great guy, but he's always been pretty affectionate and flirty."

"He is," Bex agrees. "But I think we all assumed that meant something more than it really was."

"Just be careful, Bex." I say again.

There's a knock on my door, and Bex and I turn to see Greyson pop his head in. When he sees I'm awake, he pushes the door open all the way and comes in. He's carrying a glass of water, a steaming mug, and two small brown pills. He looks sheepish when he glances at Bex. "Sorry to interrupt. I was just checking in on Jessa."

"No worries," Bex says. "I have to get ready to fill in at yoga for another instructor anyway."

She leans in to hug me before she goes. "Good luck," she whispers.

Greyson closes the door with his foot behind her. Then he turns to me and says, "Thought you might need some supplies to get you started today. Here's water,—with a bendy straw because I know you think it tastes better with one—coffee, and ibuprofen."

He's being friendly, but I can't read his mood, and that has me on edge. His eyes don't leave me as I wash down the pills with the ice water. I sip the coffee, wrapping my hands around the warm mug, then close my eyes with a sigh.

"Listen," I start at the same time Grey says, "Jessa."

We both pause and stare at each other. I suddenly feel shy wearing only Greyson's t-shirt. I pull the blankets up but it does nothing to stop feeling overexposed from his intense gaze.

"Jessa," he says again. "What's going on with you?"

"What's going on with me? What's that supposed to mean?" I ask, defensiveness overshadowing the embarrassment I was feeling moments before.

"For starters, last night was very unlike you. You were hanging all over Butler. For Christ's sake, J, Butler has more notches in his bedpost than anyone we know. Not only could you have become another meaningless notch, but you could have hurt yourself falling off the damn pool table. I've never seen you that drunk. You could barely function. That isn't you." He looks disappointed and shakes his head.

"Maybe this *is* the new me. You know I wanted to let loose more this year." I don't admit this isn't exactly what I'd had in mind with letting loose more.

"At the expense of everything you've worked for the last three years?" He asks pointedly.

"God, you sound like my mother." I say, knowing it's a low blow but annoyed enough not to care.

"That's not fair, Jessa. I'm your best friend. But you're not talking to me about any of this and I can't figure out why. You've barely spoken to me since your birthday party. We kissed, do you remember that? And you wanted me to kiss you last night, even after I found you falling all over one of my teammates. I don't even know what to think at this point. I'm hurt. I'm angry. I'm confused." His frustration is palpable and his jaw clenches and unclenches as he waits for me to respond.

"Well, you're the one who went out with the blonde bombshell last night." I blurt out, not really thinking about how it sounds. All I know is I'm hurt. I've been hurt since he rejected me on my birthday.

But when I look at Greyson, my best friend in the whole world, he looks defeated. I don't deserve him. He doesn't deserve me treating him like shit. I've done a shitty job of showing him how much I value his friendship. And he's right. Last night isn't who I am. The way he's looking at me makes me wonder if I've really fucked things up between us. That thought is followed by the thought of *us*—is *us* what I want? Is that why I've been acting like a crazy person?

"Jessa, my *date*," he says, using air quotes, "was a bust. Julia picked up vibes between us. She's the one who encouraged me to come home early to talk to you. When you weren't here, I couldn't just wait around for you to get back. I went looking for you. I wanted to tell you how I feel."

"How you feel?" I repeat, my heart hammering. I set the mug on my nightstand before my shaking hands spill coffee all over my bed.

Greyson sits on the edge of my bed and stares into my eyes. "You kissed me and then broke up with Dillon the next day. There was no mention of it afterwards. I was giving you time to process everything, but then I saw you with Butler. It made me so angry. I think I was a little jealous. Well, maybe a lot jealous. But I was also concerned. I just want you to be safe and happy."

My eyes sting with tears and my breath comes out audibly shaky. He's being so open. I owe him the same. "I hated seeing you leave with Julia. I know it's selfish of me because you deserve someone amazing. But damn, if that didn't make me feel something... Hurt? Jealousy? Both? I don't know."

Frustrated with myself, I shake my head and feel a tear slip down my cheek.

"I don't want to lose you," I say a minute later.

Grey presses his hand to my cheek and wipes the stray tear away with his thumb. "It's painful when we don't talk to each other. It doesn't feel right. We've always had the kind of friendship where we can be honest with each other. That's what makes our friendship so strong. And I hope you know, you could never lose me, J."

He keeps saying that word—*friendship*. One minute we're talking about feeling jealous, then he brings it back to friendship. Well, that's a sign if there ever was one. I think I misunderstood what he was saying. His feelings of jealousy and anger are because he's protective of our friendship. Nothing more.

I take his hand and squeeze. My smile is half-hearted but I'm sincere when I say, "You're right. Our friendship is too important to leave each other hanging. I promise to talk to you more about what I'm thinking and feeling. I appreciate you always looking out for me, Grey." He squeezes my hand and returns my smile before leaning in for a hug. I breathe in his scent. Damn, why does he always smell so good?

"Now, let's get you over this hangover," Grey says with a bit too much energy as he pulls away and stands next to my bed. "I think it's time for some fried apps, the couch, and mindless TV."

Whoa, I think. I can't believe he's letting me off that easily about Butler.

By the time Bex gets home the living room smells like fried food and regret.

The open cartons spread across the coffee table—wings, fries, and all things breaded—are dripping onto napkins that are already losing the battle. The TV is on low, a rerun playing purely for noise.

I'm sitting cross-legged on the floor, hoodie pulled over my knees, clutching a sports drink like it's a lifeline. My head still throbs, every sound slightly too loud, every light a little too bright.

Across from me, Greyson leans back on the couch, one ankle resting on his knee, methodically eating fries like he isn't the reason my chest feels tight.

"Can we all agree," Bex says, avoiding our greasy feast and looking at Oakes, "that last night was a disaster?"

Jessa groans. "Please don't recap. It won't happen again."

"I hope at least some of it doesn't happen again," says Oakes, eyes darting to Greyson with irritation.

"I owe you and Collins an apology," Greyson says, his jaw tightening at the memory of Jessa with Butler. "I was worried about Jessa but you are not responsible for her."

"No one is responsible for me, except me," I jump in defensively and then force myself to calm and continue, "but thank you for getting me out of there and home safe."

He rescued you, my brain supplies unhelpfully. Hauled you out of that party. Drove you home. Put you to bed.

I take a long pull from the bottle, averting eye contact.

"So," Bex continues, a hint of hesitation in her voice, "sounds like we are all good?"

Heat creeps up Jessa's neck as she looks at Greyson. "Yup, all good."

Greyson sets his food down carefully and gives a sheepish smile to Bex. "All good."

The room goes quiet for half a second too long.

Bex clears her throat. "Okay! Emotional honesty—bold choice."

Jessa shifts, suddenly aware of how close Greyson's knee is to her shoulder. Of the fact that he hasn't looked away yet.

The silence stretches, thick and uncomfortable.

Our phones ding at the same time. We all check our messages and in perfect sync say, "Coach." Well crap, it's never a good sign when you get a text from your coach saying your first practice of the season starts with a joint meeting with the men's team. Greyson and Monty's texts say the same.

The next day, the four of us walk over to the Blakely Center, home to Hills basketball and one of the most recognized athletic venues in America. On the way, we speculate about why a joint meeting was called and what it could be about. Monty thinks it's geared toward budget cuts and leveraging both teams for practice players. Bex thinks it's to announce a new program donor. But Greyson and I aren't as optimistic. We think it has to do with the fact that word got out that a majority of both teams were at the Hockey House party. After we left, campus police shut the party down because of noise complaints. Even though basketball players weren't the only athletes who attended, our coaches have high expectations for how we present ourselves both on and off the court, year round.

The speculation continues with our respective teams as we lug our practice gear into the locker room and restock the space for the season. I'm only half paying attention to the conversation. When we'd entered the Blakely Center, Sky Butler was standing there. Greyson hadn't tried to hold back his contempt and mean-mugged Butler until he looked away. It makes me cringe to know I'm the cause of any drama.

But by the time Bex and I take seats towards the front, I'm feeling rejuvenated. It's so nice to be back in this space, sitting amongst my teammates. The freshmen seem nervous, and Bex and I do our best to reassure them. But the second I see Coach Hayden Morris walk onto the court, my positivity dissolves. It's obvious by her 6'4 athletic frame that she is irritated. Her gate is sharper and faster than usual, which is saying a lot because Coach Morris is always sharp and fast. She stops in front of the two teams, but her posture is tense. There's none of the upbeat enthusiasm from the other first practices of the season I've been part of. Coach Morris is cold and quiet, already wearing her whistle, and keeps staring down at her clipboard.

On her left is Coach Benjamin Hayes. He's only slightly taller than Coach Morris at 6'5 but despite the muscles popping out of his blue polo, Coach Hayes looks as scary as a puppy dog next to the women's coach. His hair is standing up all over the place because he's running his hands through it every thirty seconds. My guess is if there's a Good Cop / Bad Cop theme of the meeting, Coach Hayes is the Good Cop.

All players are silent as the rest of the coaching staff trails in and takes seats in front of the teams. There's no need for an official call to order because not one of us speaks or dares look away from Coach Morris or Hayes. It's so quiet you can hear the tiniest squeak of tennis shoes in the mostly empty arena. Our two teams take up only a small portion of two sections.

Coach Morris puffs her cheeks, exhaling before stealing a glance at Coach Hayes. He nods, his mouth set in a thin line. Then Coach Morris lifts her head and projects her voice at the crowd of nervous basketball players in front of her.

"I'm sure you're wondering why we've called this meeting today. There are several reasons. The first of which I'm sure you're aware," Coach Morris clips, scowling at her clipboard. "Coach Hayes and I were contacted by campus security when the party at 724 Ellis Drive was shut down due to a noise complaint the other night."

Greyson and I make brief eye contact. Yep, that's the Hockey House address. This is one of those times I didn't want to be right. "Athletics was contacted because it's a house occupied by hockey players and had mostly other athletes present. To our disappointment, we also learned that, of those HU athletes, most of the basketball program was present."

Coach Hayes jumps in. "You can imagine how disappointed we were to learn that not only was most of the program present, but it was reported that nearly all of you were under the influence of alcohol. Now, we recognize many of you are of legal drinking age, though some are not," he says as he makes pointed eye contact with the freshman and sophomore players on both teams. "Whether it's legal or not, Coach Morris and I are incredibly disappointed to hear that this is how you've chosen to represent the HU basketball program."

They go on to talk about how much time and energy it takes to shift the narrative and reputation of the program when things like this happen. Coach Morris stresses that it will take all of us to do so. Moving forward, she and Coach Hayes expect us to hold each other accountable, not just at practice, but in our studies and *all* extracurricular activities.

We're lectured on the importance of being productive members of the Big Horn community. As a consequence, we're informed we'll be engaging in the community through volunteerism to show we're more than the drunken party animals we acted like over the weekend.

"This initiative will be led by your team captains—Monty Oakes and Jessa Blakely," Coach Morris states.

Lucky me. Not that I don't love leading the women's team, but not like this. Monty's somber expression makes me believe he feels the same way. None of us have time for this. Greyson shoots me a look and I see the same frustration in his eyes. He knows as well as I do that team morale will plummet with this punishment. Those who didn't attend the party will hold it against those of us who did. And I'm sure many will point their finger at me, considering how I was acting at the party. The shame I felt yesterday morning radiates through me.

"Next on the agenda," bellows Coach Morris, interrupting my thoughts. She glances up from her clipboard with a pinched expression. "We want to remind you of the 'no fraternizing' rule between teams, especially when in season. Yes, we expect you all to work together to get our reputation of excellence restored, but dating and engaging in other distracting behaviors is prohibited. We will, however, be working to build our relationships in a healthy and positive way. In order to challenge our limits, Coach Hayes and I will be assigning lifting partners. This will also help spread out the use of the weight room."

Coach Morris receives a collective groan and Coach Hayes raises his voice to talk over our murmurings. "Coach Morris and I have been working with the strength and endurance coaches to create a promising program for our athletes. The benefits and potential gains far outweigh what we've been doing the last couple of years." He continues to explain that our assigned partners and small groups are posted outside the coaches' offices.

Okay, I don't mind working out with the guys, but boy do I hope I'm not stuck with Butler. For his sake and mine, I think, glancing at Grey again.

"Finally," Coach Hayes says, "in an effort to bring our teams together, you will serve your punishment for your collective party behavior at a joint practice today with team conditioning."

Another collective groan echoes throughout the space. Neither coach seems phased. "You have thirty minutes to change and get back here, ready to work," Coach Morris instructs.

"You're on the clock," adds Coach Hayes. "See you in thirty."

We break and some of the players head to the locker rooms while others roam toward the offices to see their lifting partners. A few stand around talking in groups, complaining about the unfairness. Bex and I wait for Greyson and Monty to make their way down from their seats. Monty and I share we feel somewhat relieved, but also wonder why as captains we weren't in the loop on any of it. Even the coaches agenda items that didn't seem to be connected to the party at all, like the strength and conditioning partners.

"Well," I say, "The consequences could have been worse. I guess we just need to make the most out of the opportunity. Give it our all and try to build up the team connection Coach Morris and Coach Hayes were talking about."

"For sure," Monty agrees. He looks at the rest of us. "Should we go see who we got paired with for lifting sessions?"

"Yep. Onward!" I say, trying to sound positive but internally dreading the upcoming conditioning and endurance practice. We follow the crowd to the hallway near the coaches' offices. When I get close enough to the list, I freeze. I'd assumed they'd pair the captains together, but no such luck. I'm not with Monty. I'm with Sky Butler. Karma wastes no time, does it?

"Oh, hell no," comes a voice over my shoulder. I turn to see Greyson staring at my name next to Butlers. He's silent but his jaw clenches as he searches for his partner's name and retreats to the locker room. I follow Greyson's name to see he's paired with Hazel Nova, a stunningly beautiful starting guard.

Monty steps up to see he's paired with Char Jones, our ever athletic and shy starting point guard. He whistles low under his breath when he sees who I'm with, then jogs toward the locker room after Greyson. Hopefully to stop Grey before he does something stupid.

Bex grabs my arm and squeezes it reassuringly. "It will work itself out," she promises. "I've got Bryce Anders and he's friends with Butler, so maybe we can team up."

I give her a look that tells her I don't buy into her 'it will work itself out' theory. There's no time to talk about it now. We only have a couple of minutes left to get ready for practice, so we head to our locker room.

It's impressive, and somewhat humbling, to stand with both

teams on the court. Men and women together, HU has some of the most talented basketball players in the country and I'm proud to be one of them. We wait anxiously on the baseline with our Punishment Partners aka lifting partners, and when given direction, we take turns running killers until our coaches get bored. After twenty minutes, it's obvious who's been doing conditioning and endurance training in the off-season. Butler is winded and red-faced, but I'm hanging in there. For a moment, I sing my praises to Lauren Blakely for having no heart over the summer. But as we're preparing to go another round of killers, I'm overjoyed when I hear Coach Morris take pity on us. She tells us to grab a drink, then shoot ten free throws each followed by sprints for the collective misses. Coach Morris acts like this is a privilege since it gives us a break from the full running exercise. But that's yet to be determined. It could be worse if Butler can't shoot today.

Butler misses six of his first seven shots but sinks the last three. Another shout out to my mother when I make nine out of ten. Guess all that summer practice kept me sharp. Not that it's keeping me off the line running eight sprints, thanks to Butler and his off-shooting.

I guess I should be grateful we're even allowed to touch a basketball today. I'd expected our punishment to be constant running, but free throws are a nice break. I think this too soon, though, because Coach Haye's blows her whistle and instructs us to line up on the baseline again. The pattern of punishment continues for an hour until our coaches pause their frustration to show mercy. They give us a short break and we all collapse on the floor. I'm stretching when Coach Hayes blows her whistle again and announces that we get to spend the next hour in the weight room.

Welcome to basketball season.

I feel fatigued, and I'm socially and emotionally drained from having to string together words with Butler. I'm not so sure how he attracts so many women when he can't carry a conversation. Aside from his looks, that is. It's understandable that women are drawn to his olive skin, muscular body, thick hair, and deep brown eyes. But the second he opens his mouth, all that physical appeal goes out the window.

In the locker room, I'm taking a few minutes to recover before showering. Most of the team has headed home for the night, but I hear Hazel and Char chatting it up over the single shower stalls. Monty and Greyson are usually the last in the weight room. Tonight was no exception, even after the tough conditioning earlier. This required Hazel and Char to stay as well. From the sounds of their conversation, they don't mind.

"Talk about getting the pick of partners," Char gushes to Hazel. "Oakes and Hastings are two of the hottest guys on the team. Did you see Hastings's little brother is on the team too? He's just as adorable. His name is Corden."

Hazel squeals in agreement, which causes me to roll my eyes. How old is she? Twelve? Gross. Of course, Monty and Greyson would have some of my teammates drooling over them. Coach may have made it clear that fraternization wasn't okay, but I think she actually made it more appealing by making it forbidden.

"I'm pretty sure they are all three single and ready to mingle," Hazel adds, earning another eye roll from me. "Greyson, the older Hastings, wouldn't stop glaring at Butler though. It was a little weird. I thought when Butler was spotting Jessa on the bar, I was going to have to call for help to stop Greyson from attacking him."

"Yikes," Char says.

I step under the warm water and close my eyes, blocking out the rest of Char and Hazel's conversation. I'd hoped Greyson would move on from his jealousy over Butler, but life seems to be ensuring he doesn't. Why couldn't I have been paired with anyone else? Literally *anyone* would have been better. The water feels so good on my tired body, but I force myself to turn off the water and get dressed. My energy level is so low, I hardly dry my hair, so when I'm leaving the locker room, I have watermarks running down my shirt. Greyson is lying on the ground with his head propped up on his bag, eyes closed. I'm tempted to jump on him to scare him awake but that requires energy I just don't have. Instead, I kick the heel of his shoe with my toe until his eyes flutter open and land on me.

It takes a minute before Greyson rolls into a standing position and grabs his bag. Jerking his head in the direction of the door he says, "Let's go."

We're quiet on the walk home. I'm processing the first day back with our teams on the court. I wonder what Greyson's thinking about, but he doesn't hold out long. We're about halfway home when he clears his throat. "So, about Butler..."

"What about him?" I ask. Not only am I physically exhausted, but I feel like I can't escape the emotional roller coaster ride I've been on lately. The last thing I want to do right now is talk about Butler. But I knew Greyson wouldn't be able to resist bringing him up.

"I had a chat with him."

"About?"

"About keeping his hands to himself. About showing up to put the work in and not distracting you from your goals. Don't worry, Oakes and I will keep him in line," Greyson finishes reassuringly.

"I really think he's harmless," I interject.

"Maybe so, but I'm not taking any chances with you... I mean— him," Greyson says.

It's hard to be annoyed when he says things like that. Greyson may be overprotective at times, but his heart is always in the right place.

"On another note," I say with a sly smile. "I overheard Hazel and Char in the showers tonight gushing over you and Monty."

"Is that right?" Greyson's grin is cocky. "Yeah, we're probably the reason Coach keeps emphasizing the no dating within the program rule."

He's joking but it still stings for some reason. "Greyson, be serious. Don't lead them on. I know you and Monty are giant flirts, but can you take the advice you gave Butler and keep your head in the game?"

"Aye, aye captain," Grey says and salutes me with a smile.

It's hard not to be charmed by Greyson's silly moods, but there's a tinge of jealousy creeping in. What does Greyson think about Hazel or Char? *Will* he flirt with them? And Monty—will he act the same with them that he does with Bex? I'll kill him if he hurts her. The last thing I want to deal with this season is drama, especially cat fights or my friend's broken heart.

Or, if I'm being honest, my own broken heart.

11

Greyson

I can't believe we're only a week away from our home opener. Despite the first day of practice being a bit rocky, things couldn't be going better. Our team dynamic is better than I'd expected, our coaches are happy with our behavior on and off the court, and there's been no funny business with Butler. I've barely seen Jessa the last couple of weeks, except for the occasional joint practice or when our lifting schedules overlap. She's taking her role as Captain seriously and has been putting in extra training time, both to set a good example and to appease her mother. Oakes and Collins have become my personal romantic comedy reality show. Over the last few weeks, Collins "secret admirer" has committed hard. She's received a singing telegram at practice, a fruit bouquet at the condo, and so many sweet love notes inside her textbooks that I've lost count. She has no clue it's Oakes, which makes me question her detective skills. I overheard her telling some of her teammates that it's starting to freak her out. Only a stalker could know where and when to find her all the time, she'd said. Hard to say I blame her for feeling like that. I need to tell Oakes to back off or reveal his identity before Collins tells her parents and they hire her a bodyguard or something. While Collins is being mysteriously "courted" by a "stranger," she and Oakes seem to be having their own secret courtship going on. Except, they're not doing a great job of covering their tracks. On more than one occasion, I've caught one or the other leaving the other person's bedroom at weird times of night or early morning when they think no one will notice. I'm also pretty sure I've seen a few stolen kisses when they think they're alone in the living room or if my back is turned. Every time I try to catch them out in the open, they pull apart too fast. Maybe it's all in my head though.

Romance just seems to be in the air. Unless, of course, you count the air around me and Jessa. I'd thought admitting we were both jealous the night of the Hockey House party would lead us down a path of seeing what else we could be. But I'm starting to think she isn't at all interested. Maybe she's not even busy all the time. She's just avoiding me. Oake's voice breaks through my thoughts. "I'm headed out, you good man?"

"Yeah. I'll head home shortly."

I look around and notice I'm one of the last in the locker room. When Oakes leaves, I take my time getting dressed. I like the quiet of the empty locker room on a Friday afternoon. Practice was short and ended with a scrimmage against the women's team. Everyone cleared out pretty quickly after that. I'm finally showered and dressed, so I lace up my street shoes, throw on a hoodie, and grab my bag. Might as well get home and see if I can catch Oakes and Collins being all lovey-dovey, so I can finally have my gotcha moment with them. I'm headed toward the exit when the thud of a ball and squeaking shoes steers me in the direction of the court. A lanky brunette moves with grace and ease in a power move against her invisible opponent. She doesn't see me, and I don't call out to her. I just stand and watch her.

Jessa moves with a peace I haven't seen in her for awhile. We've talked before about how there's a peacefulness being on the floor alone, and I can almost feel the calmness emanating from her. She does a clean cross-over, plants her left foot and drives toward the basket, finishing with an effortless dunk. The ball ricochets off a chair and rolls my way. I jog over to grab it and that's when Jessa notices me.

"I thought everyone was gone by now," she says, her brows knit together in confusion.

"Nah, I kind of like the feeling of the locker room after everyone leaves. It's echoey, I hear my own thoughts better. Fridays are the best because everyone rushes out of here to start the weekend." I say. "Why are you still practicing anyway? It's Friday. Time to start the weekend."

She shrugs. "I had some extra energy to burn. And like you, I enjoy the peace here when there is no one else around. It's a bit eerie too, though, now that I think about it."

I toss her the ball, "Want some company then?"

Jessa catches it easily and gives me a half shrug. I take it as a yes and I follow her towards the hoop. As she starts to do the same drill as before, I wait until she's dribbled a few times, then when she's shifted her weight to the left, I move, stealing the ball. I dribble up to the basket with renewed energy, landing a left-handed layup.

"Seems to me it's a bit too easy for you with no opponent," I call back to her.

"I didn't even know we were playing until you stormed past me," Jessa huffs.

"I mean, you should always be ready on defense. You snooze, you lose." I retort, dribbling back to her.

"Fine. One-on-one?" She challenges, her eyes blazing with competitiveness.

I match her fierce expression. "It's on."

Fifteen minutes later we're both out of breath and sweaty. Jessa had given me a run for my money.

"Man, I wasn't looking to have a second practice," I complain.

"Boohoo," Jessa says, mocking me by pretending to rub tears away with her fists. "No one asked you to step in and play."

"Ouch. But fine, I give up. Stick a fork in me, I'm done," I tease, and fall to the ground with a dramatic thud. "All hail, Basketball Queen!"

Jessa rolls her eyes, but she's laughing. She sits down beside me on the cool gym floor and rolls out her ankles. After a few minutes of targeted stretches, she lays flat on her back, mirroring my position. The only sounds in the gym are our slow, soft breaths.

I'm not sure how much time passes, but I'm jolted awake when the lights above click off. The only lights are the emergency bulbs near the exits. I realize I must have dozed off and look over to see Jessa rising to her feet, bewilderment in her eyes.

"Shit," we say at the same time, bright lights shining in our faces from somewhere in the darkness.

"Who's there?" The voice is deep and demanding. Footsteps near, but we can't see with the light blinding us.

"Uh, it's Jessa Blakely. I play for the women's basketball team." Jessa says, trying to keep her voice calm, though I can hear the stress in her tone.

"And Greyson Hastings from the men's team," I say, holding my hand up to shield my face from the light.

The overhead lights click on and a jingling of keys reveals a second person walking toward us. Jessa and I are alone on the empty court, staring into the faces of two pissed off looking campus safety officers.

"You know the gym closes at ten on Fridays when there are no events. No one is supposed to be in here. What are you two doing out here on center court?" The shorter, stockier officer says in a stern voice. He sounds suspicious. "You weren't...?"

"Canoodling?" The taller, much older officer finishes.

"No, no," Jessa says, shaking her head. "We had practice, I stayed late, Greyson showed up, and then we started playing a pick-up game. We just lost track of time."

I remain silent, but it's hard to keep the shit eating grin from taking over my face. The guy called it *canoodling*? Who says that? "I see," says the shorter officer, who doesn't look a day over eighteen now that I look at him more closely. "Well, I'm going to have to write this into a report and call your coaches to let them know you were found in here unsupervised."

Well, that gets my heart racing. We do not need the coaches to find out about this. Especially if they're going to accuse us of *canoodling*. They're so strict on this whole dating other players thing, that they'll have a shit fit before we even get a chance to explain what happened. "We'll grab our stuff and head out now. Sorry," Jessa says, speaking for both of us. She's clearly thinking the same thing I am.

I pick up my bag while Jessa grabs the ball, and we both hightail it toward the locker rooms.

As we move down the dimly lit hallway past the coaches' offices, we notice a light on in Coach Morris's window.

"Shit," Jessa says, stopping in her tracks. "We need to get past without her seeing us."

I'm about to suggest bear-crawling under the window when my eyes focus in on the person in Coach Morris's office with her. "Wait," I say, grabbing Jessa's hand and jerking her back.

"What?" she hisses. "Don't do that. You about made me pee myself."

I shush her and whisper, "Look—is that Coach Hayes?"

Jessa narrows her eyes toward the window and gasps. The man in question walks behind Coach Morris's desk to where she's standing and pulls her in by the hips.

"Uh, sure is," she finally replies, incredulous.

We watch, stunned, as Coach Hayes presses Coach Morris's neck to one side and starts kissing the exposed skin. Our eyes are round and disbelieving as we turn to gawk at each other. We are not seeing this. Jessa clutches at my hand and we crouch down, both out of shock and to remain unseen. We're barely breathing, but then we hear the jingling of keys down the hall around the corner from where we're frozen on the ground.

"Let's go," Jessa whispers, and we take off sprinting around the next corner. When we're not in danger of being spotted, we poke our heads around the wall and see the older safety officer walking toward the coaches' offices. His gate is purposeful, like he can't wait to tattle on the two basketball players he just saw *canoodling* on the court in the dark. From where we stand, a corner of Coach Morris's office is visible and we see her and Coach Hayes pull apart like teenagers about to be caught making out by their parents. We take off running again.

By the time we duck into the women's locker room, we're out of breath, and I'm pretty sure our heartbeats are echoing off the walls. The women's locker room was the closest door and there's an exit to the parking lot from here. We grin at each other like we're in the clear, but then the door opens and we hear footsteps on the tile floors. "Jessa?" Coach Morris calls out.

"Hide," Jessa mouths at me. I jump into an empty shower stall and press myself against the wall, hoping the shower curtain is enough to keep me out of sight.

"Oh, hey, Coach. What's up?" Jessa's trying to sound casual, but her voice is high-pitched and she's jumpy.

I face palm my head. Jessa needs to chill or she's going to give us both away. Then we're going to look guilty as hell, even though we weren't doing anything.

"I just got done talking with campus safety. He said you and Hastings were 'canoodling' at center court. His words, not mine." Coach Morris says, smirking.

I can just see her profile from where I'm hiding. She sits down on a folding chair that is way too close for comfort and crosses her legs. If she cranes her neck at all to her left, she'll see my hiding spot.

"What's going on? You know the rules, Jessa," Coach Morris continues. Somehow—no idea how—I manage to elbow the shampoo and conditioner bottles on a shelf. I catch them before they fall to the floor, but the plastic bottles collide into each other in the process, making a clacking noise. *Shit, shit, shit!* I start hopping from foot to foot in frustration and peek out through the side of the shower curtain to see if Coach Morris heard.

Fortunately, Jessa's a quick thinker, and jumps up from where she was sitting on a bench, knocking over her duffel bag. Her voice is unnecessarily loud for normal circumstances when she protests, "Coach, I swear! I was getting in some extra shots and Greyson stopped in as he was on his way out. We played some one-on-one and then were chilling on the floor, cooling down."

"I believe you, Jessa," Coach Morris says. "But I wouldn't be doing my job if I didn't caution you to be careful. As Captain, the team is watching you. I need you to respect the rules."

"Of course, of course!" Jessa responds. She does not know how to play it cool, I laugh to myself.

Then, as if she can't quite help herself I hear Jessa blurt, "What was going on in your office with Coach Hayes?"

Damn it, Jessa! I'm pretty sure my eyes are bulging out of my head in horror. She really can't control her mouth when she's nervous. We were almost home free, I think. But now? Coach Morris doesn't say anything at first. There's a long pause and I resist the urge to look through the shower curtain crack again. But then, Coach Morris stammers, "We were... We were talking, Jessa."

"Is that so?" Jessa asks, but I can hear in her tone it's a loaded question. *Don't do it, Jessa,* I plead, hoping we've suddenly developed the ability to telecommunicate with one another. But then—she does it. "Kind of hard for him to talk when he's kissing your neck, isn't it?" I sneak a peek then, unsurprised to see Jessa glaring at her coach with her hands on her hips. Sighing, I lean against the tiled wall in resignation. I'm going to be here all night, I think.

Coach Morris must stand quickly because I hear the metal legs scratch against the tiled floors. I resume peeking through the crack because I can't stand not knowing what's going on. Coach Morris's cheeks are flushed, but I can't tell if it's from embarrassment or anger. It's hard to tell from my viewpoint in the shower. She puts a hand on Jessa's shoulder and seems to be searching for her words.

"Jessa, you have quite the imagination," Coach says, forcing a laugh. "I think you should head home and get some rest."

Jessa doesn't push further. She sighs, and it comes out sounding both weary and sharp. Coach tells her to have a good weekend, and I hear her steps retreat.

Once the door closes, I step out from my hiding spot. Jessa glares at me. I glare back.

"What?" Jessa snaps.

"What were you thinking?" I ask, exasperation marking each word. "You just couldn't let it go? You *had* to say something?"

"I was just trying to get the focus off of us. I guess I wasn't thinking." Jessa's face is red, and I can see she's embarrassed. My brain pinpoints the word *us* and stalls. She said *us*. What does that mean?

"Shit, Jessa, that was ballsy." I laugh, deciding to throw her a break. I pick up her duffel bag. "Come on. Let's go before I'm caught in the women's locker room. That would not help our argument."

We're outside the facility doors and turning the direction of the condo when I remember what I've been wanting to ask Jessa. "Hey, I've been meaning to ask you something. Do you know what's going on with Collins and Oakes? They seem to be spending a lot of time together. And are very—cozy."

Jessa's silence makes me think she knows something but isn't going to tell me. Girl Code or whatever. But she side-eyes me and says, "Bex will kill me if I say anything. But I think she's falling for him. Apparently, they made an agreement for Monty to help her 'practice' being in a relationship," Jessa rolls her eyes as her fingers come up in air quotes. "But it seems like it's gone too far and she's enjoying it way too much. The girl's on fire though. Between this thing with Monty and her secret admirer, I mean."

"Hmmm... about that. What if I told you the admirer and the 'practice person' are one in the same?" Oakes will kill me for breaking the promise to tell no one, but I feel like I owe her since she shared what she knows with me.

"You mean *Monty* is Bex's admirer? The one sending all the gifts and sweet notes? Wow, that's wild. How long have you known? And why didn't you tell me?" Jessa shrieks, grabbing my arm and giving it a shake. Boy, does her touch send a shock of electricity right through me. I wonder if she feels it, too, because she pulls her hands away like she's touched a burning stovetop.

"Oakes didn't want me to say anything. He was testing the waters; trying to gauge how Collins would react to having a secret admirer. It seems like they've both been enjoying the 'practice' time. I just keep catching them doing little affectionate things. But if they both know we know things, why are they being so secretive about it? I know for a fact that Oakes has a thing for Collins. And you're telling me Collins reciprocates…" I trail off, shaking my head. It's all mind boggling, if you ask me.

"Well, I guess that means Hazel and Char are going to have to duke it out for the one and only available man in your lifting group." Jessa winks at me and jogs ahead.

"Not funny, Jessa," I say, my voice a warning. I pick up the pace to catch up to her. No, I really don't find it funny at all. Does Jessa really believe I would go for either of those girls? How does she not feel our chemistry? Does she want me to date other people?

Maybe it's time I channel Oakes and play the role of a doting boyfriend to give her a sense of what's possible between us.

12
Jessa

Season opener week is here! It's a home game, and there's no better feeling than the high energy that pulses on campus. My mood is soaring in anticipation of the game as I head to the Hastings Center for my scheduled lift session. The only thing that brings me down a bit is remembering my mother is in town running clinics for the basketball program. I haven't seen her much yet, but knowing she's here, encroaching on my territory, is like a rain cloud threatening a sunny day.

Butler is another cloud looming above. He's being extra annoying this week and makes a pass at me when I strip down to my sports bra and shorts in the hot weightroom during one of our sessions. He's lucky Greyson wasn't there to witness it. But I'm sure it will get back to him seeing as how there always seem to be eyes on me, ready to report every tiny situation. Like Anders. He and Bex are close by when Butler comments that he'd like to take my body, which has "a lot of miles left," for a test drive. Anger short-circuits my brain for a second, and I almost lash out, but decide Butler isn't worth the attention it would bring.

"Nice. I'll go ahead and file that under 'Bullshit Feedback Nobody Asked For,' and you should add it to your running list of 'Things Normal People Don't Say Out Loud,'" I deadpan, keeping my voice low enough that only Butler can hear.

I walk away, not giving him a chance to respond. What a fucking asshole! Who openly spouts such misogynistic bullshit. I should file a complaint with the coaches.

To make matters worse, I had an encounter with my mother after her training clinic with us. She pulls me aside on my way to the locker room and tells me I look underprepared for the game. Apparently, I'm "sluggish" and might benefit from some one-on-one practice time with her before the game. I nod, wanting to avoid the argument that'll ensue if I resist. But as I make my way to the locker room, I think *Thanks Mom, you're looking great, too. I think I'll pass on that extra workout.*

My mood is shot by the time I get back to the condo. I'd thought the chilly fall air and leaves crunching underfoot would be cathartic, maybe even restore my good mood from earlier, but nope. I still feel like shit.

I try hard to snap out of it while I shower and swallow down a sandwich, chips, and one of Bex's pre-prepped fruit cups. But since I can't seem to stop my wallowing over the interactions with my mother and Butler, I resolve it's best to keep to myself tonight. Maybe I'll stay in my room and study.

I'm brushing the crumbs from my mouth when Greyson knocks and pushes open my bedroom door. He's dressed in jeans and a black t-shirt that shows off his bulging arms.

"Going somewhere?" I ask.

"We're going somewhere," Grey corrects, smiling at me.

"It hasn't been a great day," I protest. "And I've still got more fun to do." I point at the textbooks in front of me.

"Even more reason to leave." He studies me for a moment, then coaxes, "I've got chocolate chip cookies and milk."

"That's not playing fair," I say with a grin. "Fine."

I grab my sweatshirt and shoes, following Greyson and his promised bag of goodies. "Where are we going?"

"You'll see." He leads me outside, opens the passenger door, and waits until I'm inside the Jeep before closing the door. I watch him place the bag in the backseat and walk around to the driver's seat. My eyes narrow as he flexes his hands on the steering wheel and then runs one through his hair. He seems nervous. We haven't driven a block when Greyson says, "Heard Butler got mouthy today."

His tone is calmer than I expected, though I had no doubt it would come up at some point. Not with Bex standing right there. But it doesn't stop me from questioning him. "That literally happened less than a few hours ago. How do you already know?"

"Word travels quickly when it comes to you, Jessa. Especially if it's that shithead mouthing off."

That's my Greyson, I think. He just can't help himself. It's should irritate me, but somehow, I find it endearing.

"I can handle it," I say on principle.

"Didn't say you couldn't, but you shouldn't have to." he says, his tone matter-of-fact.

"Boys will be boys," I say with sardonic amusement. "It's one thing if he says that shit to me, but if says it to any of my girls, he's a goner."

"That's my girl," Greyson says. He sounds proud.

His girl. Those words spark an unexpected flutter in my chest and I replay them in my head. What would being Greyson's girl look like? I allow my mind to wander with possibilities. Before I know it, the

Jeep has stopped, and Greyson's opening my door. I look around and see we're at University Lake.

"It's a bit cold for the water," I say, giving Greyson a curious look.

He gestures for me to follow him, so I amble behind him down the hill until we stop at a picnic table near the water. He spreads a red and white checkered tablecloth over the surface, then pulls out the chocolate chip cookies,—homemade, from the looks of them—two glasses, and a carton of milk. After he pours the milk and drapes a warm blanket across our laps, he hands me a glass.

"You know what to do," he says, tilting his head toward the plate of cookies.

"Of course I do. But what is this for?" I ask, genuinely confused.

"Why does it have to be for anything specific?" Greyson asks. "It's just because. It seemed like you needed a pick-me-up." I'm still sitting there, unmoving, when Greyson adds playfully, "A sweet treat for my sweet girl."

My face feels immediately warm, despite the even colder air down by the water. *My sweet girl...*

"Well, I do love chocolate chip cookies, especially homemade ones. Did you make these? When did you do this?" I ask in a rush, trying to hide my embarrassment at his comment.

"Yup, I found some time." Greyson smiles sheepishly. "Dig in."

I grab a cookie, dunk it in the milk, and take a big bite. These are heavenly. I close my eyes to savor the sweetness.

Greyson laughs. "Good, I take it?"

"Sooo good!" I say, through a full mouth. I take another cookie before I'm even finished chewing the first.

We eat in a pleasant silence, dunking our cookies and wiping dribbles of milk from our faces. As I chew, I stare out at the reflections of the buildings on the water. It's so peaceful. After the afternoon I had, I really needed this. I just hadn't known.

"Thanks for this, Grey," I say, scooching close enough to wrap my arms around his waist and letting my head fall against his shoulder. He gives the top of my head a light kiss and then rests his own against mine. It feels natural, I think, no longer feeling the chill with my body warmed by his. We stay like that until the darkness settles in around us.

The night of the season opener, the Lady Big Horns are ready. I look around at the Blakely Center and feel a burst of pride seeing how the stadium is busting at the seams. There's a sea of rowdy Hills blue in the student section that spills across into more blue with other excited fans. They're as ready as we are to kick off the season.

One of my Lasts, I think, and am swept away by a surge of emotion. My *last* season opener. I can't believe it's here. The entire men's team is seated behind our bench, showing their support. I find Greyson among the faces, and he gives me a huge smile. "*You got this*," he mouths. I nod back him. I do. *We* do. My mother is across the court, directly opposite the bench. Like always, she's perfectly poised and looking her best. We make eye contact and she gives me a quick nod. It doesn't fill me with the same reassuring warmth I just got from Grey, but I guess it's better than nothing. Bex's family flew in for the game, and they wave with eagerness, trying to get our attention as we scan the crowd. The buzz in the air is undeniable as the starting line-ups are announced over the loudspeaker. Finally, it's time to tip off.

I wipe my shoes with my hands, bend at the waist to touch my toes for a final stretch, and get in position for the tip-off. The desire to win the tip is palpable. The whistle blows, the ball goes up, and I edge it to Char—one of the girls pining over Monty and Grey. *Not the time, Jessa*, I scold myself as I sprint toward our basket. The ball gets worked around the perimeter while I cut in and out, slipping past my defender, looking for space to be open. Hazel, Grey's lifting partner, finds an opening and bounce-passes it to me. I make a quick move to the hoop, and the ball drops in cleanly. I point to Hazel in acknowledgement as we head back toward the opposing basket.

There's a lot of back and forth between our teams, with strong crowd engagement evident in the constant cheers and clapping from both sides. We're seconds away from halftime, and it's a tie game. I've played nearly the entire half and am dripping in sweat. Coach Morris calls a time out. I guzzle water from a bottle while she draws out a play on the small whiteboard, outlined with a replica of the court, and then sends us back out to finish the half.

We take our designated places. I pass the ball to Bex as she moves forward and catches it. I cut hard from the sideline and shout for the ball without stopping to second guess. I catch the pass, take a dribble for momentum, and pull up for a short jump shot. The dribble is enough to throw off the defense. The buzzer sounds as the ball drops through the net. The crowd erupts, and my teammates high-five me as we head to the locker room for halftime with a two-point lead.

God this feels good. Our bench is deep, but the extra conditioning and endurance training, thanks to our punishment from the party, is paying off. Additionally, we're prepared for extra physicality after scrimmaging with the men's team. I'm elated as I look around the locker room, seeing all the girls' smiling faces. For the second time tonight, my emotions catch in my throat. This is my team—my girls.

We're going to get shit done this season. I resolve at this moment that we won't accept another slow start. As captain, I won't allow complacency as we go through the season. It's happened for too many seasons in a row.

Coach's voice cuts through my thoughts, and I tune in as she gives us pointers and tells us to maintain the pace of the first half. We huddle up, all hands in, and shout, 'Big Horns!' We break, reigniting our energy for the second half.

We jog out, the roar of the crowd hitting us as soon as we exit the locker room. The men's team greets us in a loose huddle outside the tunnel, welcoming us back with cheers, high-fives, and good-natured pointers. Greyson meets my eyes and nods. He knows I'm in the zone, and nothing else needs to be said. We shoot each other confident grins as my team heads back on the floor.

Late in the third quarter, we lead by a couple of points. It's clear our opponents are gassed because they're getting sloppy. As we huddle up at the end of the third, I tell my team, "Let's push the pace. We're sitting great but now let's show what we're made of."

Bex, Hazel, and Char are running and gunning, allowing Lexi Wright, the other starting forward, and me to inbound the ball and throw some impressive full court passes for easy points. I love playing basketball, but having a hardworking, close-knit team makes it a million times more fun. And we are on fire this quarter. Our lead grows and Coach pulls the starters out for the last few minutes.

Back on the bench, I wipe my face with a towel, grab a water bottle, and do a quick scan of the crowd. I love watching our fans at the end of a game. Every play causes clapping, followed by an excited ripple of chatter. The clock runs out and the buzzer sounds, ending my last season opener. And we won.

We line up to high-five the other team, some of us hugging girls we know, wishing each other good luck on the rest of the season. Another wave of emotion hits me. I'm so proud of us. Of myself.

As we break away from the opposing team and head towards the locker room, the crowd erupts in celebratory cheers. They're chanting our name and we stop to sign jerseys, t-shirts, and posters of kids standing near the tunnel. Their parents and other fans congratulate us and, though we're tired and want to shower, we know putting smiles on our supporters' faces is part of being a college athlete. We've worked hard to make this first win possible, and it feels good to eat up the recognition a bit.

After a quick team debrief with Coach in the locker room, we shower and dress in street clothes. The excited conversation of my teammates lets me know they're still high off the win. I know I am. I'm towel drying my hair when my mother enters into the locker room— *my sanctuary*. I groan. *Damn it. Why is she here?* I shake my head and continue messing with my hair.

"Jessa," my mom starts as she steps into my bubble. "Nice win."

"Thanks, Mom," I say, waiting for the *but* that will surely follow. It's best not to let my guard down. My mom typically has an agenda but always starts with a compliment. Someone must have told her it's a smart tactic at one point. I, however, think it's an overused, ineffective method that usually leaves me feeling worse.

The locker room is clearing out as my teammates head to dinner with their families or friends. A few of the girls yell over their shoulders that they'll send a team text if anything is happening later. Bex interrupts to tell me she's going to celebrate the win with her family but will see me at home later.

My mother hovers with a tight smile on her face as Bex wanders away and a few other teammates stop to compliment my game. I want to shout at her, *Go away! Can't you see I'm trying to enjoy the win with my team instead of having it ruined by your negativity?* But I say none of that, even when it's just the two of us left in the locker room.

"Jessa, overall, you looked good out there for the first game," Mom continues, as if the last ten minutes between her sentences never happened. I brace myself. I *know* that tone. This isn't the first time I've heard what's coming next, so I avoid looking at her and continue to pack up my stuff. "You were scoring, rebounding, and passing well. But you need to be quicker on defense. Limit the other team's opportunities. That's where you're needed. Fire up the defense."

"Yes, Mother," I say. It's an automatic response, something I learned long ago shuts the criticism down faster. I'm determined not to let her ruin my mood.

My mother starts moving her body around, demonstrating what she expects of my defense moving forward.

I sigh, wondering how Coach Morris would feel about my mother's micromanagement. But once again, it's easier to agree. "Got it."

"You have a high ceiling, but you need to focus on the details of your game to reach your full potential, Be a little selfish out there."

This is Mom's way of telling me to leverage my individual skills and strengths, rather than always prioritizing the team's play. Nevermind that I'm the captain, whose literal job is to prioritize the team.

I stifle down my rebuttals and hug Mom on autopilot as she says, "I love you. I'm catching an early flight in the morning, but we'll talk soon."

"Thank God," I whisper when I hear the door shut behind her. No matter how well I play, it's never good enough for her. But on the bright side, that conversation could have been worse and *much* longer.

Feeling good that my ego is only a little bruised after that nonsense, I let the post-game high propel me out the locker room door.

And right into Greyson.

"What are you still doing here?" I ask once my heartbeat has slowed from the initial shock. I hadn't expected anyone I know to still be here, especially not Greyson.

"Waiting for you, obviously," Greyson responds, laughing. He wraps me into a hug, lifting my feet off the ground. His excitement over the win is tangible, and I can't help but bask in the warmth of his support. This is how Mom should have reacted. I squeeze him back, grateful for him.

"Amazing game, J! You were on fire!" Greyson says, pulling the bag from my shoulder and hoisting it over his own. "And the team is looking great, especially for this early in the season. It's gonna be a good one. I feel it."

"Thanks, Grey. I've got a good feeling too."

"I'm so proud of you," he continues as we make our way to the parking lot. "Not to bring down the mood, but I saw your mom leaving the locker room. She acknowledged me but didn't stop to chat. Are you okay?"

"Yeah," I say and roll my eyes. "Just another Lauren Blakely constructive pep talk."

Greyson's Jeep is one of the few remaining vehicles left in the parking lot. I'm about to open the passenger door when Greyson grabs my hand and turns me to face him. There's something on his face tonight—an intensity in his eyes, a hunger in the curve of his smile—that knocks the wind out of me. I'm hyperaware of his skin against mine, though only our hands touch. His hand crawls up my arm, cupping my elbow, and the surge that runs through me liquifies my bones. *Why does this happen every time he touches me?*

Greyson doesn't seem to notice that I'm forcing myself to remain upright on sheer willpower alone. He pulls me closer until we're inches apart. His voice is lower than normal when he says, "Dance with me, J."

"What? Here?" I look around the nearly empty parking lot and fiddle with the basketball pendant around my neck. I can't look directly at him.

"Why not?" he asks, his touch gentle as he pulls my hand from the necklace and places it on his shoulder.

"You're being weird," I say with a shaky laugh. But the warmth of his body against mine is so comforting that it's hard to think of a logical reason to resist. I give in to the magnetic pull and allow my body to melt against his.

We sway together in the quiet parking lot. Grey's strong arms are firm around my waist and his large hands gently stroke the small of my back. Heat radiates through my body. With someone else, slow dancing under a streetlamp outside the Blakely Center would feel awkward, but with Greyson, it feels natural. It's romantic. Unlike anything I ever experienced with Dillon. I give in completely to the feeling, and allow myself to relax further into Greyson, laying my head against his chest. His heartbeat steadies me, and I slide my hand down from his shoulder to rest it over his heart, the rhythmic thud pulsing against my palm and ear. I hear Greyson exhale a shaky breath and wonder if he's as affected as me.

My phone vibrates in my pocket, but I ignore it. I'm sure it's my teammates, inviting me somewhere, but there's nowhere else I want to be right now. Greyson's right hand drifts to my face and brushes a still damp strand of hair out of my eyes. His fingers linger for a moment, and then he lifts my chin up to look at my face. The bright blue of his irises are a mere sliver around his dilated pupils as he stares down at me. I can't read his expression and I'm momentarily concerned I've misread everything. "What's wrong?" I ask, mesmerized by his eyes but also afraid of his response.

"Nothing. Absolutely nothing," Greyson breathes out, cupping his hand around the curve of my cheek. "You're beautiful, Jessa."

My eyes scan his face, searching for something in his eyes to tell me what all this means. We're so close right now. And his words... He hasn't said many, but each one feels weighted. I'm overthinking, and it's taking me out of the moment, dragging me to a place of doubt and fear. I force myself to forget about the noise in my head, focusing instead on the heat of our bodies pressed close, our synchronized breathing, and the growing flutter deep in my abdomen.

I'm not sure who leans in first, but I know it's me who tips us over the edge. I can't keep up the facade that I don't want this. Maybe it's messy and a bad idea, but I need to follow what feels good right now. Greyson is safe. So I lift my chin and close the distance, brushing my lips against his. It's so light that it hardly counts as a kiss, but it's all Greyson seems to need. His breath catches, and then his mouth is on mine. My eyes flutter closed and the kiss deepens, both of us surrendering to the hunger, the tension—the inevitable. Now that I've given in, I can't control it. My hands move up to Greyson's neck and face, landing in his hair. I grab a fistful and tug, just a little, but it's enough to pull the faintest moan from him. His hand finds the hem of my shirt, and then, as if it will kill him not to touch me, his fingers slip under to stroke the bare skin of my lower back. I arch my torso, melding my body into his even more, and slide my hand to his chest. Neither of us can catch our breath, and I'm spiraling into desperation, needing to release the pressure of this pent up longing. When he presses me up against the Jeep, and I feel his hardness against my hip, I gasp from the intense tightening of my body.

"Jessa," he murmurs into my mouth, and I can feel that his body is as rigid as mine. We're both trying not to lose control in this parking lot, but finding it more difficult with each kiss.

"Greyson," I whimper, and I feel his lips curve up against mine. "Let's go home." *Because I want you to do unspeakable things to me. Right here. Right now.*

With reluctance, we pull away from each other, but keep our hands clasped until getting into opposite sides of his car forces us to let go.

Greyson adjusts himself before hopping in the driver's seat, and the sight winds me up even more. We don't speak on the way home, but my mind is going a million miles an hour. *What happens when we get home? Were we just caught up in a moment? Does he want this as much as I do? Do I want more than sex? Does he? Is it worth the complications it will surely bring? Damn it, Jessa! What are you doing?* I hear Grey take a deep breath, and I'm convinced he's playing twenty questions with himself, too.

We're at the condo before I'm able to answer any of my own questions. Greyson's hand finds mine once we're out of the car, and as we make our way inside, my heart races in anticipation of what happens next. But I should have paid more attention to the parked cars outside because we're greeted by Bex, Monty, and Bex's parents, and twin brother, Aiden. They're gathered in the living room chatting and drinking wine, but all eyes swing to us when the door opens. Greyson and I drop hands just before Bex fixes her eyes on me, looking me up and down with suspicion.

"Where have you guys been?" Monty asks.

I know I'm probably blushing as I search my broken brain for an excuse, but Greyson saves me by piping up with a casual, "I waited for Jessa after the game and her mom got chatty since she leaves early tomorrow."

No one seems to pick up on the thick-as-hell sexual tension between Greyson and me, and offers us a glass of celebratory wine. Bex's dad pours us each a glass as Greyson and I share a look. I guess we're socializing instead of continuing the scene from the parking lot. We make our way to the open love seat, making sure to leave plenty of distance between us.

A week has passed since our parking lot make out session, and I've replayed the entire thing in my head at least seven hundred times. I've tossed and turned every night thinking about what might have happened if Bex's family hadn't been over. It's not like we've talked about it. Greyson and I have only seen each other in passing at home and during our weekly team scrimmages. No time for any funny business, let alone a private discussion. It feels so... Unfair? Infuriating?

Gah! I fall onto my bed, kicking my arms and legs in the air like an inconsolable toddler. *What the hell?* I think, and add a shrill scream to my tantrum, just for fun.

It makes me feel half a percent better, but I hadn't expected anyone to hear. Unfortunately, Bex and Monty are both home and hear my scream as a call for help. They run into my room with matching alarmed expressions.

"Shit," I say, offering them a lopsided smile in apology. "I didn't mean to do that so loudly."

"You okay?" Bex asks, her eyebrows knit together in worry. She's looking me over as if assessing me for injury.

"I'm fine… Just trying something new for stress release," I explain, hoping it's enough of a Bex-approved therapeutic practice to stop questioning me. Changing the subject, I ask, "Wait, why are you both here? Monty, I thought you'd already left for your game?"

"Uh, yeah, I'm about to. Just stopped by Bex's room to let her know the team is coming back tonight. Which means, I should probably tell you, too—Jessa, the team is coming back after the game tonight."

I nod. "Alright, sounds good."

Monty eyes me, still looking concerned, then turns to Bex. "Well, I'd better get going. Bex, take care of her."

Bex waits a beat until the front door of the condo slams shut before she says, "Okay, back to you…"

I don't even need to ask if Greyson is gone. He insists on being early everywhere, so I'm sure he's already at the gym waiting to load the bus.

"It's nothing," I say, "I just haven't slept in like a week. And we have a game tonight!"

"Why haven't you slept? Have we been too loud?" The words are out of Bex's mouth before she can stop them. A hint of red colors her cheeks.

"Wait, what? What are you doing that you might be too loud?" I ask, staring Bex down, willing her to make eye contact with me. When she doesn't, I jump up and grab her wrists, shaking them in excitement. "Bex? Oh my God! You and Monty had sex, didn't you? When? How was it? Tell me everything!"

"This is not about me. I came to check on you," Bex says.

"Nope, this is huge! I want to know all the things. Speaking of huge, is *he*? Wait, no, I don't want to know," I say, deciding knowing too much would make it too hard not to crack jokes in Monty's presence.

"Well, it just kind of happened," Bex says, dragging her fingernail along the thread of my comforter, still not looking at me. "We've been spending a lot of time together, and after I saw how he handled my family, there was no doubt in my mind I was falling for him. I kind of just decided I wanted him to be my first."

"And just to be clear, the *him* we're talking about is Monty?" I crack, still unsure what to think of the whole situation. Jokes are easiest to manage at the moment.

"Yes, Jessa," she replies, her tone patient like she's talking to a toddler. Which, I can't really argue with, considering I was having a toddler-level tantrum less than five minutes ago.

"Okay, fine," I huff, deciding Bex needs me to be a serious person right now. "I thought Monty was just your practice person for the kissing and holding hands stuff?"

"I thought so, too," Bex shrugs, but her eyes shine in a dazed kind of way. She looks happy. "But the last couple of weeks have felt different. I don't think it's one-sided. I get the feeling he likes me, too."

"Of course he likes you. He stares at you all the time," I say. *This is good news*, I think. I was a little worried at first, but Bex seems excited. And Monty is a good dude. "But please be warned, I'll kick his ass if he fucks and ducks you."

"Jessa!" Bex looks horrified by my word choice. "He's not like that."

"I'm just being honest," I say, shrugging in a *sorry-not-sorry* way. And then I can't help myself. I have to project my constantly cautious self onto Bex. It feels like I won't be able to be one hundred percent happy for her until I do. "Seems like maybe you two should talk. See where this is going and to make sure you're on the same page. I just don't want to see you get wrapped up in something one-sided."

Bex nods in agreement. "You're right. He's just been so caring and understanding, you know—letting me take things at my own pace."

"I'm so happy for you if this is what you want," I say, with genuine sincerity. But I can't resist and add with a cocked eyebrow, "So, how was it? Monty sportin' a nice package?"

"Oh my God, Jessa," Bex says, swatting at me while her face turns red again. "But if you must know, I think big? Granted, I have nothing to compare it to. He went extra slow because he was afraid of hurting me. And he also said I probably needed to be stretched a little before he went all the way in."

I scrunch up my face, mad at myself for asking. I don't think I'm really comfortable knowing this much about Monty. Especially because he's Greyson's best guy friend. Not to mention a roommate I see walking around half naked at least once a day. Some things are just best not to know. But Bex continues anyway, enjoying my discomfort. She knows my curiosity will win out.

"I swear I can feel it in my belly button when I'm on top. I have never felt pleasure like that, even with my damn dildo. I assumed it would feel the same," she says, with a shrug and a smile.

"Close," I say, "but not the same. The real thing is so much better."

Even though that's not entirely true. Dillon was robotic. My vibrator is definitely more fun than he was. But Greyson... *Ugh, why did I allow my brain to go there?* But that's an easy question to answer. Because Greyson is the last time I had an honest-to-God-good release. It was unlike any other time I've had sex.

The sound of Bex's voice reminds me we're still in a conversation, so I force Greyson—and sex with Greyson—out of my mind. Or as far back as I can. Basically, I'm multitasking with thoughts because my brain seems to have Greyson front and center ever since we kissed last week.

Bex is talking about her secret admirer when I tune back in. "...I just wish I knew who it was because I'd feel bad wasting his time and efforts if I officially become unavailable. What if it's some hottie from campus?"

"Better than a creeper," I say, "but I don't think you should focus on the admirer right now. Focus on what has the potential to be real." I want to kick Monty for not just telling Bex the truth. I'd tell her, but Greyson would be livid with me.

"Yes, absolutely," Bex says without hesitation. "Now, what the hell was that random scream all about? You scared us to death. My heart was in my throat."

"Guess," I scoff.

"Hmm. Fifty-fifty chance of it being about your mother or Greyson." She tilts her head and narrows her eyes at me. She knows me too well.

"It's Greyson," I sigh.

"Of course it's Greyson. When are you finally going to own up to the fact that you feel something for him?" Bex asks, not bothering to hide her irritation with me.

I shake my head, and growl in frustration. I'm tired of hearing myself whine. "I know. I don't want to, but I think I do. He's been extra sweet and attentive lately. Or had been. It's been a week since we've really talked or kissed."

"Wait, you kissed again? When?" Bex looks even more irritated to know I've told her nothing about this. But I think she knows she doesn't have a leg to stand on with the whole Monty thing.

"After the season opener we hardcore made out in the parking lot. He'd randomly asked me to dance, and one thing led to another...

I really thought we'd come back here and be together after all this time, ya know. But then..."

"And then I was here with my family, forcing you to drink with us. Oh. My. God." Bex puts her hands over her face, horrified. "You got *cockblocked* by my entire family. Shit, Jessa. I'm so sorry! I can't believe I was so clueless."

"Bex, it's fine. I mean, maybe it wouldn't have happened anyway. It was hot and heavy in the parking lot, but that's a lot to expect from one kiss." *One long, drug out, make-me-want-to-shed-my-clothes-in-public kiss that I can't stop thinking about.*

"In all seriousness, do you want to sleep with him?" Bex asks, and it feels like she's trying to stare into the depth of my soul with her intense gaze. "I mean, it's not like it would be the first time, right?"

It must be the way she's looking at me because everything I've been thinking spills out at once.

"Well, what does it say that I can't stop thinking about making out in the parking lot without wanting to jump him? I can't stop thinking about Grey, in general. At first, I thought it was just me wanting to get some, and maybe it was. Grey and I spent so much time together this summer, and it was amazing, just being together. I feel more connected to him than I ever did with Dillon. And when I'm honest with myself about it, I think it's always been that way. Now, there's no Dillon standing between us. A while back, I overheard Char and Hazel talking about Greyson, and I almost went into beast mode. I felt so much jealousy. And before that, when he went to dinner with Julia. That's why I got so drunk—trying to put him out of my mind. But lately, I've noticed sweet little reminders that he's here for me." I'm breathless when I stop, knowing I probably sound pathetic.

Bex isn't looking at me like I'm pathetic, though. She's looking at me like she gets it, which makes me feel less like a stupid girl obsessing over a boy. Bex taps her finger against her cheek thoughtfully, then says, "I think it means you and Grey need to talk about this. Like a real open and honest conversation about what is or isn't happening before it ruins your friendship. If you feel this way now, how do you think it'll be if another week goes by without talking?"

"Why do you have to be so logical when I just want to wallow in my emotions?" I pretend to glare at her. "I hate you."

"No you don't. You love me, and you know it," She says in a light, sing-song voice, then nudges me with her elbow. "Come on, let's get our stuff together and go take in the calm of the Blakely Center before the game. Maybe shoot around a little?"

"Yeah, alright. I need to get in the zone. And you are just the person to help me do it," I say, giving her a big squeeze. Bex rolls her eyes, but she's smiling. She knows how grateful I am for her.

"Five minutes," Bex orders and heads to her room to get ready for the game.

After some mindfulness practice with Bex in the quiet locker room, I feel more centered, like my nerves have unknotted. Then we crank our pre-game playlist, dancing around the locker room as the bass thumps against the metal lockers. Coach Morris pops her head in, gives a knowing smile, and just shakes her head. It's not the first time Bex and I have been caught in this pre-game ritual, and it definitely won't be the last.

As our teammates trickle in during the last of our usual songs, some jump right in with us, dancing like we're at a club instead of minutes away from tipoff. Others sing along as they smooth hair into ponytails or tie up their laces. My mood is much better than it was a few hours ago, and it hits me how lucky we are to have a team like this. If we take the court tonight with our spirits this high, there's no doubt in my mind that a win is in our future.

The game is a blowout. I think if I were a fan watching, I'd have been bored as hell and left at halftime. By the end of the third quarter, Coach puts in the bench. I'm happy to save some energy and give the freshies a chance to stretch their wings.

There's no post-game celebration since we have to work the community carnival tomorrow, but I'm jittery.

Bex is familiar with what it looks like when I haven't burned enough energy during the day, and offers to stay up with me. One look at her tired face, though, and I send her off to bed.

"I think your secret late nights with Monty have caught up to you. The guys won't be back till late, you'd better get your beauty rest while you can."

"Oh, thank God," Bex yawns. "I'd stay up for you, but if you're good on your own..."

"Bex," I laugh. "You can't even finish sentences. Go to bed!"

After she shuffles toward her bedroom with more effort than it should really take, I flip on the television and go searching for snacks in the kitchen. There's not a whole lot to choose from, so I fall back onto the couch, hoping I'll just get tired.

An hour later, I'm still wide awake. My mind won't focus on schoolwork without an impending deadline, so I decide to bake. Now, I'm not a Susie Homemaker, but I know how to make a few things for each season. Right now, I'm feeling fall vibes—tailgate snacks, spiced baked goods, and comforting scents to fill the condo.

I start mixing up Chex Mix, knowing even Bex will eat it. Once I've shoved the overflowing pan of the savory mixture into the oven and set the oven timer, I get to work on homemade pumpkin muffins, Greyson's favorite. It's busy work—alternating between stirring the Chex Mix and restarting the timer, filling muffin tins with liners and the batter, and cleaning up my mess—but it's keeping my hands and mind occupied. Once the Chex Mix is done, I spread it out over wax paper to cool, taste-testing a few warm rye chips and cashews along the way. It's delicious, so I handpick a selection of pretzels and cereal pieces with extra seasoning to snack on while the muffins bake.

I've just plopped down on the couch and am scrolling on my phone when I get a text from Greyson.

Grey: *Congrats on the win. Looks like it was a blow out.*

Me: *Blow out does not even describe it. It was the most boring game of my career. I was ready to leave. Looks like your game was better than ours.*

Grey: 😁 *Yup, we pulled out a win, though I was worried there for a while. What are you still doing up?*

Me: *Too much leftover energy from not playing a full game. Bex was tired from her late night Monty adventures, so I sent her to bed.*

Grey: *Oakes is conked out in the seat next to me. We're probably still about 30 minutes out.*

Me: *Oh, my timer is going off. BRB.*

The muffins look perfect, and the toothpick comes out clean, so I set them on a cooling rack and scoop the Chex Mix into a plastic container. I'm getting antsy again, knowing Greyson is on his way. Mindlessly munching on more Chex Mix, I settle back on the couch with the intent of catching some time with Greyson before he goes to bed.

I must have nodded off because the sound of the door jolts me awake, and I press up to a sitting position.

Greyson steps through the door and his face lights up with a huge grin when he spots me on the couch. "Hey."

I swallow, disarmed by his smile and the sight of his mussed hair. How does someone look so good in sweatpants? "Hey," I say, relieved that my voice doesn't match the shakiness in my body.

Monty follows Greyson in the door looking like the walking dead. He goes straight to his room without acknowledging me or the smells of my baking adventure. Apparently Monty is also feeling the consequences of the late night trysts.

Greyson sniffs the air and gives me a puzzled look. "Are those pumpkin muffins I smell?"

"Yep," I say.

Greyson nods his head in approval. "Nice. You've been busy tonight, J."

We move into the kitchen where Grey helps me pull the muffins from pan and into a storage container. Naturally, he keeps one for himself, peeling the wrapper off in a quick swoop before taking a huge bite. He groans in satisfaction and wanders toward the couch. I follow, trying to ignore how his sounds of pleasure remind me of... other things.

When a few crumbs land on his chest, I reach over and brush them away, my fingers lingering a second longer than they should. Flushing and feeling like an idiot, I pull my hand back, but Greyson is too quick. He grabs my hand and holds it against his chest. Heat flares beneath my skin, and I look up to find his eyes boring into me. When he licks his lips, something snaps in me.

Before I even think through the words, I say, "I'm trying to be the kind of girl who asks for what she wants, especially when she knows it will make her happy. You know how hard that is for me, Grey. And literally, all I want to do right now is kiss you again. Feel free to turn me down."

Grey cups my chin with his hand and looks at me in disbelief. "I'd have to be dead to not want to kiss you, Jessa."

That's all he has to say. I lean in, and he meets me halfway. This kiss is unhurried. Thorough. Indulgent. It's like we're pouring meaning into it, saying all the things we've held back, but without rushing. I've never experienced such a sensual kiss, or felt so physically connected to another person. Maybe I'd spent too long pining over Greyson from a distance to ever imagine something real with him. But that doesn't matter now. Not when he's kissing me, pushing me backwards on the couch, covering me with his body. This feels very, *very* real.

I edge him closer, pulling him down with one hand while my other slides up his t-shirt to feel the smooth ridges of his abs. Greyson lifts off of me to pull his shirt off, but it's long enough to take in his sculpted body. Goosebumps rise along his skin as I trail my fingers up and down his chest, back, and arms. I feel like I can't touch him enough, and every groan I elicit from him makes me want to do it again.

"Should we go to my room?" Greyson's voice is low and rough in my ear, and it's all I can do not to moan from the sound of it. I nod, and Greyson pulls me up by the hand and leads me down the hall. Neither of us bother to pick up his shirt or turn off the living room lights.

Greyson's bedroom smells like him—cedarwood and salt, like woods meet ocean. It's comfort and desire so overwhelming that I'm impatient for him to touch me again. He quietly closes the door and reaches for me, pulling me close and then backing me up to his bed. He crushes his mouth to mine, kissing me deeper and deeper until my brain can't keep up with my overloaded senses. When his hands move under my shirt, I gasp at the feel of his skin against my bare breast at the same time he realizes I'm braless.

"Shit," he breathes and closes his eyes for a second, like he's trying to pull himself together.

I smirk, and spin us until his back is to the bed, pushing him down flat on the mattress. I straddle him, knowing we can no longer hide how turned on we are from each other in this position. Even through our clothes, it's obvious I'm already wet, the damp heat pressed against his hard erection. I grind against him, and his fingertips dig into my hips, halting my movement. He's holding his breath as he watches me lift my shirt up and over my head.

Grey releases the breath he's been holding. "Jessa, you're beautiful." Then, he reaches for me, bringing my mouth to his. This time it's full of need, urgent and demanding, and I meet him kiss for kiss.

"If you don't want to do this, Jessa," Greyson says, his fingers wrapped up in my loose hair. "Tell me now."

"God, do I want this." I'm fevered, finding it hard to control my breathing as my hands skim down his stomach to the waistband of his sweats. My fingers hook under the elastic, and–

"You aren't wearing underwear," I state, giving him a questioning look.

Greyson holds his palms up in mock surrender. "Not planned, I promise. I may have forgotten to take an extra pair for after the game. I think it's working to my advantage right now, though."

I laugh, and tug down the elastic waistband to release his shaft. It bounces free from the fabric, like it's all too excited to greet me. There is a droplet already forming on the tip, and his ragged breathing tells me just how turned on he is right now. He's about to find the same beneath the fabric of my panties.

"Greyson, I need to feel you," I murmur, shimmying around until I pull my shorts and underwear off in one swoop. "I'm on the pill, and you know I don't mess around with my health."

"Same here." Greyson starts. "I mean, I'm clean and have condoms. And I need you." He reaches into his nightstand for a condom and rips it open. I snatch it from him and slowly roll it down his growing length.

"Jessa, what are you doing?"

"Mind your business," I say.

"I think *you* are minding my business," he groans, but he watches as I inch the condom down, his eyes rolling back when my grip tightens near the base.

Grey's hands guide my hips until I'm hovering over his cock. With excruciatingly slow movements, he glides me down, inch-by-inch until he's all the way in. The ribbing on the condom feels amazing where it hits me inside, and I circle my hips to take him deeper. Grey reaches for my breasts, taking one of the peaks into his mouth and massaging it with his tongue.

"You like that don't you?" He smiles against my breast, and when he pulls my nipple from his mouth, a sensual chills runs down my spine. His attention shifts to the other nipple and grazes his teeth across the peak. The contrast of his soft tongue against the light sharpness tenses my body, and my lower muscles clench around his cock, squeezing through a spasm of pleasure.

"Fuck!" Greyson cries out. "You keep doing that and I'm going to come."

"Maybe I want you to..." I challenge him, barely holding back myself.

Greyson grips the back of my head, pulling me in for an aggressive kiss, while my hips find a frenzied rhythm around his cock. He fills and stretches me, taking me to a level of pleasure that has me making noises I've never made before. Greyson's hand is on my ass, then it's between us, his fingers finding my clit. I close my eyes, the slick intensity of his hand and cock moving in harmony making my breaths come in ragged uneven bursts.

"Greyson, please don't stop," I beg. "I'm so close. Are you?" He responds with a tormented groan, and I pick up the pace, bouncing up and down on top of him, my breasts jiggling as I take us both over the edge.

We're so in sync that we cry out our release at the same time. I pound harder, rubbing my clit against him, trying to push my orgasm to the max while my pussy contracts, milking his dick through his. I collapse on top of him, and Greyson kisses my sweaty face, pulling me closer in his arms. We lay there, letting our breathing steady until Greyson takes care of the condom, wrapping it in tissue beside the bed until he gets up. He rolls over with a smile on his face and covers us with a blanket before snuggling down with his face between my breast and shoulder. I stroke his hair as we lay awake in silence, relaxed in each other's arms. Maybe we're unsure of what to say or afraid of shifting the moment, but I finally work up the courage.

"Greyson," I start.

"Hmm?" he mumbles against my breast.

"We should talk," I say, and it sounds like the start of a bad break up to my ears.

"Can't we just enjoy this for tonight?" Grey asks, propping up on an elbow to get level with my eyes.

"I want to enjoy this, but I know if I don't get it out now, I'll stress about it all night. This has been on my mind, stressing me out, ever since the night in the parking lot. It's been constant sexual tension that led us here."

"Well, I think that worked out okay," Greyson jokes.

"Greyson, be serious," I say, sitting up to lean against the headboard. I pull the blanket up to cover my chest, more as emotional support than to hide my breasts. I force myself to meet his eyes.

"Ok, ok. I'm listening," he says.

I still feel too exposed. I get out of bed and grab one of his t-shirts off a chair, slipping it over my naked body. Grey's eyes follow me, and though both of us just had incredibly satisfying sex, I see him adjust himself beneath the covers. I start pacing back and forth, trying to formulate the thoughts in my head to cohesive sounding words.

"I don't know what all of this is between us, but there is clearly *something* happening. This summer I told myself it was just because we were spending so much time together, But then you started doing all those sweet little things to let me know you were thinking of me. And now I hate it when we don't get to talk or see each other.

"But you're also distracting the hell out of me. My game, my sleep—everything. I can't stop thinking about your lips on me, the way your hands feel on my skin, how it feels when we barely even touch. Everything seems to circle around to you. Like I said, I don't know what it all means, but I'm tired of trying to make sense of it by myself."

Greyson moves toward me, taking my hands and locking his eyes with mine.

"Jessa, you don't have to make sense of it yourself." he says softly. "I want to be with you. Not just as a friend, but as your boyfriend. I've wanted this since Turks and Caicos. Maybe the timing has never been perfect. Who knows if it is right now. But I sure as hell am not going to take a chance on missing out on whatever this is."

I let out the breath I hadn't known I was holding. "Okay," I say, smiling faintly.

Grey steps off the bed and scoops me up in his arms. "Are we doing this? Are we in this?" he asks me.

My mind swirls, and I push away the doubt and fear that's trying to creep in. It's clear Greyson wants this, too.

"I'm in..."

"But..." Greyson says, raising his eyebrows at me. He knows I almost always have a but.

"This has to stay between us. I mean, obviously Bex and Monty will figure it out since they live with us, but we have to keep this private—behind closed doors—for the sake of the teams and our coaches."

"Jessa –" Greyson interjects, but I cut him off.

"No, it's the only way this will work, at least for now. Our coaches are already keeping a close eye on us. And how would it look if the team captain is breaking the number one rule?" I say. I know I sound on edge, but so much could go wrong.

Greyson listens, his eyes focused on me, while he strokes my arms. Up and down, from shoulder to wrist as I speak. His touch is soothing, and despite my cautious attitude, it's working to calm me down.

"I'm sorry. It's not that I want to keep us a secret. I keep telling myself the timing makes sense," I say quietly. "But keeping things low-key is better for the team... better for everything. If we're going to do this, I want to get it right."

I look up at Greyson, heat creeping up my cheeks. I'm halfway terrified that he'll be angry at me for putting stipulations like this on our relationship before it even begins. But what I can't bring myself to tell him is that I'm terrified of what happens if this blows up. I'm trying to take chances when they're worth it. But is he worth the risk? I'm only ninety percent sure.

It's the other ten percent that I know will keep me up at night.

"We've got this," Grey says. "I've got you. So, in public we're discreet. In private you're mine."

As proof to his statement, he pulls me back into bed and kisses me until my limbs go weak. I fall back on his pillow, loving the way it feels to be next to him like this.

Grey holds me tightly while we lay there. He feels safe—his skin warm, soft, and smooth against mine. And damn, he's arousing every one of my nerve endings. After awhile, Greyson dozes off, his breathing slow and even, his face relaxed in a boyish, peaceful way that makes my heart feel like it's going to burst. I allow my eyes to flutter closed and relish in the comfort of my best friend's arms.

<h1 style="text-align:center">14
Greyson</h1>

I'm awake, but I can't move. There's a sexy body entangled with mine—one leg draped over my groin, an arm snug around my waist, and a head full of dark hair in tousled waves across my chest. It takes me a minute to register what I'm staring at. I smile like an idiot at the ceiling—*it wasn't a dream.* Jessa Blakely, my best friend and long-term crush, is my girlfriend. *My girlfriend.* Sure, she can't be in public, but it doesn't matter. The girl of my dreams is mine.

Man, last night was great. I still can't believe Jessa waited up for me, baked my favorite kind of muffins, and then finally told me how she felt about me. And, fuck, the sex—it was phenomenal. I've never felt more connected to another human, physically or emotionally. My cock twitches at the memory of Jessa's body against mine, and I can feel my pulse pick up at the thought of doing it again. I'm willing my heart and cock to calm down when there's a light knock on the door. I shimmy out from under Jessa, moving slowly so I don't wake her. Not sure why I'm worried, though, because Jessa hardly stirs. I adjust my dick to hide my morning wood, run my fingers through my hair, and inch the door open a crack. It's Collins.

"Shit, Greyson, I'm sorry to wake you. But have you seen Jessa?"

I open the door to reveal the still sleeping Jessa curled up in my bed. I can't hide the giant smile, even as I try to play it cool. "Ohhh, well that explains why I couldn't find her," Collins says, and tries just as unsuccessfully to hide her grin. "We have the first shift at the community carnival today. We need to leave in an hour."

"I'll wake her up," I say, starting to close the door.

"Hmm... I bet you will," Collins says before the door clicks shut. Judging by the smirk and wink she gave me, I'm guessing Collins is on her way to tell Monty.

I slide back under the covers and lean over Jessa, sweeping her hair from her face before brushing her lips with a gentle kiss. She presses her backside against me in her sleep and lets out the faintest moan. The sound drives me wild. My body already aches for her, and even though her eyes are still closed, I can feel in her movements that she's awake. I press against her as she turns her face to me, our tongues finding each other. It's a sensual dance and, even though there isn't much time this morning, we get lost in each other as our kiss deepens. I let it go on for a few minutes, but then pull away, even as my dick screams at me to keep going. Looks like it's a cold shower kind of morning. No one else has ever affected me quite like this.

"Jessa," I say, my voice strained. It's taking all my willpower not to give into my dick. "Collins stopped by looking for you a bit ago. She said you have to leave in an hour for the carnival."

Jessa's eyes snap open. "Damn. Guess that means the cat's out of the bag, huh? I should probably go talk to her about our arrangement," she says as she rolls off the bed. It's already lonely and cold without her in it.

Jessa locates her discarded clothes strewn around the room, putting them on in a hurry. Before she goes, she gives me a quick kiss, then disappears out my door.

Within seconds of her leaving, Oakes barges in, uninvited, eyes bulging.

"Did I just see Blakely make the walk of shame from your room?" He asks. His excitement vibrates off of him, but I'm no idiot. I know Collins already shared what—or rather who—she found in my bed this morning.

"Yeah, though I wouldn't call it the walk of shame," I say, stretching casually but unable to mask the grin. "Things kind of progressed last night."

"Progressed? Is that what we're calling it?"

"For now," I say. "You and Collins have to keep this quiet though. In public we're not together, but in private we're trying this."

"Nice. I'm happy for you man. It's a step in the right direction."

"And she's the one who asked for what she wanted."

"Even better." Oakes grins.

"Get outta here man. I've gotta get ready for the carnival."

The community carnival is one of the last events we're expected to engage in as a part of our pre-season partying penance. But it doesn't feel like a punishment because most of us would have volunteered anyway. It's a good time and a known campus favorite. The women's team covers most of the first shift, but when Oakes and I arrive early, we see most of the men's team had the same idea. We wander around, scoping out the carnival game and food, stopping to chat with players of the women's team. We share details of our games last night, fist bumping on the double wins for HU.

Out of the corner of my eye, Jessa stands at a booth, her head thrown back in laughter at something a customer is saying to her.

She looks gorgeous with her hair pulled back in an effortlessly perfect ponytail, a make-up free face, wearing a HU hoodie and sweatpants. She looks my direction and our eyes lock. My heart thumps in my chest when her face breaks out in a wide smile, and I can only smile back like a lovestruck fool. Oakes elbows me in the ribs, and I turn to see Coach Hayes approaching us. He eyes me warily, his eyes drifting toward Jessa and back to me.

"Play it cool, man," Oakes warns. I straighten up and fight the urge to look back at my *girlfriend*. The woman I can now call mine. Well, sort of.

"Gentlemen," Coach says. "I hope we're maintaining focus on our community engagement and the season." My face warms, and I feel like a fifth grader getting caught doing something by the principal.

"Of course, Coach. Eye on the prize," I say, though I woke up with the best prize in my bed this morning. What would he say if he knew?

"Oakes?" Coach Hayes stares at him.

"Staying focused, Coach!" Oakes responds with a little too much enthusiasm. I want to elbow him and remind *him* to play it cool.

When Coach moves on, Oakes and I let out a collective breath.

"Fuck. Dude's like a spider. He's got eyes everywhere," Oakes comments.

Later that afternoon, Oakes and I are walking to meet Nova and Jones for our scheduled time in the weightroom. Our conversation is centered around Jessa and Collins, sprinkled in with talk about how well both basketball teams are doing this season. Mostly though, we're both jacked about how well things are going with the girls.

"But even with this thing you've got going on with Collins, you still haven't told her that you're her secret admirer?" I ask. Because frankly, this is concerning.

"No. But I don't know, man," Oakes says with a sigh. "There's been a shift. In a good way. So I think we're both avoiding a talk about what it is and what it means. Bringing the secret admirer stuff up seems like the wrong move."

"Well, I think it's time you two get on the same page," I advise. Not only is it the smart thing to do, but I know for a fact this is what Jessa has been telling Collins as well. *When will they listen to us?*

We let the subject drop, returning to our earlier conversation about how the women's team is on a hot streak. We're all feeling more connected—to our teams, to the program, to the hard work we're putting in. We've got a program double-header coming up before we can spend time celebrating the upcoming holidays.

Oakes and I scan the weightroom for Nova and Jones. My heart stutters when I notice something unraveling in the corner of the room. Jessa's body is taut with frustration, and it doesn't take me long to see why. It's Butler, standing next to Jessa at one of the leg stations. Judging by the annoyed expression on her face, Butler's said something arrogant that set her off. He reaches out and grabs her wrist. She yanks her arm away fast, trying to pull free.

That's all I need to see.

I'm moving before I even register the decision, cutting across the room, and shoving Butler hard in the chest.

"Greyson!" Jessa shouts, but I don't hear it—I'm locked in on Butler. No way in hell is he putting his hands on my girl. Nova and Jones rush to Jessa's side, and out of the corner of my eye I see Corden and Oakes closing in behind me.

I give Butler a second shove, and it sends him stumbling against the wall. "What the fuck, man?" he grunts.

"Don't 'what the fuck' me," I growl back. "Looks like Jessa doesn't want you touching her."

"This has nothing to do with you," Butler snaps. "It's between me and Blakely."

"If it's about her, then it's about me." I say, the words tumbling out before I can think. But I don't care. He needs to stay away from Jessa.

Corden and Oakes force us apart, but Butler keeps running his mouth. "She's not your girl. She can think for herself. But she's good at leading people on."

I lunge for Butler, fury exploding through my body. A sharp whistle cuts through the weightroom. Everyone freezes, including me. I glance at Jessa and see the panic written across her face. Coach Morris and Coach Hayes storm across the weightroom, both flushed and furious.

"What the hell is going on?" Coach Hayes yells. I've never seen his face so red.

"Ladies, are you alright?" Coach Morris asks.

"You four," Coach Hayes barks, pointing at me, Oakes, Butler, and Corden. "My office. Now."

"Ladies—my office," Coach Morris says more softly. "Everyone else, get back to work."

Damn it. Everything had been going so well. The carnival marked the last of our penance punishment, but now this. Because I couldn't keep my temper in check. But no way could I just stand by and watch Butler put his hands on Jessa. Or any of the girls, for that matter.

Coach is calmer than I'd expected, all things considered. I have to give him credit for letting us each share our versions of the story. Then, he asks Coach Morris to bring the girls in.

What a shit show. It's obvious Butler wants to get with Jessa, and is butthurt about her flirting with him at the party but showing no interest since. Today, he crossed a line.

An hour later, I'm still vibrating with anger. Butler's keeping his distance, but he shoots me the occasional contemptuous look from across the locker room. Coach sent us here while he and Coach Morris discussed what should be done. The girls were already sent home.

The coaches decide Butler and Jessa will be reassigned lifting partners. Oakes and Corden are off the hook since their only crime was trying to break things up. Butler and I get a two-game suspension, but we're required to attend practice and come early for extra conditioning. The extra conditioning is supposed to "work off our hostility."

Coach stops me as I'm leaving. "Hastings," he says quietly. "I hope she's worth it." The look he gives me is part warning, part knowing.

At home, Jessa won't even look at me. I understand she's upset that I almost outed us, on the first day of our relationship, no less. I'm sure she thinks I don't believe she can handle Butler herself. I mean, isn't it enough that I have a two-game suspension and extra workouts? Did she think I could just let his behavior slide? This is more than just about Jessa. It's about boundaries and respect. She's not wrong to be upset with me, but damn... this is brutal.

We literally went from friends, to secret lovers, to now being cockblocked by tempers and pride.

The first of the two-game suspension is our program double-header at home. At least we still get to sit on the bench with the team, but man, this sucks. Basketball has been my life. Jessa has been my life, even when we were only friends. I've always wanted to do whatever makes her happy.

With this suspension, I can't help thinking about life after basketball. I want to get married and have little ballers, and maybe coach someday. Sports broadcasting doesn't feel like my path. I want to stay directly involved with the game. I need to stop living off the high of our high school state championship and the dream of winning one here. I need to figure out what comes next. Maybe that starts with figuring out this thing with Jessa. Who knew a suspension would push me into such deep thoughts about my future?

I focus my attention on the women's game unfolding in front of me. Jessa is intentional, deliberate, and powerful as she runs the court—cutting between defenders, rising for shots. Watching her play defense against bigger opponents might be my favorite. She makes it look so easy. Her face is set in determination; she's locked in, completely in the zone. Muscles flex as she moves with force and grace. I've never seen her look so strong. All the off-season work shows.

The opposing team's center has been throwing elbows like a crazed chicken all night. Suddenly, her elbow flies out and connects hard against Jessa's temple.

Jessa drops to the floor, crumbling in slow motion, and her head hits the floor with a sickening thud. The crowd gasps and goes deadly silent. I can't move. I can't speak. My heart stops.

Jessa was just sprinting down the court. Now, she's lying on the floor, unmoving. Her teammates rush to her, yelling her name in a panic. Trainers and the on-scene medics run in. Everyone is moving around, reacting, but I'm still frozen in place. My teammates are all in the locker room getting ready for our game, so I'm alone with my panic.

Jessa's loaded onto a spinal board and the medics place an oxygen mask over her nose and mouth. I still have not seen her move. I can't see her emerald eyes. *Oh God. Not Jessa.* They wheel her through the tunnel where an ambulance waits. Coach Morris and the rest of the women's team look rattled. Someone must have alerted Coach Hayes because he's standing with the women, seemingly trying to comfort them.

Suddenly Oakes is at my side, guiding me toward the locker room. It's only then I realize my face is wet. I've been crying without even noticing. Oakes is talking, trying to bring me back to reality, but everything is muffled. Our team still has a game to play, but I can't think about that. All I see is Jessa's head hitting the floor. Her body still as she lays on the floor. "I have to go," I croak out. I think Oakes tries to stop me, but I'm already leaving. I need to get to her. Now.

This is Jessa. A force of nature. Tough as hell. Why didn't I force her to talk to me when she shut me out after the weightroom incident?

I get in my car and somehow drive to the hospital. *She has to be okay.*

Jessa

I try to open my eyes, but everything is blurry. My head throbs, and it feels heavy, like someone swung a bat at my skull. I attempt to sit up and immediately feel a wave of nausea.

A moan escapes me.

My right hand is pinned beneath something heavy and warm. I try to move it, but it barely budges. I switch to my left hand and feel along my face and scalp. It all feels normal. There's no blood anyway because my fingers come away clean.

Greyson's voice pierces through my skull. "She's awake!"

Why is he yelling? I squeeze my eyes shut, trying to block out the sharp pain that followed his deep voice.

"Jessa?" Greyson says. His voice is shaky now, but at least he's softened it. He squeezes my right hand.

I groan in response, but keep my eyes shut. Footsteps move about the room and then cold fingers touch my wrist. There's a thermometer pressed into my mouth.

I breathe deeply, trying to quell the nausea. It takes too much effort, but I manage to whisper, "Where am I?"

Greyson's soft voice comes through the darkness. "You're in the hospital."

Well, that explains the thermometer and cold hands.

He continues before I gather the energy to speak. "You were unconscious for a bit, J. I've been so worried. You took an elbow to the temple during the game and hit your head on the court. Hard. You weren't moving. I just saw you lying there, and—" His voice cracks.

I peel my eyes open and squint up at him.

"There was nothing I could do. It was awful. Coach Morris and the team came by, but you weren't awake."

Wait, how is Greyson here if this happened during my game. The men play after us. Grey must see my confusion because he adds, "I followed the ambulance."

"When can I go home?" I say, swallowing hard and wincing at the ache in my head. The nurse in the room ignores my question, guiding me to lie back. She explains they've run scans and did neurological checks, but they want additional cognitive testing to assess the concussion.

It's all too much. Everything is too bright, too loud, too muddled. "I want to go home." I whisper, and begin to cry.

Greyson squeezes my hand again. My eyes are closed again, but I'd bet anything Grey is pleading with the nurse with his intense blue eyes. Begging her to bend the rules. Anything to stop my tears. I squeeze his hand back in gratitude.

The nurse finally says, "I'll send in the doctor to chat with you."

After I calm down a bit, Greyson reaches for his phone. "I'm going to update Collins and Oakes. Let them know you're awake. I called your mom, too, and left a voicemail."

That makes my stomach twist. I'm sure she was watching the game and is probably already on a plane. I must nod off, because the sound of shuffling footsteps startles me awake. A low voice follows.

"Ms. Blakley, I'm Dr. Pfeiffer. How's that head doing? Feeling any pain or nausea?"

"Hard to lift my head. Nauseous." I grunt.

He nods and tells me it's to be expected after a head injury. "We'll get you some Tylenol and anti-nausea medication."

As he's leaving my room, Dr. Pfeiffer says, "Given that you lost consciousness, we'd like to keep you overnight for–"

I tune him out. Standard protocol, *blah, blah, blah*. I don't need hospital observation. Can't he see I've got an overprotective best friend here and an overbearing mother on her way?

It's late. I'm exhausted and uncomfortable, but each time I drift back from a restless sleep, Greyson is there. He jolts awake with every move I make. The one time he left my side to pee, he was back at an impressive speed.

We're both awake when the door swings open flooding the room with harsh light. I wince. Not just from the light, but because I can hear my mother's voice in the hallway.

"Jessa, I've been calling and texting since I landed!"

Oh God.

"She was knocked out during the game," Greyson says, saving me from having to respond. "I'm sure her phone is still in the locker room. I left you a voicemail but never heard back."

I squeeze his hand gratefully. Even exhausted, Greyson steps in to be a buffer between me and my mother.

"Mom, I'm fine," I say, grimacing with each word. This head pain is no joke. "It's just a precaution to keep me here overnight. You didn't need to fly in."

"Jessa, you're my only daughter. Of course I came." She flicks her eyes to Greyson. "I'm here now. You can go."

I inhale, ready to object, but Grey beats me to it.

"With all due respect, Mrs. Blakely, I'm not leaving." His tone is stern, leaving no room for argument. "If Jessa's here, I'm here."

My mother gives him a disapproving look, but Greyson doesn't flinch.

"I'm going to get an update from a doctor," she huffs, storming out of the room.

We're an odd trio in this small hospital room. Greyson and my mother are silent, sitting on opposite sides. Which is probably for the best. Greyson takes the chair directly next to my bed, which seems to irritate Mom, but she says nothing. Eventually, she dozes off on the small couch adjacent from the bed, snoring softly.

Morning comes, the light fortunately muted by the blinds. My head still hurts, but at least I don't want to vomit every time I move or speak. Greyson's phone dings a few times, jarring him awake.

"Bex, Oakes, and Coach Morris are here if you're up for a visit," he says.

I nod. A few minutes later, they knock softly and enter, immediately filling my sterile room with warmth. "Glad to see those eyes again, Jessa," Coach says. "You gave us quite a scare last night. Good to see your mom made it."

My mom woke up with the sound of their voices, and is now sitting on her makeshift bed, smoothing out her sweatshirt and hair.

For the first time, I notice that Bex is hovering behind Monty. She looks close to tears.

I hold out my arms to her. "Hey, Bex."

I sound weak, and that seems to be what breaks her. She bursts forward, hugging me tightly. Pain shoots through me, and I grunt in pain. "Ow, too tight, Bex."

Bex jumps back, horrified.

"I'm fine, just not ready to be jostled too much," I laugh, and that seems to make her feel better because her shoulders relax.

The doctor walks in and scans the crowded room.

"Ms. Blakely," he says, nodding his head at each of my guests in greeting. My mother stands up as if he is addressing her. He continues, keeping his eyes on me. "How do we feel this morning?"

"Much better," I say, shifting against the pillows to get comfortable in a sitting position. "I can at least open my eyes without pain and nausea."

"Excellent. Sounds like we're headed in the right direction. How do you feel about blowing this popsicle stand?" the doctor jokes.

"Yes, please!" I've never heard a better idea in my life.

He smiles, but his tone is serious. "Okay, but here's the deal—your body and brain need to heal. If I let you go home, I need you to stay hydrated, relaxed, and rested. No screens or reading for at least a few days. I'd also like you to have someone with you around the clock for the next couple of days. Just to ensure you follow my instructions. Someone will also need to bring you back in a few days for more cognitive testing. Clear?"

I nod. *Whatever I need to do to get out of here.*

Greyson jumps in. "There are three of us who can take shifts at home. Jessa won't be alone."

"I'll stay with her," my mother interrupts. *Dear Lord, if my mother stays and plays nurse the next couple of days, I will go insane.* I look at the ceiling, as if emphasizing how serious my prayers are. Coach must read my expression and steps in like an angel.

"Lauren," she says, her tone soothing yet firm as she steps closer to my mother. "I'm sure you've got a lot going on at home. Between Jessa's roommates and the team, Jessa will be in good hands. We'll make sure you're updated daily."

My mother bristles, looking first at me then around the room. "Jessa needs me. Of course there's things I need to do back home, but this is more important."

"Mom, I'll be fine," I say. "You'd hate sleeping on our couch or staring at me while I rest. I have plenty of help."

Please, please, please, I plead in my head.

My mother exhales, defeated. "Fine. But I expect regular reports. And I'm not leaving until she's settled."

"Now that we've settled that, let's get Jessa out of here and into her own bed," Coach Morris says with a clap of her hands.

Greyson offers to drive since Mom Ubered from the airport. Poor guy. Once again willing to step into the line of fire. Bex and Monty go ahead of us to make sure I'll have everything I need at the condo. Coach follows them out, continuing to reassure my mother.

Hours later—because hospitals move at glacial speed—we finally pull into the driveway. Greyson helps me out of the car, his hold gentle around my waist. Once in my bedroom, Greyson steps out so Mom can help me into my most comfortable clothes. She tucks me in like a child. I can't remember the last time she's done that, but it feels nice to have her acting so nurturing.

"Thanks, Mom," I say, a little unsure how to act around her in this space where I can't pick up a basketball.

"You rest. I'm headed to the airport to see if I can get an earlier flight on stand-by. It sounds like Coach Morris has things under control here. As long as you let me know if I'm needed back here. You'll be good as new in a few days."

Mom slips out of my bedroom, and I hear her say something to my roommates. Undoubtedly a prepared lecture about how to properly care for me. I nestle down into my cozy bedding, letting sleep take hold now that I'm in the softness of my own bed.

Greyson

Thank goodness Lauren Blakely is gone. Her lecture implying we're all incompetent boobs was next level. It gave me more joy than I'd admit out loud to when she had to eat her own words when she saw our well-organized plan. Collins, Oakes, and I detailed out tasks and assigned shifts for Jessa's care. I volunteer for the first night shift. Jessa slept most of the day after coming home, so I assume she'll be awake part of the night. I also want to talk to her about the weightroom incident with Butler, and I'm hoping this gives us the chance.

I ease through Jessa's bedroom door, careful not to wake her, and sit on the edge of her bed. She's a bit pale and her hair is matted to her head, but she still looks like my Jessa. God, what a terrifying ordeal. I don't even want to think about how it could have been worse. I reach out to brush stray hairs from her face, and at my touch, she snuggles into my hand. It's a simple thing, but it makes my heart feel like it could burst.

How did I go from burying my feelings just a few weeks ago to becoming a possessive asshole?

The slow rise and fall of Jessa's chest hypnotizes me. She looks so peaceful. I text my siblings to give them an update. Soren and Corden love Jessa and have been as worried about her. *Love.* It's such a strong word, yet it doesn't scare me as much as it used to. Jessa is loveable and deserves the kind of love she wants but doesn't get from her mother. She understands me, knows basketball is a part of me but not all of me. She sees my insecurities before I can even name them. From the beginning, Jessa has seen me for more than my family's money or the superficial relationships I've had over the last three years because of my name.

Tears roll down my cheek as I continue to watch her sleeping soundly.

"I love you, Jessa."

It feels like an out-of-body experience.

"Mmm... love you Grey." It's so quiet, it's almost inaudible. I stiffen. Did she just say she loves me? A stupid big smile spreads across my face before I can stop it. I know she's half-asleep and maybe not coherent, but damn, hearing those words feels good. I walk to the other side of the bed and slip into the open space beside her. Facing her, I gently stroke her hair until sleep pulls me under too. When I wake up, Jessa is staring at me in confusion. "Grey, what are you doing in here?" she mumbles, her voice raspy.

"I figured you wouldn't sleep all night, and I didn't want you to wake up alone or confused," I say, reaching for her water bottle on the nightstand and passing it to her.

She takes it gratefully. "What's with the big smile? You should not be smiling when I feel like I've been hit by a truck."

"Nothing in particular," I say. "Just glad you're awake and making sense. Did you know you talk in your sleep?"

"Do not," Jessa argues.

"Do to," I retort back.

"Shit. What did I say?"

"You don't remember?"

"If I did, would I be asking?" she fires back.

"Guess not. Doesn't matter," I say, crestfallen.

I knew I shouldn't get my hopes up that she was ready for more. Hell, we haven't even talked about the Butler fight because she got hurt, and here I am professing my love like an idiot. Damn it, Greyson. Get a grip.

"Why do you look so pissed all of a sudden?" Jessa asks.

"Not pissed," I say, plastering a smile on my face. "How are you feeling? Do you need anything?"

"I'm okay," Jessa says, searching my eyes. "Will you just hold me for a bit?"

"Always," I say, leaning against the headboard and pulling her into me.

The fact that she wants me to hold her makes me feel gooey inside. I love her. I thoroughly and fucking completely love her. I'm in trouble.

Over the next day, things go smoothly. Collins, Oakes, and I are excellent caretakers, if I do say so myself. A few of her teammates stop by, and she seems a little better. We eventually move her to the couch for a change of scenery since she's restless in her room. She's still supposed to avoid screens, so her only real entertainment is us and whoever comes to visit.

The next afternoon, when Oakes and Collins head off to practice, I stay behind since I'm suspended anyway. Coach is pissed about the whole Butler situation, and honestly, my mind is nowhere near basketball right now.

With no other distractions, it's probably the best chance I'll get to talk to Jessa. She's half sitting, half lying on the couch, using me like a personal body pillow.

"Jessa?" I whisper, gauging if she's awake.

"Hmm?"

"I wanted to say that I'm sorry about the Butler outburst the other day," I say. "I realize I was reactive and overprotective. I know you can handle yourself. I just... I don't want you to have to do it alone."

She shifts to face me fully. "Grey, I appreciate the apology. I know you care. But I don't feel in control of much in my life, and I don't need rescuing—except maybe from my mother." She sighs. "And we only just agreed to see where this might go. No one can know about us, and that almost blew up in our faces day one. Maybe this isn't going to work."

Her eyes hold mine, and my stomach drops.

"No," I blurt. "We can make this work. We will make this work. I almost lost you the other night—do you know how terrifying that was? Seeing you on the court, not moving? I couldn't get to you. I couldn't do anything except watch them load you into the ambulance."

Tears burn behind my eyes, and I swallow, forcing my voice to come out steadier than I feel. "I don't know what I would have done if you hadn't woken up."

I pull her back into me. She wipes away one of the tears I didn't manage to hide. Neither of us speak for a long time.

The tension sits in the air around us. There's uncertainty left in the things unsaid, and I worry I've ruined everything. Occasionally, one of us sniffles or wipes a tear from our face.

Jessa reaches up and nuzzles my neck. I look down to see her eyes on me, and I trace the curve of her jaw with my thumb. Her lips part with a soft gasp. Our mouths meet like a magnet drawing them together, and Jessa guides one of my hands up the smooth skin of her stomach until it meets the swell of her breast. I rub my thumb over her nipple, and it puckers beneath my touch. Her tongue swipes over my lips, and I let her explore, matching her stroke for stroke. My body buzzes, caught up in the feel of her soft skin. Jessa's breath is ragged as she tugs my shirt over my head and pushes me against the couch. Our emotions are palpable, intertwining around our moving bodies.

"Jessa," I say, a lukewarm attempt to stop her.

She quiets me with a finger to my lips, lifting herself up to straddle my lap, a gorgeous muscular leg on each side of me. Her hips shift, causing friction between her body and my growing erection. Her eye contact doesn't break, even when she licks her lips in a way that makes my heart hammer.

"Everyone knows me for basketball. If I died tonight, that's what they'd remember me for, but I need more than that." Jessa is still looking into my eyes like they're windows, like she's trying to let me see her clearly.

"Your head," I croak. My skin is hot and the yearning to break this tension is almost unbearable. But the logical voice in my head keeps reminding me she has a concussion. "You need to rest."

"I'm already feeling much better," Jessa says. Her hands place mine on her thighs. I can't help but rub my palms up and down them. Jessa pulls me to her, her rough kiss deep, causing my erection to jump beneath her. Her nipples brush against my chest, and I hiss as she pulls down my waistband to release my cock. My head drops back as she begins to stroke it.

She pauses, watching the lust on my face, looking smug. Her hands circle my dick and pump up and down.

"Fuuuck! So– good, Jessa," I groan.

She smiles, but it isn't a sweet Jessa smile. It's a wicked grin. I lift my head to look at her, but she drops to her knees, still holding my length in her palm, and slides her tongue over my tip. Her fists pump up and down in short strokes, faster and faster, while her sucking gets harder and harder. I'm thirty seconds from coming.

"Christ. You have to stop," I pant with pleasure.

But she doesn't stop. Jessa looks me straight in the eyes before taking me all the way to the back of her throat. My hands go to her hair, spreading my fingers along her head, and groan. *Fuck.* I remember her head injury and shift my hands to her shoulders, guiding her up and down my length. My hips twitch, involuntarily thrusting towards her mouth. I can't stop anymore, not when she takes me in like this, like this is all she wants to be doing. My dick pulses and my control snaps. With one more thrust, I pull Jessa up. "Going to come..."

Jessa moves her hand between my legs, cupping my balls and circles my head with one last sensual lick. My stomach tightens as the waves of pleasure take over. She watches as my release comes, pooling on my abs.

I don't have words. I stand up, no way done with her.

Jessa stares as I slowly help her up from her knees. "What are you doing, Grey?"

"You are a dirty girl, J, and now you've made me dirty." I pick her up, and she wraps her legs around my waist, arms circling my neck. I walk her toward her bathroom. "Time to get clean."

I gently set her down in front of the shower, and close and lock the door.

"Strip," I say to Jessa after I turn the water on and watch as she obeys, still eyeballing the erection straining against my shorts. I hope she sees what she does to me.

Her clothes drop to the floor, and Jessa steps into the shower, leaning her head back to let the water run down her hair and breasts.

I join her, my eyes on her fingers, pinching her hard nipples. It's too much to bear, so I pull her wet body into mine, covering her mouth with a kiss that tells her everything I want to do to her. My dick is already so hard, and I can't believe I feel this much need after she was just on her knees.

I lift her up, setting my dick against her opening and a trail of kisses down her neck. She jerks against me, trying to force my tip in further, but I resist, nibbling the skin at her collar bone until she moans.

"More. I need more," Jessa says desperately.

My mouth pulls in her nipple, sucking and tugging lightly with my teeth. She hisses.

"You like that?" I tease.

"Y-ess," She says between jagged breaths.

"The things I want to do to you, Jessa."

"Please."

I smile wickedly—my turn to make her lose control— and trail kisses down her stomach, until I reach the sensitive spot between her legs. I place a kiss there, and then move my fingers between her folds.

"You're so wet," I breathe.

"That is what you do to me, Grey. Keep going."

"Yes, ma'am," I say, and plunge two fingers into her warm, wet pussy. I push in and out, and her body moves against my hand. Her inner walls tighten around my fingers, and she moans, rubbing her nipples again as rivulets of water trickle down her breasts. *Shit. That's so hot.* I add a finger to work her clit, and a soft whimper escapes her.

"I've got you, J," I say, moving my fingers faster, enjoying how she squirms in response.

Her moans get more desperate when I swap my fingers for my mouth, parting her legs further, and flattening my tongue against her clit. I lick up from her opening until I almost reach her clit, then I stop, doing it again. Each time, I apply a tiny bit more pressure and stop millimeters before hitting that sensitive bud. I can tell by her writhing body that it's driving her crazy. After a few more swipes, she yanks on my hair with one hand and hits the shower wall with the other.

"What... are... you... doing?"

I smile against her opening, then continue licking her most sensitive spot. God, she tastes good and is so fucking wet. I want her to come as hard as I did when she had me in her mouth, so I make an O-shape with my lips and suck her clit into my mouth. Jessa cries out, and I can feel her legs shaking, barely able to hold her body up.

"Grey, please," she begs. "Stop teasing. I can't take much more."

I know the feeling. I might explode just from tasting her.

I continue sucking on her clit and drive two fingers inside of her. Pumping them in and out, I add a third finger and put pressure on her g-spot. Her strained, breathless moans make pre-cum burst from my dick. Her body rocks back and forth in synchrony with my fingers, and she presses her body down, trying to get more pressure on her clit. In a matter of seconds, she changes her tactic to pulling my hair and grinding her pussy against my face. She tenses, and her pussy contracts in tight spasms as she climaxes. As she's losing control, I keep going with my tongue and fingers, but slow my pace. I want her to ride this wave of pleasure for as long as possible.

When she's finished, I stand up, but she pulls me down for a kiss, getting a taste of herself in the process.

"Uhh... seems like we have a new problem." She giggles, still flushed and out of breath, and looks down at my rock hard dick. It still feels ready to burst, but giving Jessa that much pleasure is well worth a little blue balls.

"Let's finish showering, and I'll take care of this after you hop out," I say. I can't believe I'm ready to go again. Jessa got me off like fifteen minutes ago, and here I am, ready to blow. Only Jessa can do this to me.

We shift to something almost as intimate, me gently massaging shampoo and conditioner into her hair. I use this opportunity to continue to touch her and lather the body wash, using my hands to gently massage the soap into her skin. I take the handheld shower head and with the still hot water thoroughly rinse the bubbles from my dirty girl.

Content and relaxed, Jessa gets out, wrapping herself in an oversized bath towel as she waits for me to finish my shower.

17

Jessa

I feel dizzy, but it has nothing to do with my concussion. We didn't even have sex, yet he left my head spinning with pleasure. What the fuck is he doing to me?

I'm in fresh clothes, hair brushed, and settled on the couch while Greyson starts dinner. I can't even begin to think about dinner when all I see in my head is us pleasuring each other. It was so hot. If I don't stop running it through my head in a loop, I'm going to be wet all over again. Tomorrow, I go back to the doctor for my final tests. Hopefully I'll be cleared to practice. Coach already warned me I wouldn't play in the next game. I'm not happy about it. Sitting on the bench won't get me to my goals.

Bex and Monty get home just as Greyson finishes dinner. "Smells good," Monty says, headed straight for the kitchen.

Greyson swats him away. "It's not ready yet, dear."

Bex drops down on the couch next to me. "You're looking so much better. We missed our fearless leader at practice though. The team's a mess without you."

Great. Nothing like confirming one of my biggest fears—letting my team down. Bex must see something on my face because she quickly adds, "But practice was good. We're getting ready for the game."

She leans over and gives me a hug. I know she's feeding me a white lie, but it does make me feel slightly better. What would I do without her? I glance at Greyson, and he's watching Bex and me with a smile. I can't help but smile back.

"Looks like you two made up," Bex says under her breath, following my gaze to Greyson.

"Something like that," I mutter. She raises her brows and scoots closer to me. "I mean, he made me feel much better."

Bex giggles, and I smack her arm before the guys notice and ask what we're talking about.

"Oh, I talked to Coach about skipping weights tomorrow to take you to your appointment," Bex says.

"Great, thanks."

"I—I was planning to take her," Greyson says, setting a plate in front of me.

"I've got it," Bex says.

"No. I'll take her," Greyson says, a little too intensely.

Bex flinches. "Okay... you take her," she says, looking at me.

I shrug. No clue what that's about. "Well, at least you don't have to miss weights, Bex. Thanks for the offer," I say trying to lighten the mood.

No clue what that's about. Greyson's been weirdly possessive lately. I think he feels more responsibility for me since we said we'd try this boyfriend/girlfriend thing.

That night as I'm getting ready for bed, I mentally plan for the return to normal life. There's so much to catch up on. My mother has been unusually quiet since she went back to Connecticut. I appreciate her silence, yet it makes suspicious at the same time. I'm sure she'll pounce once I get the all-clear at my appointment.

Greyson appears in my doorway, pillow in hand, wearing only a pair of shorts. He tosses the pillow at me. "I'm here for the slumber party."

"Greyson, you really don't have to. I feel so much better."

"Well, if you don't want me here, I'll take my pillow and go." He reaches for it dramatically.

I roll my eyes, and he drops the act, kneeling beside me on the bed and pulling me in. "What's going on? You seem stressed. The appointment will go well, I'm sure."

"It's not that. Well, I guess it kind of is, but it's more so thinking about how I'm going to be able to make up for the last couple of days—missing workouts, letting my team down, waiting for my mom to insert herself." I sigh and look away from him.

"Jessa, you've got this. It's only been a couple of days, and you're missing one game. Show up and be the best damn bench coach they've ever had."

I give a small smile. "I don't deserve you."

"Come here," Greyson says, wrapping his arms around me when I rest my head on his chest.

"Relax. Sleep. We'll deal with everything tomorrow."

I fall asleep faster than expected, safe in his warmth.

The next morning, the doctor says I'm lucky considering how hard I was hit. I'm improving fast, but setbacks are still possible. I can ease back into basketball and school. He hands me a note for my professors, coaches, and trainers explaining how I might feel over the next couple of weeks and to keep an eye out for anything concerning.

"I'm cleared," I say with relief, climbing into Greyson's Jeep.

"That's not exactly what the doctor said," Greyson reminds me.

"Close enough. I can play basketball. That's all I needed to hear."

"I think that's all you heard," he says. I stick my tongue out at him as he pulls out of the parking lot.

Greyson drops me off at the Blakely Center to update Coach Morris. When I walk into her office, she and Coach Hayes appear to be reviewing game film, but they jump apart like guilty teenagers when I enter.

"Uh— am I interrupting?" I ask.

"Jessa!" Coach Morris says too brightly. Her face is flushed. "It's good to see you up and around. We were just reviewing a game."

Coach Hayes heads towards the door. "I'll just be in my office. Good to see you, Jessa."

I stare at Coach. "What was that all about? I know I had a concussion, but that was weird."

Coach waves it off. "Nothing. Just surprised to see you."

Right.

I hand her the doctor's note and tell her I'm cleared to play. She still insists I don't dress for the next game, but wants me on the sidelines to support the team.

The next day, Coach lets me dress for practice, but only for non-contact drills. I feel like a fucking failure. The team seemed pumped to see me, but they couldn't hide their disappointment when she said I was out for the next game.

The next couple of days are a slow, headache-inducing blur. Reading takes forever, but I try to push through. I stay cheerful around my roommates, especially Greyson, because I don't want them to worry or suspect something is off. He means well and is only trying to be protective, but Greyson is smothering me. I'm not sure I can handle much more before I snap on him. I love sleeping next to him, but I'm still cautious outside the condo, which makes things feel... off. And as I predicted, my mother has started back in with her regular calls and texts, reminding me I need to be at peak performance.

The team won the last game, and I somehow survived not playing in it. I nearly lost my voice, yelling from the bench. It was close, but a win's a win. We're all exhausted from balancing classes, weights, practice, and games. Thanksgiving ends the semester, but winter athletes barely get a break. We'll play through Christmas, get a couple days off, then we're back to finish the season. And, fingers crossed, make the NCAA Tournament.

And then there's graduation looming. The WNBA draft. My entire future. Everyone keeps asking what my plans are, and suddenly I realize I don't really have any. I'm usually more on top of this stuff. Now I feel behind on everything.

As captains, Oakes and I meet with the coaches to discuss how we can build up the teams' spirits during the holidays. It's easy to be antsy and homesick when the gym and campus are closed. Oakes and I agree to host the teams at our condo for Thanksgiving.

"It'll be fun!" I say, at the end of the meeting, but really, it's just another thing on my plate. My already *very* full plate. The one without future plans on it.

"You good Jessa?" Monty asks on the walk home. "You seem a bit distracted. How's the head?"

"I'm good. Just a lot on my mind."

He smirks. "Is Hastings one of those things on your mind?"

He sure is, and he might die in his sleep if he keeps hovering like a mother hen. "What?" I say, but then I sigh. No point in hiding it. "Oh, shit, of course. Him and a million other things linked to my future that I currently have no bandwidth for."

"Right there with you." He pauses. "It's actually really overwhelming, now that I think about it."

Shit, I don't need to bring Monty down with me.

"Sorry to be a downer," I say, forcing a laugh. "In happier news, how are things with Bex?"

He lights up. "So good."

I grin. "That's all I get? 'So good' and a dreamy look? Are you going to tell her you are the secret admirer? I know that activity has slowed a bit, but she still thinks about it."

"Yeah, I need to find the right time. Things are just so good with us. I don't want to risk ruining it," he says.

"Maybe over our break?" I suggest.

"Maybe," Monty says, but it's clear he's lost in his own thoughts.

"Have you noticed anything weird between Coach Hayes and Coach Morris?" I ask, gauging it's time for a subject change.

That gets his attention. "What do you mean?"

"When I went in to have my all-clear conversation, they got jumpy when I walked into the office. They were all red and flustered. There's been a couple other instances too."

"Maybe you are still recovering from that head injury?" Monty laughs.

Maybe he's right. No one else knows about what Greyson and I saw with our coaches earlier this year. It's none of our business, really, unless you count the fact that they're so strict with the players. Something is going on. I know it.

But I should focus on my own life. Easier said than done, but a break might help. Then I can refocus on basketball and figure out my future.

18

Greyson

Practices, games, exams, final papers, projects, and planning Thanksgiving for both teams at the condo might actually do me in. On top of that, it's work just staying under the radar with Jessa. We're both athletes—she's a star—so people notice when we're out together. I've tried to tell her it's nothing new for people to see us hanging out, but she's paranoid, especially now that she feels she has something to prove coming back from her head injury.

My parents are riding me about my future and have turned my siblings into their spies. I swear Soren calls me twice a week to "chat," which actually means snooping about me and Jessa. I've caught Corden eyeing me suspiciously at practice and whenever he's at our place. Seriously, are my siblings getting paid to report back? I love my family, but everything is fine without them butting in. At least, I think everything is fine. I've been too focused on Jessa, school, and basketball to think much about what comes next. To get my parents off my back, I promised I'd spend time over break exploring job opportunities. Graduation will come fast after the season is over, especially if we make the NCAA tournament. A guy can dream about making March Mania, right? But for that to happen, we've got to get our shit together. We shouldn't have as many losses as we do. But our starting point guard, Mr. Monty Oakes, has been distracted by the lovely Ms. Bexley Collins. That doesn't help.

Oakes seems to be having the opposite effect on Collins's game. She's been on fire the last few weeks, which is par for the course when it comes to the women's team. I have to admit, I'm a bit jealous of their performance so far this year. They are kicking ass, with Jessa leading the way. As much as she stresses about how she shows up, especially after her concussion, she's still light years ahead of her teammates. Which is no small feat since they're some of the top players in the country.

My chest tightens as all of this spins through my mind.

I try to clear my head in a hot shower after our last practice before Thanksgiving. We have a lot to do before we're prepared to host the teams for a meal, so we'd all made the last minute decision to shower in the locker room instead of at home.

Oakes, Corden and I head into the hallway and find the girls already there. Collins sits on the floor with Jessa's head in her lap. Jessa's face is covered with her sweatshirt, her body sprawled across the hallway.

"Is she okay?" I ask, nodding towards Jessa.

"She may have overdone it a bit at practice but is too stubborn to admit it," Collins whispers.

"Shit. Maybe you should take her back to the condo. We can finish the shopping." I say.

"I can hear you, ya know. I'm fine. Just a bit tired." Jessa slowly pushes herself up and glares at us. "Let's go to the store."

The store is nuts. We split up to get our remaining supplies so we can get the hell out. There are stressed out people everywhere I look—fighting over the last ham, glaring at empty shelves and picked-over veggies, abandoning carts in aisles. The workers look frazzled with fake smiles, barely hanging on.

Thank God we just need seasonings, drinks, whipped topping, and cleaning supplies. The meat is already thawed, and we bought the main ingredients earlier in the week for this exact reason. Sometimes having Type A roommates pays off.

We regroup with everything on the list, take one look at each other, and book it for the exit. We breathe in relief as we cross the parking lot to my Jeep, stuffing both groceries and bodies inside. On the drive home, Jessa and Collins go over the to-do list for the night, handing out assignments so we can get it all done quickly.

At home we crank up the music, crack open drinks, and get to work. A few hours (and drinks) later, we're almost done with the prep. Corden decides that's his cue to bail.

"Of course you leave when it's just clean-up work to do," I call to my brother as he heads towards the door. He just smiles and presses a finger to his lips, shushing me as he slips out.

I turn and see Jessa curled up in a chair, fast asleep, and Collins passed out under a blanket on the couch.

"Practice must have done them both in," I say to Oakes as we clean the kitchen. "Guess we'd better set our alarms since I'm guessing the Queens of Planning fell asleep before they could."

Oakes and I try to wake the girls so they don't spend the night on the couch and have sore backs in the morning. Oakes manages to get Collins up, but he has to guide her to her bedroom.

Jessa isn't budging. She's out.

Well, it's not the first time I've had to carry her. I slide one arm under her back, the other under her knees, and pick her up. Oakes shakes his head as I walk past with her in my arms. I lay her on her bed, tuck her under the covers, and hesitate for a second. I want to climb in next to her, but she needs real sleep, so I leave her and head to my room.

The next morning, I wake to my alarm and the buzz of the blender. Collins must be making her usual smoothie. The smell of fresh coffee hits me, and I know Jessa is up.

I knock on Oakes's door to make sure he's up, then we both shuffle to the kitchen in search of caffeine.

"Morning, gentlemen," Jessa says, handing us each a mug of steaming coffee made to our liking. We grunt our thanks in return. "I think I'll let you wake up a bit before we put you to work."

Once the coffee kicks in, the morning flies. The condo fills with the smell of roasting meat and spices. Pies and desserts line the counter, the fridge is stuffed with salads and veggies, and the stove is crowded with bubbling dishes. We're dressed and ready by the time the last of the Thanksgiving Day Parade is playing.

Our teammates arrive in a steady stream—freshly showered, starving, talking over each other as they come in. The coaches are here too, admiring the condo and the spread, impressed by how prepared we are.

Everyone files through the line filling their plates with juicy meat, fluffy potatoes and a buffet of other side dishes. They squeeze around the tables we've crammed into the space. We might not be with our families, but our teammates feel like the next best thing. We have a lot to be grateful for.

After the meal, people are sprawled everywhere. Some are watching football, others are napping, and a few of the senior girls are in Jessa's room watching Christmas movies. It's become part of their

Thanksgiving tradition at HU. We all agreed to give our stomachs a rest before dessert.

I'm wandering around, clearing plates and checking on people, when I feel Jessa's eyes on me from across the room. She arches a brow in a *come here* way, then slips down the hall towards my room.

I drop the garbage bag in the kitchen and follow, trying not to look suspicious. My bedroom door is cracked open, and Jessa is sitting casually on the bed, a condom already sitting next to her. I step inside, close the door, and click the lock.

"Greyson," she says in a husky voice, curling her finger and motioning to me. "Come here."

Every time she says my name, I'm a little less mine and a little more hers. I'm surprised how effectively we've kept things low-key in public. No one's called us out for the way we look at each other. Or how I always find excuses to touch her. I move toward her. "You like sneaking around with me, don't you?" Jessa asks. "It turns you on. Knowing our teammates are right out there. Anyone could hear us."

"They're going to notice we're gone," I say, trying to be rational.

"Then we'd better be quick." She smiles in a slow, sexy way that makes me rush forward. There's no time to waste.

Jessa reaches for my zipper, but I'm going to be in charge this time. I push her back until she's lying on her back, and I pull her jeans down, flinging them to the floor. I kneel on the floor, scooting her down until her bottom is on the edge of the bed.

"You're already wet," I say, pulling her panties to the side. I work her with my tongue, running it up and down her slit before thrusting it in and out of her opening, over and over, feeling her squirm as my pace quickens. Her moans are soft, but getting louder, so I pause and lift my head.

"Jessa, we have to be quiet."

She nods, and puts the corner of my comforter in her mouth, biting down as I keep going. Watching her hold back is so fucking hot. I add a low hum and push my tongue down harder, swirling it in and out as she bucks her hips up toward my mouth. Then she's coming apart, her body tensing, trying not to cry out.

I pull back, wipe my face with a towel, and kiss a dazed Jessa before helping her get back into her jeans. After I freshen up in the bathroom, I return to the group to find everyone in pretty much the same positions as when I'd left. It seems no one noticed our absence—except maybe Corden. He gives me a look, and a few seconds later when Jessa returns with flushed cheeks, his eyes narrow and flick between us. Jessa sees as well, and quickly looks away, heading into the kitchen.

"Who is ready for dessert?" she calls, holding up a slice of pumpkin pie. Our teammates, now recovered from their food comas, crowd into the kitchen for round two.

Thank goodness our coaches give us a long weekend free of practices because we all need to recover from overeating. After everyone leaves, the four of us plus Corden clean up. Corden's joining our traditional Black Friday shopping trip in the morning. We've decided to venture thirty-minutes to Raleigh in hopes of escaping running into people we know.

"I'm exhausted, but what a great day. I can't believe we pulled it off." I sink into the couch and let out a long breath.

"Ya sure it was just the food and socializing that wore you out?" Corden jokes, looking between me and Jessa.

"What are you talking about, Corden?" Oakes asks. "We were up late and then up early. I'm beat too."

"Why don't you ask Grey and Jessa?" Corden smirks.

"Jessa? Grey? What's going on?" Collins asks, looking up at us from where she's lying on the floor.

"Nothing," Jessa and I say at the same time. Great. Real subtle. I sigh. "Fine. Oakes and Collins already know Jessa and I are seeing each other on the down low. And judging by your questions, I'm guessing you've figured it out too."

Corden shrugs, not looking at all surprised. "It's about time you admitted it. Not sure how you thought you were going to keep it from me. I spend a lot of time with you. Plus Soren's been asking questions. But," he says, a little embarrassed as he adds, "That isn't what I'm talking about, and you know it." The last thing I want to do is discuss my sex life with my brother, but Oakes and Collins are still staring.

"Okay, okay," I say. "J and I may have snuck off for a few minutes between dinner and dessert."

Jessa throws a pillow at me, her face bright red.

"Damn bro. That's gutsy, even for you!" Oakes says, laughing.

"Jessa!" Collins says, eyes wide, but Jessa just gives a tiny shrug.

"Alright, change of subject," I say quickly. "We're leaving early, so we have time to grab coffee before shopping. Jeep leaves at five a.m. sharp."

Everyone groans, but the next morning they're all up, ready and anxious for the coffee shop on the way to Raleigh.

By the time we get to the shopping center in Raleigh, we're hopped up on caffeine. Even Collins, who usually opts for more natural energy sources, is practically bouncing off the walls. It feels good to hang out as friends instead of always being in grind mode. Jessa seems more relaxed today, too. Maybe being away from all the eyes on campus helps.

As we move from store to store, Corden swears he sees Coach Hayes. We chalk it up to early morning and tell him to get his eyes checked. But a few minutes later, Jessa spots someone who looks a lot like Coach Morris. That feels too coincidental. Plus, after the weird touchy-feely moments we've seen over the season, Jessa and I exchange an affirmative look that says *we're going on a hunt*. Our friends won't let us out of their sight, so we fill them in and they tag along. I'm not sure what we look like, five large athletes crouching behind racks and people, but it's definitely not subtle.

We're about to give up when Collins spots Coach Hayes. "There he is," she hisses.

"Wait, wait. I see Coach Morris too," Oakes says. The crowd parts, and there they are—hands clasped, Coach Morris holding onto Coach Hayes's arm, their faces turned inward as they laugh intimately.

"What the....?" Corden trails off.

"Where do they get off telling us we can't date each other when it's pretty obvious they're together?" Collins sounds miffed.

We're all still watching them as Coach Hayes plants a kiss on Coach Morris's head. Now, I love my brother, but sometimes he doesn't think before he acts.

"Hey, Coach!" Corden calls, half jogging towards them.

Coach Hayes looks up, and he and Coach Morris pull away from one another. Maybe they could've played it off with just Corden, but then they see the rest of us behind him.

"*Shit*," I see Coach Morris mouth to Coach Hayes as we approach. "What's up, Coach?" Corden says. Both coaches look at the five of us with sheepish expressions.

"Looks like you all had the same idea as we did—getting out of town," Coach Morris says.

"Sure did," Jessa says, studying her coach. "Looks like you two are having a good time together."

"Uh, yeah," Coach Morris sidesteps Jessa's comment.

Coach Hayes seems to realize there's no point in avoiding it and angles his head at Coach Morris before gesturing to the rest of us. "Let's find a table and talk." They lead us to a table, and we wait patiently as Coach Hayes takes Coach Morris's hand in his.

They seem to be taking their time collecting their thoughts when Coach Hayes finally speaks. "So, as you have probably guessed, Coach Morris and I are together."

"No shit," Jessa blurts. I nudge her with my foot under the table and shoot her a glare.

"Jessa, it's more complicated than that," Coach Hayes says. "Not that we owe any of you an explanation of our personal lives, but you seem to have 'caught' us a few different times now, so it's easier to come clean. Ben and I reconnected over the last eight months. We were together in college for a time, and it didn't go how we would have liked. We decided to set boundaries for our players, so you didn't have to figure it out the hard way like we did. It was quite the surprise when we both ended up coming back to coach within a couple years of each other and found our way back to each other."

"How is that fair?" Corden asks. "We're adults. Maybe we *are* capable of making things work."

I'm not sure if I'm proud of my brother or wondering why this matters so much to him. As far as I know he doesn't have his eyes on another player... but maybe I'm wrong.

"That's fair, Corden," Coach Hayes agrees. "You have to understand, we really thought we were doing what was best for you all."

"Ben's right," interjects Coach Morris. "Back then, this was the one boundary we could agree on for the good of our teams. We were still holding a lot of anger toward each other. It was easier to set a rule than to deal with all the gray areas."

"Hayden and I ended up spending a lot of time together traveling for conferences and recruiting. And with our joint efforts to rebuild the program's reputation, we were together constantly. We realized we were stronger as a team than trying to avoid each other."

"That led to us rekindling things from college before we had to make decisions about our futures. We found it was almost harder to stay apart than it was to just be together. By that time it was too late to go back on our team expectations and boundaries, so we decided to just keep things on the down low. Hence why we left town this weekend."

"Well, that explains the weirdness in your office," Jessa says.

"You knew about this and didn't tell me?" Collins asks, looking at Jessa with a hurt look on her face.

"I swear, I didn't actually know anything was going on," Jessa explains.

I interject with, "I mean nothing was confirmed, just suspected."

Oakes and Corden both jerk their heads toward me. "You knew too?" Oakes asks.

"They may have caught us in an embrace a few months ago, but we never confirmed nor denied anything," says Coach Morris. "I feel better getting this off my chest to at least a few of you. Hiding sucks and people are bound to find out eventually."

"We'd appreciate it if you all kept this to yourselves for the time being, until we can tell everyone ourselves," says Coach Hayes. "The University already knows, so there is no issue there, but we want to be the ones to share it with our teams."

We all nod, agreeing it isn't our place. I think we all walk away stunned. Coach Hayes and Coach Morris were college sweethearts who let the game tear them apart. That's not going to help my case with Jessa, even if they came to their senses and got back together. I hope she doesn't spiral before we have a chance to talk about things.

By the time we're home from shopping, we're physically and emotionally wiped. The crowds were insane by midday, but we pushed through. For D1 athletes, you'd think we wouldn't be this tired from shopping, but we all drag our bags inside and collapse on the couch, zoning out to a movie we've seen a million times. We all eventually make our way to bed.

The long weekend without practice goes way too fast, and I know the short break from classes will too. Practices, weights, games, travel, and some holiday stuff will keep me busy, but I'd promised my parents I'd think about my future.

I roll over and look at Jessa sleeping beside me. She's gorgeous like this. Relaxed, not buried under everyone else's expectations.

I can't get comfortable and am wide awake, so I sneak out of bed and grab my laptop. I guess there's no time like the present to plan my future.

Where do I want to work? Do I want to do sports broadcasting? Where do I want to live? Should I move back to be near family in Oklahoma? Connecticut wasn't bad. At least not in the summer. Do I want to stay in North Carolina? These last three and a half years have been the best of my life—but would it feel the same without my teammates? And where does basketball fit in all this?

The team isn't doing great. I'm playing fine, but I know I'm not getting drafted. I've been playing since I was six. Maybe it's time to hang up the sneakers.

And then there's Jessa. I know exactly what I want her to be to me, but she's so hot and cold. Will she ever go all in? I want a relationship like my parents have—loving, caring, supportive, kids, maybe a dog. Is it naïve to believe I can have it all? Job, wife, house, kids, friends? I'm so deep in job searches and what-ifs that I don't hear Jessa get up until her arms slide around my neck from behind, making me jump.

"Jumpy, are we?" Jessa teases. "What are you doing over here? Quite the list of questions... not a lot of answers."

"I know," I say and close the laptop, feeling defeated. "Just got some thinking to do."

I lead her back to bed where she snuggles into my side and falls asleep quickly. I lie awake, wondering what the hell comes next.

19

Jessa

Ever since Coach shared her college relationship story and explained how basketball contributed to the downfall, I can't stop thinking about it. It doesn't help that Grey has been in his head lately, working out his future.

Seeing my name on his list of questions the other night was jarring. *What is Jessa's role in my life?* What kind of question is that? Is he second guessing this thing we started? Wondering if this is even worth it? If I'm messing up his basketball? Ever since I saw it, that one line has been running laps in my brain. Maybe I should talk to him... or maybe I don't want to hear the answer.

Coach has been encouraging us to use the break from school to focus on our game and future. She wants us to decide our own path. We shouldn't let media speculation about our abilities to continue with a basketball career control our choices. It makes sense, but it's hard not to let the pressure eat at you, especially when our team is doing so well. A few more games before Christmas and we could move into first in the conference. We're under a microscope between our coaches, trainers, the media, and other teams. And then there's my mother. She's watching me closer than all of the rest combined. While I've bounced back quickly from my concussion, she accuses me of being complacent. Fans and the media still refer to me as the Lady Big Horn's "defensive powerhouse" and "top scorer," but she doesn't see it. She's even tried using Bex as a channel to send me nutrition tips. Nothing says adulthood like your mom using your best friend to micromanage you.

At least she knows nothing about Greyson. Yet. I'm sure she'd be on the next flight here to move me out of the condo if she had. Dating is a distraction, she says. Especially in season. At least Coach has stopped harping about the no-dating rule lately. *Crap, what time is it?* I check my phone and realize it's time to head over to the weightroom. I grab my water bottle, headband, and phone, then yank an oversized hoodie over my head. The rest of my stuff is already in the locker room. I yell for Bex that I'm ready to go, and she pops out of her room, water bottle in hand, munching on a baggie full of seeds.

"Are you eating seeds? Like a squirrel?" I ask, unable to keep the disgust out of my voice.

"Sure am. Pumpkin seeds. Want some?" she says as if that is the most normal thing in the world.

"No, thanks. I'm good," I say as I turn toward the living room. "Ready?"

"Yup, I'll let the guys know it's time to go." But they're already in the living room, waiting for us.

I smile at Bex. "I think we're the slow ones."

Greyson gives me a peck on the cheek, and Monty looks like he's about to do the same to Bex but hesitates. Instead, he gives her an awkward fake punch to the arm like I've seen him do to Grey. It's like he's transitioned to treating Bex like one of the dudes. Weird. I look at

Greyson, but he only shrugs and walks out the door.

Butler's in the weightroom when we enter. He hasn't been an issue lately, but we keep our distance from him, and he wraps up and leaves. I was never actually reassigned a new lifting partner, so I plan to just stick with my roommates and their partners until I'm told otherwise. "Damn, look out. Blakely is in full out beast mode today," Hazel jokes, watching as I meet a PR on the bench press.

I do kind of feel like a beast today the way I'm in the zone. I'm moving to the squat rack when Coach Morris calls me into her office. "Sure, Coach. Be right there," I say, and put my weights away.

"Have a seat, Jessa," she says when I step into her office, sitting in the chair opposite her. "How are you doing?"

"I'm good."

"Glad to hear it. I want to talk to you about where you see yourself and the role of basketball in your life after graduation."

Coach Morris keeps a Zen garden on her desk, and since I'm unsure if I'm excited or dreading this conversation, I pick up the little rake and drag it through the sand, contemplating.

"Jessa, you are a high-energy player," Coach continues. "You're not afraid to take the tough shots. You're also a fantastic defender and you have the blocking and rebounding stats to back that up."

"I'm always working to improve my game," I say with confidence.

"You're a leader both on and off the court. Not everyone is capable of the pressures that often come with that." Coach assesses me for a moment before she continues. "I'm sure you've seen the media reports with their projections of you being a high-round draft pick. But I want to talk about *your* view of your future after college basketball. It's time to ignore outside noise and consider what you want. If going pro is a goal, we can be more focused and intentional in the rest of the season. We have a strong coaching staff and trainers who are committed to helping you reach your goals. And you know I'll be here to help prepare you, too."

There is a long pause as I process everything she's said. I take a deep breath and try to be as honest as I can with her. "I guess I've been avoiding even thinking about all of this. I always hoped it was a real possibility to play after college, but I was never sure of how realistic it would be. I'm still not. There are so many unknowns. I love basketball, but I worry about wasting my education. And I love my friends."

Coach nods during my pause, but she seems to know I'm not done verbally processing.

"There is also so much pressure to live up to everyone's expectations, especially my mother's. I have my own goals and records I want to break, but sometimes I feel stuck in the shadow of Lauren Blakely, college Hall of Famer. I've really only just started to consider real possibilities and the doors that could be opened for me with basketball."

"I understand all of that, Jessa. I want you to know, we will support you no matter what direction you take. I assume your mother will do the same. If basketball is the path, we'll do what we can to help you along the way. If you choose to go into a different career, so be it. Obviously, there's a deadline if you want to declare for the draft, so thinking about that should be your next step."

My heart races and my head spins at the thought of the possibility of declaring. I've put in so much work to open up this opportunity. Coach Morris goes on. "Well, as you probably already know, to be eligible for the WNBA draft, players must be at least twenty-two during the draft year or set to graduate within three months of the draft. The deadline to declare is ten days before the draft, or within forty-eight hours of your final game if we make it to postseason play—which is a high possibility this year. You have some time to decide, but

I want you to really think it through. I'm here if you want to talk more once you've processed. And, remember, this is your decision, not mine or your mother's."

"Got it, Coach. I have some thinking to do," I say as I slowly get up from the chair.

Coach Morris smiles at me. "You do, but I know you will make the decision that is best for you. I just ask you to keep me posted on how we can best support you in this process."

"Will do," I say. I'm in a panic as I walk back towards the weightroom. At the last minute, I take a detour to the locker room, needing to be alone with my thoughts for a bit. But after a while, I worry I made a terrible decision. Stewing on such big life choices that have a drastic impact on my future is making me sweat. My hands are clammy and I might throw up.

I pull out my phone and text Bex.

Me: *Need you in locker room. NOW.*

She runs in without responding to my text. "Are you okay? You don't look so good."

It feels hard to breathe, and Bex doesn't wait for me to answer her. She gets me a bottle of water to sip on and helps me lay back on the massage table the trainers keep in the locker room. "Focus on your breathing, Jessa. In through the nose and out through the mouth."

I listen to Bex's soothing voice, letting it ground me. "Now, what happened?" she asks, once she sees I'm breathing more regularly. Her gentle hand comes to my forehead.

I tell her.

Bex shrieks. She shrieks so loud that I have to shush her. I stare at her, now jumping up and down with excitement, and wish I was reacting the same way. I can't seem to think beyond the panic.

When Bex calms down, her expression changes. "How do you feel about this?"

I repeat what I'd said to Coach Morris, and Bex asks what it means if I choose the draft path. "I think it means my focus needs to be basketball... and saying good-bye to Greyson. Coach said basketball and relationships don't mix. I don't know how Grey and I could possibly be together if I don't know what my future holds and he's working so hard to finalize his." I flashback to Greyson's question about how I fit in his future.

"You have to tell Greyson. That's a big leap to break things off with so many unknowns *and* without letting him have a say," Bex rationalizes.

"Yes, I have to tell Greyson but not right now," I say, jumping down from the massage table. I feel better, thanks to Bex. I just need to push through. "I need to go shoot around for a while. Thanks for coming to my rescue."

"You sure you don't just need some time to sit with this?"

"Nah, I'll be fine, but not a word to anyone," I say seriously. Bex responds by miming the zipping of her lips and throwing away the key.

I warm up by shooting free throws, which turns into a quick game of Around the World with one of the practice players. Afterward, I take a short break and run a few timed killers. By the time I'm done, I'm sweaty, out of breath, and most of the panicky energy from earlier has faded.

The lifting group finally filters into the gym. It's obvious none of them are in the mood for a real workout, so I'm glad I got mine in— they've already pulled out practice jerseys for a pickup game.

"You in, Blakely?" yells Anders, the men's starting guard, from across the court.

"Absolutely!" I jog over to them, still catching my breath. Bex hands me my Hills blue and gold practice jersey.

"Thought you left us," whispers Grey while Anders and Hazel come up with the teams. "Nah. Just wasn't in the mood to lift after talking to Coach," I say.

"Yeah... what *was* that all about?" Greyson asks, peering into my eyes.

I brush him off. "We can talk about it later."

Somehow, I end up on the opposite team from all my roommates, the youngest Hastings, and Lexi Wright, our starting forward. I'm teamed with a few of the strongest guards from both squads—and Butler—which honestly works in my favor. We've got ball handlers and outside shooters for days.

I forget how fun and competitive these pickup games can be. Grey and Monty definitely aren't thrilled with me; I've already blocked several of their shots, and anytime their team manages to put one up, there are no second chances because I'm crashing the boards hard.

"Yeah, Blakely!" yells Anders after I rebound one of the other team's missed baskets.

"Damn it!" Corden shouts. I flash him my biggest smile as I turn to help him up after knocking his ass to the floor while boxing him out.

He glares at me, ignoring my outstretched hand. *Yikes, okay*, I think, but I don't have to coddle Corden. I run down the court, and we play for another 20 minutes until everyone is worn out. We stop mid-court to high-five, and most of us stick around to stretch.

"I think it's safe to say you are back at full strength, Blakely," Anders says, whistling to show how impressed he is. Then he jerks his head in the direction of our most recent opponents. "Those guys are pissed."

Back at home, we've all showered and are vegging out in the

living room. Everyone is in a surprisingly good mood, leaning into the holiday spirit. We talk about how we want to deck the condo out with Christmas decor. Eventually the conversation lands on me.

"So, what was up with Coach Morris calling you into the office during weights?" asks Oakes.

I hesitate and glance at Bex. The tension I'd finally shaken off creeps back into my shoulders.

"Was I not supposed to ask?" Oakes adds quickly. "You don't have to tell me, just curious."

Greyson leans forward. "Yeah, what's up, Jessa? You dodged me earlier."

"I didn't avoid you," I say lightly. "I got picked and moved to my team, that's all."

"Okay, so...?" Grey presses not picking up on the tension the question has brought into the space. "And why aren't you more curious Bex? Wait... you already know, don't you? Bex knows, but we can't. Rude!" He jokes lightheartedly.

The guys are perched on the edge of their seats waiting for my answer. Bex gives me an anxious look—she knows I'd hoped to keep this to myself a bit longer. I take a deep breath and let it all spill out, my gaze glued to the floor.

"She asked if I'd been following any of the WNBA draft predictions, because apparently I have a high probability of going in an early round." The words tumble out faster. "She said the basketball staff is willing to prep me if I want to go for it, but I need to make the decision on my own, without pressure."

I can't bring myself to look up, but suddenly the room shifts. Greyson is on his feet, rushes me, and lifts me clean off the ground, spinning me around.

"Fuck yeah, Jessa!" he shouts. "I'm so proud of you!"

"This is unreal!" Oakes adds, crossing the room to pull me into a second hug.

I blink at Bex, dazed. She smiles at me in an *I told you so* way and looks ecstatic to finally be in a room with other excited people.

Maybe I shouldn't be surprised by their reactions, but I am. Do they really think this is something I could do? I didn't—not until Coach said it out loud. And shouldn't Grey be worried about what this means for... us? For any future we haven't talked about but keep hinting at?

"Why don't you look more excited? This is a BIG deal!" Grey blurts, concern slipping into his voice. He takes my hands in his.

"I mean, I am excited," I say, "but... it's a lot. This is my future we're talking about—the thing that's going to shape everything else."

Later, after Bex and Oakes mysteriously have somewhere to be— together—Greyson and I find ourselves alone. He gives me that look, the one that says he's been holding back questions.

"What's really going on, J?" he asks quietly. "Why aren't you more excited than this?"

"I swear I am. Or at least I want to be." The confession breaks something in me. Tears pool despite my attempt to blink them away. I turn my face from him, embarrassed.

"J," he says softly, "we're at that point in our college careers where we have to think about what comes next. About what all this work has been for. I'm right here too—trying to make adult decisions that feel heavier than they should. But we're here." He hooks a finger under my chin, urging me to meet his eyes.

A tear escapes anyway. I swipe at it, frustrated. The more I fight it, the harder the rest fall. How is he so calm? So steady?

"I saw my name on your list for the future..." The words come out broken, choked. "It said, 'What is her role in my life?' You're already questioning what does and doesn't make sense with us."

"Jessa," he says, shaking his head and putting his face in his hands. "No, you've got it all wrong. I mean, yes, that was some of what I noted, but I also wrote *'Will she ever take the leap and be all in?'* I'm definitely not questioning you or your role in my life."

His voice softens and he bumps his shoulder against mine. "I'm considering the impact you have on my future. And what I should consider because you are a part of my life, and I hope you continue to be."

"Even after what our coaches shared about their relationship and basketball not working?" I sniff. "You have to do what's right for you, and then we go from there. I don't want to be the reason you don't do something."

"Damn it, I knew that would get in your head. I should've asked you how you were handling that sooner." He shakes his head.

"We aren't them," he emphasizes. "Plus, I'm coming to terms with the fact that basketball isn't in my future. I'm not going to be drafted. I'm not pursuing it further. That is one thing I've made up my mind about. I'll put in my time with the team the rest of the season, but realistically, we aren't going to make the tournament, so this is where my career ends. And I'm okay with that. Basketball is *your* future. If that's what you want."

"Oh, Greyson." My chest tightens, and I feel a little bit like a jerk. "Why didn't you tell me you decided this was the end of your basketball career? That's a big decision. Here I am whining about an amazing opportunity, and you've already made a hard choice."

"We knew the time was coming where we had to adult. We've clearly put it off as long as possible." Greyson chuckles. "Life has a funny way of everything happening at the same time, like a sick joke."

"Yeah, I guess so," I say.

"Jessa, you need to make this basketball decision for you. Yes, this is an amazing opportunity, but only if you want it. If you want to break the records and have a successful season and be done, no one will fault you. Well, except maybe your mother, but we can deal with her later."

"You said *we*." I look up at him, searching his expression. "Of course I said *we*," he says, his eyes softening. "We're in this together. This is your decision, and I'm here to support you in whatever you choose. We'll figure out the rest as we go."

"I don't deserve you, Greyson."

"You may eat those words when you're supporting us on your W salary," he jokes. I can't help but laugh. I feel lighter after this conversation.

"You realize this means I'm going to be eating and breathing basketball more now than ever, right?"

"I know." He squeezes my hand. "But I've got you. *Always*."

I reach for the basketball charm around my neck, "*Always*."

20

Greyson

Today was our last practice before Christmas. The women have a game tonight with a chance to move into first in the conference with a win. All eyes are on them. All eyes are on Jessa. Word spread like wildfire about the possibility of her getting drafted. Needless to say, the energy around the team is crazy right now. Jessa's been handling the added pressure by performing during games. It's like something released in her, and she's rising to every challenge placed before her. I'm in awe of her.

Since deciding I'm done with basketball after this season, a small weight has lifted. I still want to finish strong, but without the pressure to perform for a future I no longer want, the game feels more fun than it has in years. And honestly, the extra time I put into basketball now? It's for her. It's always been for her.

The guys and I will be front and center tonight, hyping up the women's team. Our season's over, but theirs isn't—not even close. We've always seen ourselves as one program, the HU Big Horns. We push each other, we show up for each other, and we want the women's team to go all the way.

We ran into Jessa and Collins earlier. They were already locked in, heading to the Blakely Center for their pre-game routine. That left Oakes and me with way too many hours to kill before tipoff. We cleaned the condo, finished the Christmas decorations, even baked the rest of the cookies Jessa and Collins had prepped. Anything to distract ourselves from the waiting.

Ninety minutes still to go.

"Fuck it," I say. "Let's just go,"

"Agreed," Oakes sighs. "I don't know how the girls handle all this pressure."

"Maybe that's why they're where they are," I say with a smirk.

"Fair point," Oakes agrees. "Let's get outta here."

When we step into the Blakely Center, I'm glad we came early. Fans in Hills blue and gold flood the seats, buzzing with anticipation. The vibe is palpable, and people are still streaming in.

I glance out at the court, trying to gauge their energy. The women are shooting around, and they all look sharp, focused, and loose. They look good. Really good. Judging by their movements, tonight's going to go well for them.

Jessa catches my eye, and I give her a smile and a small wave—hopefully encouraging, not distracting. Across the court, Collins and Oakes lock eyes and Collins blushes. Those two are so obvious.

Just get together already, I think, shaking my head. Maybe that's what people think about Jessa and me, but I'd like to believe we're doing a decent job keeping things quiet. Being longtime friends and roommates helps—no one questions why we're together so much.

Jessa and I have fallen into an easy rhythm during break: practice, extra shooting, weights, at least one meal together, old game film, then ending up in each other's bed every night. It's comfortable. I'm falling for her harder every day. Every second with her makes me crave more. I'm applying for jobs and trying to figure out my future, but honestly? The only part that feels certain is wanting her in it. She's been more open with me lately, less guarded. Fingers crossed she feels the same.

I glance away from the court as the rest of the guys arrive, loud and restless, ready to cheer the women on. This—team spirit, camaraderie, that electric buzz before a big game—is what basketball is supposed to feel like. We hate that it's not *our* team playing for first place, but at this point our season is about growth, not rankings.

Oakes is joking around with the guys, fully in hype mode. I'm quieter, my stomach tight with nerves. This game means everything to Jessa. Watching her play always ties my insides in knots. I shake out my shoulders and focus my energy toward her, willing her to feel supported, not stressed.

The lights dim slightly and the announcer starts his intro. "And now, let's get ready for the Big Horns to take the floor! Here are your starting five..."

The crowd erupts. Finally: "And number 51, your captain, Jessa Blakely!"

Jessa runs out grinning, immediately scanning the stands until she finds me. I wink, and she beams before turning back to her huddle.

HU wins the tip, and they look sharp on the court. Jessa is everywhere—clean finishes near the basket, huge rebounds, relentless defense. She's moving better than she has all season, and the other team is feeling it. A timeout is called just as the announcer drops the news: Jessa is now HU's all-time rebound leader. The crowd loses it. Her teammates swarm her. This is her moment—and hopefully just one of many.

The women head into halftime up twelve. The guys immediately start googling stats.

"Blakely could tie the record for double-doubles tonight," Anders says. "Did you know, Hastings?"

"I knew she was close," I say, proud enough to burst. If she keeps her pace, she'll tie it in the third quarter.

My excitement dies fast when I spot Lauren Blakely heading straight toward me. I knew she'd be here, but I was hoping to avoid her. It looks like she's on a mission for me though.

Oakes notices and nudges me. "Good luck, man." He quickly pulls Corden into fake conversation.

"Greyson. A word," she says, stiff as steel.

"Uh... sure." I climb down a couple of seats to meet her.

"I want to make sure Jessa keeps her eye on the prize," she says, glaring. "She can't afford distractions." She looks me up and down like I'm something she stepped in. "Especially *you*."

"What?" I stammer. "She looks great out there."

"She does, because she put in the work," Lauren snaps. "But it's very clear who could derail her. *You*." She jabs a finger into my chest.

I step back so she stops prodding me. Out of the corner of my eye I see the team returning to the court. The last thing Jessa needs is to see her mother cornering me, so I rush to end this.

"I'll do everything I can to help her stay focused," I say evenly, revealing nothing.

Lauren seems satisfied and stalks off in the opposite direction. I exhale hard. The nerve of that woman. She's the one piling pressure on Jessa, no one else. Especially not me. I calm myself before heading back. Jessa checks for me often from the court or the bench, just a quick look to see that I'm there. And I am. I always will be.

Oakes slaps my shoulder when I sit down. "Well, shit. What was *that* about?"

"Nothing I can't handle," I assure him. "Just Lauren Blakely trying to be in control."

The buzzer sounds for the second half, and we're glued to the game in front of us, waiting for Jessa to get the record-breaking double-double. It takes less than five minutes. She comes out on fire, pumps her fist, grinning through sweat as her teammates swarm her. I beam with pride. Below, Lauren Blakely barely nods, like it's just another stat line.

The energy doesn't dip, even with a 17-point lead heading into the fourth. The other team gets scrappy and pulls within seven. Coach Morris calls a timeout, rallies them, and whatever she says lights Collins up—she gets two steals back-to-back and scores uncontested on both. The lead jumps to 11 with under two minutes left. Coach subs in the bench to finish the game. The place erupts as the starters come out—smiling, exhausted, victorious.

They're now first in the conference heading into Christmas break. NCAA contenders.

When the final buzzer sounds, the court floods. Courtside media immediately grabs Jessa and Collins for the post-game interview. I know it will be a bit before I can talk to Jessa. She'll have post-game media expectations, but there's no way I'm leaving without congratulating her in-person. Oakes has the same idea and says he's staying with me.

Since we're players, we slip into the hallway by the locker rooms. Coach Hayes is killing time by shooting on the mini hoop in his office. He waves us in, and we burn nearly an hour playing HORSE before the girls finally come out. We erupt in loud cheers, celebrating their win and all the milestones.

I hug Jessa a little too long, caught up in the emotions from the game and the pride I have for her. Oakes does the same with Collins, and someone clears their throat. We pull apart to find both coaches staring at us. *Shit.*

But the throat-clearing wasn't from one of the coaches—there's another presence behind them.

Lauren Blakely. Awesome. Back to haunt me with her presence. "Jessa. Bexley." She says, then acknowledges each of the coaches with a nod. "Hayden. Benjamin." Oakes and I get no words, only looks like we're gum she found on the bottom of her shoe.

"We will just be outside," Oakes mutters, dragging me away. Collins hesitates, unsure if she should stay or save herself. Jessa tells her she'll meet her outside. Collins practically sprints after us.

"God, I hope her mother isn't shitty to her tonight," I say to Collins and Oakes. "She already cornered me, but come on, tonight couldn't have gone better. Nothing to criticize about Jessa or the team."

"You know that no matter happens, it's never enough for Lauren Blakely," Collins says with an eye roll.

"No wonder Jessa's such a perfectionist and overly anxious whenever something isn't just right," Oakes adds.

Another forty-five minutes pass before Jessa finally emerges. I'm about to tease her for taking so long—then I see her eyes. Red. Shit. She's been crying. My stomach drops. Lauren must've ripped into her.

I go to reach for her, but she walks right past me and straight to Collins, who hugs her tight. They turn toward the condo, and Oakes and I look at each other then follow. This tells me a lot about what happened tonight. I hope she's willing to talk when we get home.

At the condo, Oakes and I pour big glasses of wine for the girls. We're not sure if it's celebration or damage control, but he and I are ready for either. Jessa sets her glass down and wraps her arms around me. "I'm sorry. I didn't want my mother seeing me walking home with you and making things worse. I know I shouldn't care, but she has so much control, or at least thinks she does. I didn't want to rock the boat."

"I get it. We had a run-in earlier too. It's fine. I'm ignoring her."

"Earlier? Like at the game?" Jessa asks.

"Yes. Not a big deal. I handled it." I rub her arm, trying to be reassuring.

"Fuck! That woman is maddening." Jessa rubs her hands over her face. "I will not let her dictate my future." The last part seems to be more to herself than anyone else.

"Moving on," Jessa declares, climbing onto my lap.

My dick reacts instantly, and I squirm under her fantastic body.

Oakes clears his throat. Right, we are not alone.

"I want to offer a toast," he says, lifting his glass. "To the amazing people here with me. May we continue to have each other's backs, and for you ladies to continue to kick ass for the rest of the season."

We clink classes, and I assume Oakes is done, but then he says, "And... Bex." Jessa and I exchange glances.

"Bex," Oakes repeats, turning to her. "You've become an incredible friend and partner. Your laughter, your joy, your energy... I cherish it. And I want more of it."

"More?" Collins asks, eyes wide. "What are you saying, Monty?"

"I'm saying I'm falling for you. And I want us to stop pretending there's nothing going on. Everyone knows it—even Blakely and Hastings." He laughs nervously. "Let me romance you the way you deserve."

Collins bursts into tears. Jessa squeezes my hand so hard it might break. Oakes goes on before she can answer. "And I'm your secret admirer. The one who left the notes and treats."

Collins's jaw drops. "You? Really? Honestly... now that you say it, that makes sense. Thank God. I couldn't handle two men. I'm so relieved it's you!"

She launches herself into Oakes's arms, spilling both of their glasses of wine.

Jessa leans in to kiss me. Across the room, Oakes and Collins do the same. Then Jessa starts giggling.

"What?" I ask.

"I was just thinking how this feels like a junior high make out party in here," she says.

"What kind of parties were *you* going to in junior high?" I tease. "Because that was not my experience."

I lift Jessa off my lap to stand, then scoop her up in my arms. Oakes laughs and does the same with Collins. We head down the hall in opposite directions, ready to celebrate the night the *adult* way.

21

Jessa

Christmas when you are a basketball player isn't like a normal Christmas. Most people go home to their families; we stay near campus because there's no time to travel.

This year is different—Greyson's family is coming here. Since both he and Corden are away from home, the rest of the Hastings clan decided to bring Christmas to them.

Monty and Bex have been on video calls with their families all morning. Meanwhile, I've been praying my mother doesn't call. Ever since Monty and Bex made things official—at least with us—they've been adorable, giggling through embarrassing childhood stories. Bex is already all in, and I know Monty will take care of her heart.

Greyson and I spend the morning waiting for his family and debating what to tell them about us. While we obviously don't want my mom or coaches to know, I know it's killing Grey to keep it from Soren.

"Soren loves you, Jessa," he says. "Just think, she already looks up to you like a sister. My parents have always loved you, so they'll just be excited to know I'm in a grown-up relationship with you."

Hours later, his family arrives straight from the airport. Soren bursts in first and beelines to me instead of her brothers.

"Geesh, Soren. What are we, chopped liver?" Corden calls out, and she sticks out her tongue. Her parents are close behind but instead beeline for the boys. They make their way over to give me hugs as well.

"We're so glad you could make it," I say. And I mean it. They couldn't be any nicer, and they've raised some really great kids. "Bex and Monty will be out soon. They were just on video calls with their families." Grey's mom, Dr. Judy Hastings, is an impressive pediatrician and Bill Hastings, Grey's dad, is a sports attorney. They are remarkably busy people, yet always prioritize their family.

Judy waves her hand as if they can catch up with them later. "How are you? We watched the game on television the other night. You broke records and now you've moved into first in the conference?"

"Of course she's great, Judy," Bill jumps in. "She's currently one of the most talked about draft prospects, isn't that right, son?"

"Yup, Jessa is doing some impressive things," Greyson says. He wraps his arm around my waist and my fingers automatically reach for the basketball charm. "There's something else we wanted to share with you too."

His parents look at each other, and Soren giddily jumps up and down.

"I knew it! I knew it!" she says, bouncing on her toes.

"Jessa and I are together," Greyson says proudly.

His mom pauses. "Oh... How nice. You two have always been close."

"Well, that's great news," Bill piggybacks, trying to sound upbeat, but I can tell it's forced.

Greyson and I exchange confused looks. Their reaction is

underwhelming. Maybe even concerned. Soren squeezes me tightly, but I can't stop analyzing his parents' faces.

I excuse myself, so Greyson and Corden can have time with their parents and Soren. And to be honest, I need time to process.

The moment I lie on my bed, I hear raised voices, then hurried shushing.

I crack my door.

"What's your problem?" Greyson snaps. "Your reaction to me and Jessa was disappointing. I thought you'd be happy I'm with her."

"Jessa is a lovely girl, who has lots going for her," Judy starts. "We just worry about your future, you know that."

"What if Jessa is my future?" Greyson shoots back.

My heart stops.

"We love Jessa," Bill says. "It's just if she gets drafted you have no idea where she could be landing and for how long. There are a lot of things up in the air with professional athletes."

"Don't you think I know that? There is a lot of uncertainty, but I'm navigating it. I'm applying all over for a variety of things. I'm okay being in the unknown. Basketball isn't my future—but it's Jessa's. And I want to support her."

"How serious are you about this girl?" Bill asks.

"Dad, Jessa isn't just a girl. She's my best friend, and I love her." Greyson defends. I quietly shut my door before I break. I slide to the floor, back against the wood, palms pressed to my face. He loves me. And his parents think I'm bad for his future.

I don't know how long I sit there. Eventually there's a gentle knock.

"Jessa? It's me."

I wipe my face and open the door. Grey pulls me into a tight hug.

"I'm sorry about my parents," he murmurs.

"I'm sorry too," I whisper.

"What are you sorry for?" he asks, pulling back.

"It feels like I'm making things harder for everyone. Clearly your family wants you focused on your future. A future where I'm not holding you back."

"No," he says immediately. "You're not backing away from this, from us."

"Greyson... I have to." Fresh tears sting my eyes. "We've spent more time talking ourselves into this than being in it. It's too complicated. Too hard. The cards are stacked against us. Even your family thinks so."

He grips my arms, searching my face. "Jessa, I know you want this. I saw you looking for me during the game. Every time you came off the court. Every time you sat on the bench. I know you feel this too."

I swallow hard. I did feel it. I do. But the panic hit the second I heard him say he loved me. It made everything suddenly too real, too big, too terrifying.

"I think it's best if we go back to the way things were," I force out. "Before we complicated things with sex."

Pain flashes across his face. I can't look at him. After a long moment, he leaves my room without a word.

I fall onto my bed and let myself break.

Again.

22

Greyson

The holidays and break go by in a blur. Soren is devastated that, right after learning Jessa and I were together, she got the news we'd broken up. Glad my parents are the ones dealing with her moodiness over it.

I'm still talking to my parents, but I'm frustrated with their reaction to the news of Jessa and I. Corden keeps checking on me like I might shatter, but I'm coping by throwing my energy into making future plans. A future without Jessa. She's going on with her life, so I need to do the same. That's how life goes sometimes, right? But who am I kidding? I'm gutted by all of it. I've done a decent job avoiding Jessa, despite living across the condo from one another and sharing a basketball schedule. At least basketball gives me an excuse to see her and make sure she's okay. As angry as I am about her decision, I know this isn't actually what she wants. She's stuck in her head and unsure how to navigate the challenges. I'm convinced she believes she doesn't deserve more than one good thing at once, including me. Jessa always deserves so much more than she thinks she does.

The new semester and the final stretch of the basketball season begins with an announcement: our coaches are together and got engaged on New Year's Eve. How fucking romantic is that? A friends to lovers story, reunited after years of being apart. Meanwhile, I spent New Year's Eve locked in my room, trying not to think about how I should be kissing Jessa at midnight.

Everyone's still reeling from Coach Hayes and Coach Morris's news, and its spurred announcements from a few other couples who are making it public they're together. The coaches couldn't really keep up their no-dating rule after getting engaged, could they? Jessa and I should have been one of those couples. Instead, we're not speaking, and it's obvious people have questions but aren't asking them.

I'm not ready to give up on Jessa. But I know she needs space to figure things out for herself. That doesn't mean I can't find subtle ways to remind her what she's missing, though. She said we could go back to being best friends like we were before things got complicated, so that's where I plan to start.

I text Oakes and Collins to meet me after practice. Before I head for the locker room, I spot Jessa shooting alone, determination and focus clear in her expression and posture. I see she's wearing the necklace I got her with the *Always* engravement. She wears it every day. That has to mean something, right? I'm glad to see she's continuing to put in the work to be draft-ready. She's going to be incredible wherever she ends up.

After a shower, I meet Oakes and Collins at our favorite coffee shop. They slide into the booth across from me, waiting for an explanation.

"What's going on?" Collins asks. "Your text sounded urgent."

"Yeah, man, we've been worried," Oakes adds. "But figured you needed space."

"You're right. I needed time to think and process. Now, it's time for some action," I say.

They both look confused.

"I'm obviously still in love with Jessa," I admit. "But that's not what she wants to hear. She said we could go back to being friends, so that's what I'm doing. No pressure. Just us, the way it was before labels complicated it."

"Okay... so, what does that mean?" Collins asks.

"I want Jessa to trust in our relationship, whatever it is. If I can make her see that being friends isn't that much different from being a couple, maybe she'll see that the rest isn't so scary."

"I don't get it," Oakes shrugs, taking a sip of his coffee.

"I think she focuses so much on making others happy that she doesn't focus on her own happiness. It's like she wants to prove herself, but worries about her decisions altering someone else's decisions," I say.

Collins nods slowly. "So you're just going to show up—no expectations—and let her remember what you two had before. Because from what I can tell, sex was the only difference."

"Exactly," I say. "And I need you both to treat it like nothing's weird. Just a normal thing to be friends with me."

"You really think this will work?" Oakes asks, skepticism written all over his face.

"I have to try."

They exchange a look.

"Alright, buddy. We've got your back," Oakes says, reaching across the table to shake my hand.

"Same," agrees Collins. "She's cranky as hell. Getting her out of her head will do all of us a favor."

When we get home, I prep some of Jessa's favorite snacks and meals for the week. It's a small thing, but it's something we always did for each other. I leave a note so she knows they're hers. No pressure. No conversation required. Just something to make her week easier. The next day I get a text from Collins.

Collins: *Taking care of the hangry girl.* ✓ *She hasn't stopped talking about the snacks and the meals that will make her life easier as she continues extra gym time in addition to school and regular practice and games.*

Me: ♥

As I put my phone down, I notice several unread emails—from universities and organizations I applied to before the holidays. I open the first about a Director of Player Development role.

Greetings Mr. Greyson Hastings,

Thank you for your interest in the Director of Player Development position for men's basketball at Mount Oread University (MOU). We were extremely impressed with your application. We'd like to schedule an on-campus interview. Please confirm your availability at your earliest convenience.

We look forward to connecting with you and learning more about your qualifications.

Sincerely,

Mount Oread University Men's Basketball

More emails follow. Player Development. Basketball Operations. Even the NBA wants to forward my resume to a few teams.

What is even happening right now? I cast a wide net hoping someone would bite. I had no idea I'd get so much interest. I almost call Jessa. She'd lose her mind, but I remember the boundaries I'm trying to maintain. So I text my family instead.

Corden responds first.

Corden: *Hell yeah, Grey! This is so exciting!*

Then a response comes from Soren.

Soren: *That's great, but how are things with Jessa?*

Finally, my parents respond.

Mom: *How exciting!*

Dad: *Stay focused. Hard work pays off.*

Not exactly the celebration I'd wanted. I text Oakes, hoping he'll be a little more enthusiastic. Like Jessa would be.

Me: *Good news! I've been invited to interviews for basketball jobs— both college and potential NBA.*

My phone rings almost instantly. It's Oakes.

"Hey, Oakes!" I blurt.

"Interviews, as in plural?! This is so awesome! We need to celebrate. I may have just walked out of my class when I got the text, so I'm free."

I laugh, picturing Oakes just walking out mid-lecture. "Let's grab lunch since you have sudden availability."

"You got it. Pick me up on the South side of campus."

23

Jessa

It's conference tournament time, and I miss Greyson. I told him we could go back to being friends, but I haven't followed through. I've been too busy and too afraid to sit in the same space with him like nothing happened. Even though we live across the living room from each other, we're miles apart.

And yes, Greyson keeps showing up.

First, he meal-prepped for me during a brutal week. Then he dried and folded my laundry when I'd left it in the washer. He sends Bex and Monty to check on me, posts draft prediction updates on the fridge (especially when they are really positive about me), and he's still cheering me on at games whenever he can. He's been finding ways to give me subtle nudges back towards our friendship. Little signs that tell me he isn't going anywhere. Do I regret breaking things off? I don't know. I thought it was the right thing so he could focus on his future, but it sucks missing out on this last semester with him. Basketball has been my focus, and thankfully, that part's paying off.

"J, did you hear that Greyson has multiple interviews with college basketball teams? And maybe the NBA?" Bex asks.

"What?" I exclaim, shocked but not surprised teams are interested in him. "Why didn't he tell me?"

"You haven't exactly been talking to him," Bex points out.

"Right... he doesn't owe me anything," I say, hating that this is the new normal with him. "I was always the first person he told these things to, even when we were just friends."

I turn to her. "Bex, do you think I did the right thing?"

She exhales. "I honestly don't know, J. I think you believed it was the right thing at that moment, and that it was the best thing for Greyson. But... was it the right thing for you? Did you give it a fair shot? Are you sure you weren't running away because you were scared? Because you didn't know how to balance a relationship with basketball?" Her questions hit too close. I go silent, letting it crash over me.

What the hell did I do? Can I fix it? Do I even know how? All I know is life is harder without him in it. Greyson filled all parts of my life. There's too much space without him.

"You okay, Jessa?" Bex presses.

"Sure..." I lie. Badly, judging by Bex's skeptical expression before she leaves me to think.

I find myself drifting across the condo toward Greyson's room. I knock softly, only half-hoping he's there. There's no answer, so I push the door open. His room is empty.

I grab the notepad on his desk and scribble a quick note to let him know I'm thinking about him and proud of him. Nothing heavy. I leave it on his pillow. It's enough, I tell myself.

I head back to my room to get ready for our trip to Greensboro for the conference tournament. Five days, five potential games. Five days to keep my head straight.

24

Greyson

Oakes and I return after practice to an empty condo. The girls are probably already headed to Greensboro for the conference tournament. After Oakes wins at Rock, Paper, Scissors to determine who gets the first shower, I head to my room to check emails. I pull off my shirt as I walk in and toss it to the floor, blowing a piece of paper along with it. I pick it up and see Jessa's handwriting scrawled on it.

Grey – Heard you have some amazing interview opportunities coming up! Congrats! Can't wait to hear about them. – J

I blink down at the note, smiling stupidly. From anyone else, this isn't a big deal. But Jessa doesn't leave *thinking of you* notes. This is a huge step. Oakes walks by with a towel around his waist, pausing when he sees me standing there. I glance up at him and smile. "It's from Jessa."

"No shit? What'd she say?" Oakes asks.

"She knows about my interviews and wants to hear about them."

"Is this her way of extending an olive branch?"

"I think it is. At least I hope it is."

The note was enough to snap me into action. I look at Oakes. "I'm going to shower. Then we need to get on the road to Greensboro to cheer on my best friend and *your* girlfriend."

25

Jessa

I try to focus on pre-game warm-ups, but my mind keeps drifting to the note I left for Greyson. He's probably read it by now. Maybe I shouldn't have done that.

I'm still overthinking in between practice shots when I see him. Sandy blonde hair, muscular frame, and a shirt with my number on it. God, he looks good wearing my number. He catches me staring and his icy blue eyes squint into a smile. At that moment, I manage to throw up an air ball that bounces in his direction. He picks up the ball, and I jog over to retrieve it.

"Might wanna work on that before the game starts," he teases, tossing it back before heading into the stands with the rest of his teammates.

He's here. Of course he is. Greyson always shows up.

I keep glancing up at him like a lovesick puppy. Bex notices me and jumps into my line of sight. "Head on the floor, Blakely. Not in the stands."

Right. We're here to get that conference title. I need to focus.

We breeze through the first and second rounds, advancing to the quarterfinals. The guys make the short trip back and forth between classes, so I've only seen Greyson from a distance. He texts sometimes, checking in about games, but is careful not to push. He's treating me like a skittish puppy, which sucks but is... fair.

Bex and I are roommates during the tournament. She spends a lot of time glued to her phone, texting Monty. I can't lie, I'm a bit jealous. Here I am, lying on my bed pretending the book I'm reading is interesting, and Bex is texting her person.

She finally looks up from her phone. "Monty and Greyson are planning to head back for the Quarterfinals tomorrow. They booked rooms for the whole weekend."

My stomach flips in anticipation. That means I might actually have to talk to Greyson, in person, for the first time in months.

I don't see the guys before tipoff, but I feel Greyson is in the arena. It's like static in the air. Unfortunately, I feel *something else*, too. This *something* fills me with impending doom, and I glance toward the entrance to see my mother walking in.

The Lady Big Horns win the quarterfinals easily. Next stop, the semifinals. So close to sealing our invite to the NCAA Tournament.

Riding the high from the game, I'm ready to have a conversation with Greyson. The guys plan to swing by our hotel to hang out. When there's a knock on the door, Bex leaps up to greet Monty and Grey, but it's not them.

It's my mother.

Bex slips out with an excuse of going to Hazel and Char's room. I assume she texts the guys because they never come by. So much for a celebratory evening.

No one kills a win quite like Lauren Blakely. She's skilled at turning anything good into not enough. I've started to accept I'll never meet her impossible standards.

And this weekend, I need to block her out of my mindset completely.

26

Greyson

I'm looking forward to finally talking to Jessa. But as Oakes and I head toward the girls' hotel, Collins texts.

Collins: *Jessa's mom just showed up.*

So much for that.

I tell Oakes to go ahead without me. There's no reason he should miss time with Collins just because plans changed. I could go hang out with the other girls, but that's not why I'm here. I came for Jessa. She's still my priority no matter what she thinks.

I text Collins to let me know how Jessa is afterward. Lauren Blakely has a gift for destroying confidence, her daughter's most of all. I've spent years trying to pick up those pieces.

The next day, a bunch of us drive over to catch the women's semifinals game. I'm hoping I'll get a chance to talk to Jessa tonight, but I also know I shouldn't distract her. She's on the edge of something huge. So I text and tell her we'll talk Sunday night after the final. She thanks me for understanding and apologizes about her mom ruining last night.

Unsurprisingly, the women make it to the conference tournament finals.

Because Hills is so close to Greensboro, the crowd is packed with Hills blue. The first half of the game is sluggish. The women are showing tournament fatigue, but they're too close to give in now.

The women come out ready to fight in the second half. Jessa comes out firing in the third. Hustling, battling in the paint, racking up rebounds like it's nothing. She's closing in on another double-double, but I can see how gassed she is. The fourth quarter is war. In the game of basketball, three minutes can feel like an eternity. This is especially true when two strong teams are head-to-head. It's a battle of wills to see who will come out on top. The tension in the area is thick, and the already slow game slows even more with timeouts and official reviews. The lead shrinks, grows, and shrinks again. There are no remaining timeouts and a three-point lead, when the other team shoots and is fouled.

I inhale and hold my breath. There's one minute left, and a made shot will tie the game. Anything can happen at this point.

The shot is made—tie game. Fuck. I watch with clenched fists. The ball is inbounded and dribbled down the court. HU beats the full court press and the ball is a lob pass to Jessa in the paint. She fakes, goes up strong, and finishes through a whistle. She's hammered to the floor but still scores. The crowd explodes. She gets to her feet with help, steps to the line, dribbles once, twice, three times, and sinks the free throw. A three-point lead with thirty seconds left.

Don't foul, don't foul.

A long two-point shot goes up and drops through the hoop. Now it's a one-point game; twenty seconds left—no shot clock.

Will they hold the ball and finish with a one-point lead or attempt another shot?

Jessa flashes open again, takes the pass, but the defense collapses, forcing her to kick it back out. Five seconds left.

Hold it, I think. *Just hold onto the ball.*

Four... three... a pass... two... one—

"THE BIG HORNS ARE CONFERENCE TOURNAMENT CHAMPS! They just sealed their automatic bid to the NCAA Tournament!"

Pandemonium ensues.

The crowd rushes the court, quickly becoming a sea of Hills blue. The players are hugging and shaking hands, some of them hysterical with happiness. Coach Morris is dabbing her eyes. I look on, so proud of Jessa and the entire women's team for all the time and energy put in to pull this win off. I push into the crowd until I reach Jessa, pulling her into a bear hug. It's steady, safe, and familiar. For a second, it feels like nothing has changed between us.

Jessa is swept away with the team for interviews and the trophy presentation. They'll announce Conference Player of the Year, Defensive Player of the Year, Sixth Player of the Year, Coach of the Year, and Freshman of the Year.

The crowd is cleared from the court and sent back to their seats for the awards.

The announcer starts, "Congratulations to the Hills University Big Horns on being Conference Champs and on their automatic bid to the NCAA Tournament. We can't wait to see the great things you'll do in the coming weeks!"

Coach Morris accepts the trophy and hands it off to the team. The girls take turns with the trophy— kissing, touching, and lifting it up with exhilaration. The crowd watches on, cheering loudly.

Once the crowd settles down, the announcer comes back with, "And now for our Conference individual awards..."

They announce the winners for the Sixth Player of the Year, Freshman of the Year, Coach of the Year, and then they finally get to Defensive Player of the Year.

"Your Conference Defensive Player of the Year *and* Conference Player of the Year go to Hills University's Senior Forward... Jessa Blakely!"

I'm yelling and cheering as Jessa gets passed from teammate to teammate, pushed to the front to accept her *two* trophies. She's pink-faced, embarrassed, and absolutely glowing. She looks beautiful, I think.

Take that Lauren Blakely. She did this.

27
Jessa

Holy crap. Hearing my name called for not one but two conference awards feels unreal. My teammates shove me forward, and I accept them still sweaty and red-faced. All eyes are on me, so I lift both trophies, say a simple thank you, and get pulled into a quick interview.

Broadcaster: *Congratulations Jessa! Conference Defensive Player of the Year AND Conference Player of the Year. This is so well deserved. You've been described as a dominant, versatile, and determined player. Fans have had a treat watching your growth over the last four years, yet this year when most maintain, you continue to grow. You just didn't stop. What do you attribute this to?*

Me: *I think it's taken our entire coaching staff and my teammates to get me here. Without their support with extra workouts and challenging me in practice, it would be easy to be content where I am. My hope is that I can be 1% better every day, and I've been putting in the work to get there.*

Broadcaster: *You are typically a calm and collected player, though you are known for being aggressive on the boards and in your power moves to get off shots. How do you handle pressure in a game?*

Me: *Again, I really think it comes down to the trust I have in my teammates, and they have in me to do what each of us is intended to do and have each other's backs all the way. The pressure isn't just put on one person's shoulders. It's about how we show up and move forward together. We are all better together.*

Broadcaster: *Thanks, Jessa.*

The interview ends and my teammates swarm me with hugs before security ushers us toward the tunnel. As we approach, I spot Greyson. Our eyes meet. I detour straight into his arms, and he lifts me like he always does.

"You did it. I'm so proud of you," he murmurs, squeezing tight. His scent hits me and, for a split second, I'm back in every moment we've ever shared. I pull myself together and jog off to sign autographs for a group of little girls.

Greyson is outside when the bus pulls up at the Blakely Center. Coming home after a week in the tournament bubble is overwhelming, but seeing him waiting by his Jeep calms something inside me. He grabs my bags before I can protest, but this way I can balance my hardware. His hand rests against the small of my back and leads me to the car. The gesture is so small but my traitor of a body reacts. It misses his touch. He loads my stuff, opens the door for me, and we drive home in comfortable silence. When he parks, he finally turns toward me.

"I've missed you Jessa. It's lonely without my best friend. I miss our talks, just hanging out without having to say anything. I miss seeing you. Do you know how impossible it is to avoid someone you live with?"

I laugh softly.

"I may have some idea about missing someone. Bex told me I've been crabby. I didn't realize how much I missed... all of this." I gesture between us. "And everything you did while we weren't talking—you didn't have to, but you did. Why?"

He exhales. "Because I want us to enjoy these last months together. No labels, no pressure—just... us. In whatever form you want. Say yes to what makes you happy, J. Right now. Not later."

I put my trophies in my lap and reach for his hands, giving them a squeeze. "Thank you for being you and never giving up on me." I smile at him warmly. "You are a true best friend."

I lean over the console and trophies to hug him. Suddenly everything feels right in the world, even if I keep insisting we're just friends. I'm afraid I might panic again if I consider anything else. Maybe I just need the safety of the friendship for now.

"Let's get inside. I'm dying to be in my own bed," I say.

Inside, the lights are out and Bex and Monty are nowhere to be seen. We were talking for quite a while, so we suspect they went to bed. Feeling vulnerable and a little brave, I say, "Will you sleep in my bed tonight?"

His eyebrows shoot up. "You want me to sleep in your bed?"

"Just to... not feel alone. Cuddle buddies."

"I know what you mean, Jessa." He smirks and I smack his arm.

"Gosh, I hate you," I say, but I'm smiling.

"Of course, I could use a cuddle buddy tonight. I'll throw my stuff in my room and change, then be in."

Later, lying side by side, neither of us can sleep. I catch him looking at me.

"What?" I whisper.

"I just need to tell you that I leave tomorrow for an interview at Mount Oread University, so I'll be gone for a couple of days. It kind of snuck up on me."

My stomach dips. "MOU? That's huge, Greyson."

"And then NYC for the NBA, then Orange. I'll be home one night this week." His eyes are bright with excitement. "It's a lot."

I turn away so he doesn't see my face fall. "That's... really amazing."

"I've also got to find time to go to Bruins University and then a few other locations a bit closer."

I can tell he's excited. I'm happy for him. I am. But I also feel the distance already forming. He spoons behind me, warm and steady, and I fall asleep wondering if this is the beginning of losing him for good.

I wake up alone the next morning. Greyson is probably packing for his trip. My chest aches. I'm disappointed he's not in my bed and even more so he'll be gone all week. I don't have classes today, so I throw on shorts and a t-shirt and shuffle to the kitchen for breakfast. Greyson walks out of his room rolling a suitcase, wearing a crisp blue button-down and navy pants that make his eyes look unreal. He smells like cologne, adulthood, and possibility.

"I thought you'd left," I say, embarrassed to have been staring.

"I wouldn't leave without saying good-bye," he says, stepping close. "But I didn't want to wake you since I know your body is probably recovering from the tournament. I've got to get to the airport, but I'll let you know when I'm there."

He pulls me into a strong hug, fingers brushing my hair. He kisses my cheek and then he's gone.

I'm still standing there, staring at the door like an idiot when Monty and Bex emerge from her bedroom.

"You okay?" Bex asks.

"Yep, fine," I respond, but a tear betrays me.

They head out for coffee, after I assure them I'm good, and I curl up on the couch, sinking down to eat my breakfast and overthink. I begin a mental checklist of life goals. Some I've hit. Others... I'm not even close.

I was lucky enough to pursue basketball on a D1 scholarship away from my mother and have broken several basketball records, stepping out of her shadow. Found best friends and had an amazing college experience.

But, I still have work to do:

☐ Live out a romantic love story

☐ Stop trying to get Mom's approval

☐ Say yes to more than basketball

☐ Be genuinely happy

☐ Don't sit around waiting

☐ Win NCAA Tourney

☐ Build my HR firm

I've made progress, but I'm also the one standing in my own way. That much I can see from my own list.

I need help. And clarity. And someone honest enough to call me out.

So I head to Coach Morris. She doesn't look surprised to see me.

"Ah, Jessa, to what do I owe the pleasure?" starts Coach.

"Well," I say, feeling nervous now that I'm here. "I've been thinking."

"What a dangerous thing that can be," she says with a knowing smile. I take in the large, sparkly diamond on her left ring finger, admiring how it catches the light.

"I don't have class today, so I thought I'd take a recovery day. I started thinking about my goals, where I am with them, and what I want to do with my future," I start.

"Whew, sounds kind of heavy for a recovery day."

I exhale. "You're right about that."

I open up to Coach Morris in a way I never have before. She's a good listener. We talk about so much—about goals, timing, how life rarely unfolds on our schedule. About regret. About relationships. About choosing for yourself instead of choosing out of fear.

"Coach, are you happy?" I blurt out at one point. Somehow knowing this makes me feel like I'll have a better idea of what I want.

"Yes, I am happy, Jessa. But it took me a while to find my way here. It's not always easy to look beyond the choices in front of you and how they'll fit into your future."

"Are you talking about Coach Hayes?"

"He's definitely a part of that. He was one of the missing pieces when I chose basketball, and later, when I started my coaching career. I made up my mind too early, and never gave us a real chance back then. I regret the lost time." Coach Morris studies me for a beat, then says, "What's this really about?"

I don't say anything. I'm not sure if I should bring Greyson up.

But then Coach Morris says something that knocks the air out of me. Greyson has been visiting with her and Coach Hayes regularly—getting advice, asking questions, using their contacts to line up interviews in every city I might land. He told them both that he wants a job that keeps the door open for *us*. Whether it's now or way out in the future.

Something in my chest cracks open right there in Coach Morris's office.

28
Greyson

I take a steadying breath as I step off the plane. This is my first professional interview. It's surreal, but I feel good about it. An MOU assistant coach meets me at baggage claim, warm and enthusiastic, which is exactly the energy I'd hoped for. We talk basketball, player development, and what it's like transitioning from athlete to staff. Every word reinforces that I'm where I'm supposed to be.

The day moves fast. I meet players, sit in on practice, and attend a dinner with the coaching staff. By the time I return to the hotel, I'm exhausted, but I text Jessa anyway. Just a quick message to let her know I've been busy since I landed and will try to catch up with her sometime tomorrow. She doesn't reply before I crash for the night.

I'm up early the next morning, though there's still no answer from Jessa. Interviews run smoothly and better than I expected. Talking player development suddenly feels natural. It's even fun. Maybe this really is my lane.

The same coach who picked me up from the airport is the one to drop me off.

"Well, what'd you think about MOU men's basketball?" he asks. "Could you see yourself here?" I keep my tone neutral but honest. "You all made me feel at home right away. Thanks for having me, Coach. Best of luck in the coming weeks."

"We'll be in touch," he assures me, shaking my hand before I head through the airport doors.

I check in for my flight and get through security with a few minutes to spare. Before I board, I check my phone. Still nothing from Jessa.

I text again before takeoff.

Me: *Boarding my flight back, hope to see you tonight when I get home.*

The typing bubbles appear but then disappear. My stomach drops, and I'm suddenly overthinking all the reasons she isn't messaging me back. But they call my group, so I put my phone in my pocket and board.

It's late when I get home. The condo is quiet and dark. I grab a snack and push open my bedroom door, then freeze in the doorway. Jessa is curled up asleep on top of my bed, a book open beside her, like she tried to wait up for me. She looks peaceful.

I forget about the snack, change quickly, and lie beside her, careful not to wake her. It's calming being in bed with her, and I let her slow, even breaths lull me to sleep. I wake up the next morning to Jessa's alarm. She fumbles for it, startled to see me awake.

"Shit, I'm so sorry."

"No problem," I say, my voice scratchy from sleep. "I wasn't expecting to find you in here last night."

I try to adjust my morning wood without her noticing.

"You good?" She asks, eyeing me while I squirm. "Yep. I've got to get up anyway and repack."

She looks me over, flustered. "I planned to be awake when you got home. I wanted to talk. Maybe after I get ready?"

"Sounds like a plan," I say.

She disappears to her side of the condo, and Oakes pokes his head in my room. "How'd it go?"

"It was great! Better than expected."

"Does that mean you will be trading in Hills blue and gold for the blue and crimson?" he jokes.

I groan. I hadn't thought about trading colors by working at a different school. "Guess we will wait and see. I'm off again today. Be back Saturday." I say with a shrug.

I shower, repack, and realize there's no way Jessa and I will get a moment before I head to the airport. So I move to the kitchen and make her a quick breakfast—her usual on-the-go peanut butter English muffin and smoothie.

When she emerges, hair damp, backpack slung over one shoulder, she freezes at the sight of it. Then looks at me like I've sprouted two heads.

"What's this?"

"Your breakfast."

She just stares at me. "Right," she finally says.

"You okay? I saw you were running late, so I made it since I had a minute." I know I sound a bit defensive.

"All good, just unexpected," she says, swallowing hard, like she's holding something back.

"Jessa..." I start.

She grabs the food, gives a quick "Good luck this week," and bolts.

It feels off, but we don't have time to fix it.

At the airport, I text Collins.

Me: *Jessa okay? She seemed off this morning.*

Collins: *She's quiet but says she's fine. Probably stressed about the bracket announcement.*

Probably. But I can't shake the image of her asleep in my bed, then acting like she didn't know what to do with me in the morning.

New York is on another level entirely. A private car takes me from the airport to a fancy dinner to the hotel then to the interviews the next morning. The interviews with big NBA names for amazing opportunities make my head spin, but it's also exciting to think I could work there. I'm taken on a stunning tour of Manhattan, and it's hard not to revel at the expansiveness of the city. Before I head home, I fly to an interview with Orange University. At the end of it, I'm exhausted but proud of the steps I'm taking for my future. And still, after every meeting, every handshake, every hotel room, every *"we'll be in touch,"* my mind returns to Jessa.

I miss her. Not only Jessa, my best friend. But I miss the intimacy, too. Several times I find myself hard, sexual frustration settling in with a vengeance, until all I can do is fist my dick thinking of her. Jessa fingering her clit, thrusting against me, making those sexy noises she makes when she climaxes.

By the end of the week, I feel positive about how I interviewed at MOU, the NBA, and Orange University. I'm grateful for the opportunities. I want to be excited. But the thing I want most still feels out of reach.

I touch down at the airport on Saturday and text Jessa.

Me: *Back in town. Hope I can see you today.*

As I drive home to the condo, all I can think about is finally being in the same room. We need to talk and figure out what we are now. Or what we could still be.

29

Jessa

I receive a text from Greyson telling me he's on his way home. It's taken everything in me not to respond this week. I want him to walk into a surprise without any warning. After a week of him being gone and me avoiding everything that distracts me, I'm ready to talk. Like to really talk—about us. Before Selection Sunday when things will get chaotic.

Tomorrow is the program's Selection Sunday watch party. By Wednesday, we'll be wherever our region is scheduled to play. The agenda is jam packed once we get there with media interviews, meet-and-greets, and pre-game prep for the first round. It's a little overwhelming, considering we haven't had a ton of breathing time since the conference tournament.

I snap back to reality, realizing Greyson will be here any minute. Bex and Monty have been life savers since I shared my vision. They've helped me clean the condo, make a meal from scratch, and create a romantic ambiance in the living room. They sneak out just before I hear Greyson's Jeep pull up.

The room is unrecognizable. There are candles flickering everywhere, warm light bouncing off rose petals scattered across the floor. The air smells like garlic, chocolate, and a dozen spices we definitely never use. Photos of Greyson and me from the past four years are framed and arranged around the room.

I smooth the hem of the silky gold dress I chose. It falls above the knee and has a hit slit all the way up to the crease of my hip. It's nearly strapless, with a single piece of fabric over one shoulder. My hair is in soft waves and I'm wearing simple gold earrings and the basketball necklace.

The door opens and Greyson is here. He's on the phone and his mother's voice comes through the speaker loud and questioning. When he spots me, his eyes don't stray from me as he tells her he'll call her back later.

He steps inside and closes the door, looking around the living room.

"What's all this?"

He starts to say something else, but I step forward and press a finger against his lips. I guide him by the hand further inside, and I feel his eyes sweeping over me hungrily. "We haven't had a chance to talk, so I made dinner. I wanted it to be special," I say, pulling him towards the kitchen table. I wave my hand toward the table, showing him it's already set with two plates.

"Wow, Jessa. This is pretty over the top for us to catch up," he says.

His eyes move down my dress, and I see his jaw tighten when he notices the high slit running up the side, showing off my muscular thigh. He swears under his breath.

"I'm not sure what your plan is, but I think I might be getting the wrong idea." His tone is rough and serious, and he glances down where he's obviously hard.

That didn't take long, I think.

"Well, that's exactly the effect I was hoping for," I say, laughing. I absolutely wanted him to look at me like I was something ravenous. It's exhilarating, seeing his reaction match the one I'd envisioned in my head.

I push him down in a dining chair and straddle him, the slit riding up more, revealing my lack of underwear. He groans as my center lines up with his growing erection, and I breathe in his scent, trying not to move and ruin the moment. His hands grip my waist instinctively. Before I lose my courage or control to my pussy, I sputter out, "Greyson, I've been a huge idiot." He opens his mouth to speak, but I put my hand up to silence him. "Please, just listen. Let me get this out." I repeat, "I've been an idiot. But only because I didn't want you to mess up your future plans because of me. The longer we're apart, the more I crave you. You're the reason I get up in the morning, and you're always my biggest cheerleader. I'm yours, too. I'm sorry I never gave you a chance to tell me what you wanted for your future. I made the decision for both of us, without listening. I was afraid, but I don't want to do any of it without you. Coach told me you've talked to her and Coach Hayes, and she helped me see that what you're doing with the interviews is making it possible for us to be together while I'm pursuing professional basketball, or wherever the future leads."

I pause for a second, knowing that I'm rambling, but haven't said the one thing I really need to. "I need you. I want you. I love you." For a moment, Greyson says nothing. Shit. What if I'm too late? What if Coach was wrong?

Then Greyson grins, cupping my face with his hands. The movement makes his dick twitch against me and I resist the urge to let my eyes roll back. "Do you have any idea how long I've waited to hear you say those words?" Greyson asks, laughing. "I can't count the times you said it with a concussion."

"I did what?" I ask, holding my hands over my face. "Why didn't you tell me?!"

"That's not important right now. What is important is that you love me, and I love you," he says, pulling me closer to him. "God, I love you so much, Jessa. I've hated being apart."

The conversation ends with the most sensual kiss I've ever experienced. When he pulls away, my lips tingle with need. I moan, pressing my mouth to his and slipping my tongue between his lips. My body is losing control fast and I can already feel the wetness between my legs.

"Jessa," Greyson teases. "You're not wearing panties, are you?"

I shake my head, and he drops his head back, and pulls my hips down against the hardness beneath his pants. I roll my hips and Greyson thrusts up to meet me. Our hands are all over each other, and I feel like this cloud of ecstasy won't last long. I'm already close.

Greyson stands and I wrap my legs around him. He carries me across the room and sets me on top of the counter. I can't help but shriek a little when my bare bottom makes contact with the cold granite. He laughs at the sound, but I recover quickly, yanking his zipper down and pushing his pants and boxers down to his ankles. My knees fall open, and Greyson looks down between the silk fabric where I'm fully exposed.

"You are so sexy. You make me so hard. I got off the other night just fantasizing about you touching yourself," he says in my ear, his voice low. The thought of him touching himself in a hotel room is enough to make me moan and twist against his dick. Greyson stops abruptly. "I don't have a condom."

"I'm okay without one. I'm protected—and I trust you."

Greyson lets out the breath he'd been holding and just as quick as he stopped, he sticks the tip in and holds it there, pushing me back when I try to take him in further.

"No fair," I say. "I need all of you inside of me."

He ignores my pleas and pushes the tip in and out, in and out until I'm writhing against him. Just when I think he's going all in, he pulls out completely. I whine in response, but he distracts me by kissing the sensitive skin on my neck, his hands falling down to stroke himself. He swipes at the precum and slides his finger along my clit. I groan and press into him, needing him to fill me. My hard nipples push at the silk of my dress, and even that feels like it could push me over the edge. I unbutton his shirt so I can admire his body, a beautiful expanse of smooth skin truncated with dips and valleys of hard muscle. Finally, he pushes into me, and I cry out from his massiveness. I squeeze my pelvis, making more room and making Greyson groan from the pressure around his cock. "Shit, you have to slow down, or I won't last," he rasps. I don't stop, though, and he glides in and out of me until I involuntarily tense up, my pussy tightening around his dick. Pleasure rocks me, pulse after pulse vibrating through me.

"Grey, I'm coming."

"I know," he says, a lilt to his tone. He smirks at me, pleased he pushed me over the edge first.

He maintains a steady pace for a few seconds but then loses control of his pleasure. He slams into me, harder and faster, until his body tenses beneath my hands. I squeeze him with my pussy, milking him until I feel the warmth of his release deep inside of me. We stay connected, both of us enjoying the aftershocks until I find another small release in the tiny movements and cry out once again. He shivers, and I feel his body collapse against me. It takes his core strength to keep us both upright on the counter. We're half-dressed, sweaty and sticky, but satisfied.

"I think our food might be cold," he says, setting me down on the tile.

When I don't respond, he looks at me, cupping my face with his palm and gazing into my eyes. "You good?"

"Never better," I say. Then I steal another kiss.

30

Greyson

Well, that was quite the unexpected welcome home gift. I'd hoped to come home and hang out with a friend, but instead I walked into a living room covered in candles and rose petals. And a girlfriend. I am on cloud nine. Jessa told me she loved me, and showed me in every way she could.

We're tangled naked on the couch, me kissing her shoulder and playing with her basketball charm, when the apartment door unlocks. We jolt apart, grabbing the nearest blanket just as Collins and Oakes step inside.

"I assume this means you made up? For real this time?" Collins asks, eyeing Jessa's unmistakable post-sex glow.

"Good," Oakes adds, "because I'm not sure how much more I could take if you two weren't actually together."

We grin at each other and, still clutching the blanket, announce in unison: "He loves me!" "She loves me!"

"That's more like it, lovebirds," Oakes says, steering Collins toward his room. "We'll leave you to... whatever."

Once they disappear, Jessa laughs. "Maybe we should move this party elsewhere."

"Agreed. You hungry? Maybe we should warm up the dinner we didn't eat."

"Starved," she says dramatically.

I wake the next morning in her bed, our limbs knotted together, her breath warm on my chest. Last night was the best night of my life. The relief of finally saying the words—of hearing them back—settles deep inside me. We're not hiding anymore. We're moving forward together.

I kiss her forehead, careful not to wake her, and text my sister.

Me: *Hey Sis! You better be planning to watch Selection Sunday today. It's a big day for our girl, Jessa.*

The response is almost immediate. Soren's phone might be permanently attached to her hand.

Soren: *Of course! Our girl? Do you mean...*

Me: *Yup. I mean when I got home from my week of interviews, Jessa surprised me with a romantic candlelight and rose petal covered living room, a homemade meal, and told me she loved me!*

My phone rings almost instantly.

"Seriously?" Soren screams into my ear. You couldn't even call to tell me. You thought a text was good enough?! Is she there with you right now?"

"Shh—yes, she's sleeping," I whisper, glancing at Jessa just as she stirs. "I didn't want to wake her." Jessa rolls toward me, squinting her eyes. "Good one, Soren, you woke her up."

Jessa reaches for my phone, smiling at me. "Hey, Soren."

"I can't believe you are, like, my future sister-in-law!" Soren shouts.

"Woah, woah, woah," Jessa says with a grin. "We just said we love each other. Let us enjoy that first."

"Ok, that's fair," Soren agrees. "But a girl can dream."

After I hang up, Jessa searches my face like she's memorizing it.

"It's real," I whisper, brushing my lips over hers. It's meant to be gentle, but she pulls me in deeper. Our kisses are hungry, hands roaming, breaths quickening until we finally pull apart, laughing and breathless.

"We should probably get ready," Jessa says reluctantly.

"At least we get to spend the day together."

"It's going to be a good one," she says, slipping out of bed. I grab her waist, dragging her back for one more kiss before she escapes to the bathroom, giggling. I follow her in.

Jessa turns the water on, but I can't wait for the water to warm up. My hands circle her waist and pull her in, the still cold water making her gasp. I pull off our now wet clothes, and the shower steams around us. The moment her hands find my shoulders, the playful teasing melts into something urgent. Water slides over her skin as our mouths collide. I press closer, chest to chest, every line of my body insistent against hers.

I frame her face with both hands, kissing her like I'm claiming air. I drag my mouth along her jaw, her throat, tasting water and skin until she tilts her head back with a sharp inhale.

Her fingers thread through my hair, tugging, guiding, demanding. Our now ragged breaths are somewhere between desperation and surrender. We shift, stumbling against the slick wall. I lift Jessa so her back is against the wall, pinned beneath the weight of my body.

Her eyes are lidded as she stares into mine, and we move together—sliding, gripping, pulling—like we can't get close enough.

When we finish, we hold each other for a moment, taking each other in. We don't speak it, but there's an overwhelming certainty hanging in the misty air. We're exactly where, and with who, we're meant to be.

By the time we walk into the Blakely Center, hand in hand, our smiles give everything away. Collins and Oakes trail behind us, and several teammates erupt in applause as soon as they see us. Even the coaches look somewhat relieved to have us out in the open.

As we enter the space further, I see Jessa's mom at the same time she does. They make eye contact and Lauren Blakely's scowl is unmistakable. Of course she's here without telling Jessa. But I won't let her ruin this day.

The teams help set up because the doors are open to the public to watch the selections with us. It's a thank you for their continued support, and the atmosphere they bring makes the day more exciting. With our women's team doing so well, it's unsurprising when more fans than usual crowd into the center.

It's almost time to start, so Jessa breaks away from me reluctantly and joins her teammates in the front row. As the men's bracket is wrapped up and the broadcasters move on to discuss the women's, I watch Jessa. Her knee bounces and she's threading her fingers together nervously in her lap. I refocus as the announcement comes:

"Hills University, the number five seed."

The place erupts. The women's team jumps to their feet, hugging, crying, cheering. A five-seed. This is huge.

The announcer's voice can hardly be heard as they continue, "HU will play the number 12 seed Heartland University in Birmingham Region Two."

When Jessa makes her way back to me, I pull her into a fierce hug.

"Damn," I say, "Out of 64 teams in the first round HU is number five!"

She nods, in disbelief.

"I'm so proud of you," I tell her. "Oakes and I already made spring break plans with some of the other guys. We'll be there to support you. The rest, we'll figure out."

Relief softens her shoulders. She leans her forehead to mine, smiling.

Together feels like the easiest decision we've ever made.

31

Jessa

The last few days in our home gym before the tournament pass in a blur. Between school and practice, Bex and I pack and repack, making sure we have everything we'll need for at least the first two rounds. There's no way of knowing when we'll get to stop at home again.

Since Birmingham is an eight-hour drive, the team gets to fly. The guys, of course, are road-tripping for the "full spring break experience," as they put it. We arrive Wednesday, enjoy open practice, and meet fans. Coach keeps a tight bubble around us, which fortunately limits my mother's access to phone-only. I keep tabs on Greyson and Monty's locations as they make their drive but otherwise stay focused on my team.

We load up on carbs at the hotel ballroom and loosen up with games after dinner. Back in our room, Bex and I text the guys, listen to music, and do anything we can to distract ourselves from the nerves. Lights out just after eleven—breakfast, shootaround, and our first NCAA Tournament game await.

The arena buzzes even during shootaround. I take a moment, fingers wrapped around the basketball charm Greyson gave me, trying to steady my nerves. Before tipoff, I find him in the crowd. He forms a heart with his hands and points at me. I can't stop beaming.

Once the game starts, we find our rhythm quickly. At halftime we lead Heartland University by 17, and we finish them off 83–53.

With a few days between rounds, we use the time to practice and watch some incredible basketball. We learn we'll face the four-seed, Terrapin University, in the round of 32.

True to their word, the guys show up again, cheering us on louder than ever. At half, we trail by six. We surge in the third, leading by two, and somehow hang on through a chaotic fourth quarter. We win 91–86.

After showers and media, we meet up with fans and settle in to watch the next game. The guys get ready to head out—they're driving to Gulf Shores before returning for our Sweet Sixteen matchup against number two seed Wellington University.

"Great game, Jessa," Greyson says, hugging me tightly. "We were on the edge of our seats the entire time."

"Tell me about it. Try playing in that game. We pulled it off though," I say. "I know you guys are anxious to get going. So be safe. And don't do anything I wouldn't do."

"Trying to get rid of me already?" Greyson teases. "But what exactly does that leave that we shouldn't do?"

I punch him playfully and narrow my eyes at him.

He holds his hands up in surrender, "Woah, kidding, kidding!"

"I'm serious, be safe and behave," I say as I look into his ocean blue eyes and hold both of his hands in mine. "I know how spring break trips can go."

He catches the unspoken memory—our spring break in Turks

and Caicos. "Okay, fair. But this is just the guys. We'll probably do something stupid, but nothing you'd kill me for."

I pinch him. "You'd better not."

"Ow—okay, okay! No women. Oakes and I will keep everyone in check. We wouldn't want you and Collins to kick anyone's ass."

"Good." I smirk. "Now go before I hold you hostage."

He leans in. "Don't tempt me. I might like that. Especially if—"

I smack him before he can finish. He laughs, holding up his hands.

"I love you, Jessa."

"I love you too," I manage before Monty drags him away.

Bex and I return to the arena to sit with our team.

With a few more days off before our next game, we hold long team meetings to study our past game tapes and watch games of potential future opponents. We fit in light practices and even visit the Alabama Sports Hall of Fame and the Civil Rights Institute.

Greyson keeps sending photos of the guys building sandcastles and goofing around. There are no women in sight, which both amuses and reassures me.

Reality sets in early in the week. Friday could be our last game as a team. Another one of my Lasts. My throat tightens as I fight away the tears threatening to fall. No. Not today. We're not done. We have four more games in us. We're going all the way. I breathe through the negative thoughts—one day, one game at a time.

We've reached the Sweet Sixteen. The guys text that they'll arrive just before tipoff. Greyson knows me well enough to keep me updated so I don't spiral.

In the locker room, Coach Morris calls us in and tells us to sit.

"You've put in the work. All that work has led up to this key moment. You earned your place here. Now make this moment count, then the next, then the next. You are four games away from being National Champions. Let that sink in. Hands in. Big Horns on three."

"One, two, three—BIG HORNS!"

I lead us onto the court. My eyes scan the stands, but I can't find Greyson. Panic flickers, but Coach sees me looking and points him out. He's sitting beside Coach Hayes. Relief floods through me.

"Head in the game, Blakely."

"I'm ready, Coach!"

Wellington's defense is relentless. We'd heard they had an aggressive style of play, and knew we'd need our offense to be on point. But they move like lightning and dominate the defensive boards. They suffocate every offensive look we try. I rack up fouls early and sit, irritated. By halftime, we're down 25.

In the locker room, Coach lays out adjustments, but the team looks defeated. There's no spark, no energy like before. Something in me snaps, and I know I need to do something fast. I stand.

"Ladies, we're down—but not out. We need to be more disciplined on defense and more aggressive on offense. Not just you, me too. We play OUR game, *together*. They're aggressive? Who cares? So are we. We want this more, and this game is ours. Let's go win it."

My speech must have ignited something in us. By mid-third quarter, we've cut the lead to eight. I'm pulling down boards for second shots on offense, blocking shots on defense. I've finally found my groove in this game. And I think both teams know it.

The crowd is alive with the direction change this game has taken. Wellington looks frustrated and their coach calls several time outs. We enter the fourth down by just two. I'm on my way to another double-double and have the potential to break my own rebounds per game record. I catch Greyson's eyes. His arms are raised, his mouth open as he cheers. Seeing his support pushes me even harder.

Wellington completely unravels. Their players rack up fouls, frustrated, while our team pushes and pushes. The momentum is all ours. We dominate the last quarter and secure the win 82–59. And I finish with a double-double and set my new personal rebounding record.

Postgame is a whirlwind of emotions, interviews, and a press conference with Coach Morris. When she and I make it back to the locker room, the rest of the team greets us with spraying water. This is an amazing feeling. We're headed to the Elite Eight.

After showers, the team grabs snacks and settles in to watch our potential next opponent. Greyson, and his devastating smile, find me.

"Winning looks good on you, J," he says with a wink.

I beam at him. I'm buzzing with pride, but I've missed his calming energy. "Gulf Shores looks good on you. You're so tan."

Then my mother appears.

"Congratulations, Jessa," she says, stiff and clipped. How is she always so robotic? Her gaze sweeps from me to my teammates then lands on the guys with clear disapproval. God forbid they come to show us support. "Thanks for coming, Mom." I say. I'm cordial but cool, hoping she'll take the hint I'm in no mood to chat.

"Of course, dear. It's a big moment for your team and the program. It's been years since they've come this far."

"And we plan on going further," I say with a bite to my tone. She always drags this side of me out.

"The next game is starting. I best get back to my seat, but I'm staying in town for the game on Sunday."

"Sounds good. See you then," I say, watching as she leaves.

Greyson exhales. "I wish she wasn't so condescending when congratulating you."

"Me too," I say. "But she doesn't get a say in my life anymore, so it doesn't matter."

We watch the next game together, analyzing both teams because we'll play the winner next.

Bruins University wins by one. Free throws really can win games.

32

Greyson

The girls have been playing unbelievably, and Jessa is shining like the star she is. Pressure doesn't crack her. She seems to thrive on it. And based on what I've heard from the other girls, Jessa gave a fiery halftime speech that pulled them out of their heads to win that last game.

The time in the Gulf Shores was better than I'd anticipated. Somewhere between beach days and late-night talks, the guys surprised me with how supportive they are about my future with Jessa. I told them all about the interviews I've had so far and the ones coming up. None of them envy my impending decisions, but having them listen meant more than I'd expected. I haven't told Jessa about the interviews next week. She has so much on her plate as it is. They're scheduled for early in the week, at least. And one is in Indiana, the same state as the Final Four where I fully expect the girls to be. Timing is on my side for once.

My parents are warming to the idea of me and Jessa, but they're still a bit miffed about how I've gone about job searching. Soren's been the voice of reason, somehow. I never thought I'd put those two things together in the same sentence. My whole family plans to be in the stands if the Big Horns make it to the Final Four. Collins's and Oakes's families, too, if all goes right. It'll be one hell of a surprise for the girls.

It's finally time for the Elite Eight match up versus second seed Bruins University. The arena is alive with fans, bright lights, and noise vibrating around the court. The opposing team looks calm, like it's just another game, not one with potential to send them to the Final Four.

The girls are in sync from tipoff. Their defense is tight, their ball movement is smooth and quick, and they push the Bruins until they can't breathe. I'm amazed at how our girls get sharper with every game. The Bruins throw everything they have at them—a full court press, traps, tough man-to-man—but the Lady Big Horns never lose their rhythm. They win 77-62.

On to the Final Four!

The girls look stunned, hugging and crying. Even through their excitement they pause to shake the hands of the Bruins University players. There's a mutual respect for the grind, grit, and sacrifice it takes to make it this far.

Even after cooling down, Jessa's cheeks are pink when she spots me. She runs and jumps into my arms, wet hair leaving a cold patch on my shirt. I don't care. I hold her tight as she buries her face in my chest.

"I don't even know why I'm crying right now," Jessa says, her voice muffled as she sniffles into my chest.

"This is a big deal," I murmur into her hair. "All the relief, excitement, and overwhelm are understandable."

I squeeze her again. I want to memorize this moment.

"Alright, everyone," Coach says, doing her best to corral her excited team. "Bus to the airport leaves in twenty. It's time to head home." Before I gather the guys for the road trip back, I shoot a quick text to my family.

Me: *See you at the Final Four.*

It's late when Oakes and I drop everyone off at home and get to the condo. The girls had texted when they made it back hours ago, and Jessa's message made my heart tick with anticipation.

Jessa: *I'll be waiting in your bed when you get home. I've missed you.*

When I open my bedroom door, she's curled around my pillow in one of my shirts, asleep. She looks so peaceful. God, I've missed her. I peel off my clothes and slide into bed. She stirs, sees me, and immediately shifts closer. I brush my lips over hers. It's meant to be gentle, but she pushes her body closer, pressing hard into me like she's starved for touch. Maybe she has been. I know I have. Our mouths collide, hungry for each other after so much time apart. We're breathing fast, tangling our fingers in each other's hair like we can't get enough. I roll Jessa on top of me and she melts into my body.

"I love you so much. I've missed you so fucking much," I pant between kisses. She responds with a sound that goes straight through me. She's grinding on my thigh, and that's when I realize she's not wearing anything under my shirt. I grip her ass, lifting her slightly. She moans into my mouth.

"Greyson," she says, lifting up to take my t-shirt off. "I'm so wet. I need you to fill me."

"Fuck, Jessa," I swear. "That's so fucking hot. Tell me what you want, baby."

"If you don't take those boxers off, I'm coming before you even touch me." We shove them down together. Her stomach grazes my cock and I almost lose it right there. She wraps her hand around my cock and I swear I see stars. She smiles at my reaction.

"I can't take it," I warn, voice ragged. "Baby, I—"

She straddles me, dripping onto my skin, then sinks down inch by inch. I come the moment I'm fully inside her. It's one of the best orgasms of my life. Deep, uncontrollable, and comes in waves. Jessa gasps, riding me through her own orgasm, unable to steady herself as her body clenches around me again and again.

We stay like that for a while, still connected. I've never experienced anything like this. It's more intense than anything I expected. Looking at her face, I suspect it's blowing her away too.

I get up for a washcloth and help her clean up. Then I pull her back into my arms for a long kiss before we fall asleep holding onto one another.

I wake refreshed from what could be the best sleep of my life. My body aches in all the right places, and Jessa's body is still wrapped around mine. "Whatcha thinking about?" she murmurs, eyes still closed.

"How amazing you are," I say without missing a beat.

She laughs softly, followed by a sigh. "I wish we could stay like this forever."

"Maybe once school and basketball are done," I say.

She stares into my eyes for a moment, then kisses me. It deepens until I force myself to pull back before we end up repeating last night. She hums in protest.

"I know we were hoping to spend more time together this week, but I have to go to Indiana."

She brightens. "Of course you do. We're in the Final Four!"

"Well, yes—but also another interview."

"Oh, I didn't realize," she says. A flicker of worry crosses her face, but she masks it quickly.

"I'll be there on game day. I promise."

Relief washes over her face. She doesn't want to be needy, but sometimes I need her to be.

The week flies by. Between coordinating flights for my family and focusing on school, I'm juggling too much, but it'll be worth it when the girls are surprised in Indianapolis.

On Wednesday morning, I kiss Jessa goodbye and wish her luck then Oakes drives me to the airport. I haven't even walked through security when my phone dings.

Jessa: *I love you. Safe travels. You're gonna kill it.* 🫶❤️

I'm still smiling down at her text when my phone rings. It's not a number I recognize, but I answer anyway.

"Greyson Hastings," the voice says. "This is James Brady calling on behalf of Mount Oread University Men's Basketball. Did I catch you at a good time?"

"Hello. Yes, now's a good time," I say, my heart stuttering. I hadn't expected to hear back so fast. "Well, Greyson, we really enjoyed getting to know you during your visit and think you'd be a great addition to our program. We'd like to offer you the Director of Player Development position at MOU."

"Wow, thank you," I say, too overwhelmed to even know what questions I should ask. "Can I have some time to think the offer over?"

"Of course. We will send an email with the details and the official offer."

"Thank you. I'll be in touch."

Later, when the wheels touch ground, I see I have several voicemails. Orange University wants to talk again. The NBA has a few team opportunities and wants to follow up with me. It's too much, too fast. Just a few weeks ago I'd worried no one would want me. And now... Now I have options. I remind myself to breathe. Naturally I want to talk to Jessa about all of this, but it can wait. She needs to focus. And I have the interview with Heartland University to get through.

Like the first few interviews I've had, Heartland University is busy with dinner, introductions, interviews, and a low-key practice. It went well. Better than well, actually. By the time I'm dropped off at the hotel, I'm buzzing with energy. I text Jessa.

Me: *Thinking about you. I love you. Hope tomorrow feels magical.*

Her response is brief. She's probably at a team dinner.

Jessa: *Thanks, and I love you too.*

33

Jessa

While we practiced here yesterday, I'm still in awe looking around Gainbridge Fieldhouse—home of the Pacers and the Fever. The idea that pros might be in the building makes my heart pound. What even is this life I'm living right now? It feels unreal.

Bex and I move through our pre-game ritual, something sacred at this point, and a few teammates join in like always. It hits me that this could be the last time we do this... but no. I refuse to think that way. One moment at a time.

My phone is blowing up with good-luck messages, but I silence it. Greyson texted last night; I don't expect more from him today. I need to be fully present.

When it's time, we step out of the tunnel into a packed arena. The energy hits hard. Fans from both schools roar in the stands. We all look around for a moment, taking it in. I scan the stands and freeze when I find Greyson. He's not alone. He's sitting with his whole family. And beside them is Bex's family, including her twin, Aiden, and Monty's family. They all grin and wave at us like they've planned this together. Bex and I stare at each other, wide-eyed. This we hadn't expected.

Our team huddles, breaks, and then begin warm-ups. The Storrs University Norse, the three-seed, looks sharp and ready. So are we. We didn't make it this far just to go home.

From the opening tipoff, it's war. Both teams are dialed in, trading baskets and pushing pace. This is a true battle of talent and wills amongst two evenly matched teams. By the start of the fourth quarter, we're still tied. Everything comes down to these last ten minutes.

Commentator One: *Folks, you can feel the tension in the air! We're tied at 68 with just two minutes left in the final quarter. Possession goes to the Big Horns.*

Commentator Two: *This is where coaching and execution become absolutely critical. Every possession counts and both teams are looking for an edge.*

1:58: *The Norse point guard brings the ball up the court, looking to set up the offense. They run a pick-and-roll at the top of the key.*

1:50: *The point guard dishes the ball to their power forward, who attempts a jumper, contested by Big Horns number 51, Jessa Blakely.*

1:48: *The rebound goes to the opposing team, the Big Horns, number 51 Blakely.*

Commentator One: *Great defensive stand there by the Big Horns! Now they have a chance to take the lead.*

1:45: *Big Horns point guard, number 23 Char Jones, quickly pushes the ball up the court.*

1:40: *Jones drives to the basket and gets fouled by the Norse.*

1:38: *Jones steps up to the free-throw line. First shot...good! Big Horns take a 69-68 lead. Second shot...also good! The Big Horns now lead 70-68.*

Commentator Two: *Huge free throws from Jones! Ice in her veins!*

1:35: *The Norse inbound the ball to a guard.*

1:30: *Feeling the pressure, they take a quick three-pointer.*

1:28: *Misses the shot! The rebound is snagged by the Big Horns center, number 51 Blakely.*

Commentator One: *That was a risky shot from the Norse, but sometimes you have to take chances in these situations. Big Horns Blakely continues to dominate the boards, leading the NCAA in rebounds and double-doubles after breaking several school and conference records this season.*

1:25: *The Big Horns look to extend their lead. They work the ball around the perimeter.*

1:20: *The Big Horns shooting guard, number 11 Bexley Collins, gets open for a mid-range jumper.*

1:18: *It's good! The Big Horns now lead 72-68.*

Commentator Two: *Collins with the clutch shot! The Big Horns are pulling away!*

1:15: *The Norse call a timeout.*

Commentator One: *The Norse need a big play here to stay in the game. They must execute perfectly coming out of this timeout.*

1:00: *Coming out of the timeout, the Norse run a play designed to get the ball inside.*

0:55: *They get the ball to the post. She makes a strong move to the basket.*

0:53: *She scores! The Norse cut the lead to 72-70.*

Commentator Two: *Excellent post work! That's exactly what the Norse needed.*

0:50: *The Big Horns bring the ball up and try to run out some clock.*

0:40: *The Big Horns number 34 Hazel Nova tries to drive but is met by a tough defense.*

0:35: *The Big Horns are forced to put up a desperation shot as the shot clock expires. It misses.*

Commentator One: *Great defense from the Norse! They forced a tough shot and got the stop they needed!*

0:30: *The Norse have the ball back with a chance to tie or take the lead.*

0:25: *The point guard drives to the basket, trying to draw a foul.*

0:22: *No call! She puts up a contested layup, but misses.*

0:20: *The Big Horns number 51 Blakely grabs the rebound.*

Commentator Two: *Oh, what a heartbreaker for the Norse! They thought they had a foul there, but the refs saw it differently.*

0:18: *The Big Horns are now just looking to hold on to the ball and run the clock out.*

0:10: *The Norse foul the Big Horns number 11 Collins to stop the clock.*

0:10: *Collins steps up to the line. First shot...good! Big Horns lead 73-70. Second shot...misses!*

Commentator One: *A sigh of relief for the Norse! They still have a chance!*

0:08: *The Norse inbound the ball and immediately look to their hot shooter.*

0:05: *She catches the ball on the wing and puts up a quick three-pointer.*

0:03: *It goes in and bounces back out! Blakely grabs the board and holds onto the ball to run out the clock.*

Commentator Two: *UNBELIEVABLE! The Big Horns win the game!*

Commentator One: *What a finish! This is what March Mania is all about folks. The Big Horns, number five seed, advance to the Championship game on Sunday.*

I jump up and snag the rebound, holding it tight for the last few seconds until the buzzer sounds. We did it. We freaking did it. We beat Storrs University and are going to the 'ship! My teammates tackle me to the floor. I'm laughing and crying all at the same time as the bench rushes out to peel us apart and hug anyone within reach. Coach Morris has tears in her eyes as she moves to the opposing team bench to shake hands and then embraces the team.

It's surreal. Another dream unlocked after four years of work. We have one day to celebrate before the biggest game of my life, but right now I'm floating. Nothing is bringing me down—not even my mother.

She approaches, and before she can say a word, I pull her into a hug. She freezes for a second, surprised, and then the moment is swept away as I'm suddenly surrounded by everyone who came here for us.

Greyson finds me first, kissing me with a grin I can feel against my mouth. We break apart smiling like idiots until Soren tugs him back.

"Stop hogging Jessa," she scolds as she hugs me tight.

Corden hangs back, unsure, so I pull him in too. He's been part of this whole journey.

Then I see Greyson's parents, and my stomach flips. The fact that they're here supporting me and the team means a lot, but I'm still hesitant. The last time I saw them, I overheard them worrying about my effect on Grey's future. I square my shoulders anyway. They rush toward me, beaming.

"Jessa! That was incredible," Dr. Hastings says.

"Unbelievable game. We're glad we planned to stay all weekend," Mr. Hastings adds.

Their enthusiasm throws me, but I smile. "Thank you. I'm really glad you're here."

Before I know it, they both have me in a hug, and Greyson, Soren, and Corden are watching, equally stunned and relieved. When his parents pull away, Grey slips an arm around my damp lower back like he wants me close no matter how sweaty I am.

By the time I've made the rounds with the Hastings and my mother, Bex's family makes their way over to me after smothering Bex with love. Aiden reaches me first. As we're hugging, I whisper that Bex may need rescuing from Monty's sisters. He glances over and sprints off to save his twin.

The support here is overwhelming. Even Coach Hayes circles through the team, shaking Grey's hand and then pulling me in. "You did it. You made it to the 'ship. Never a doubt. Soak it in, Jessa."

I hug him back. "Thanks, Coach Hayes!"

Finally, Coach Morris gathers us for locker-room debrief, showers, and our schedule through Sunday. We stay to scout the next game, still pumped full of adrenaline.

We're one win away from everything we've worked for.

34
Greyson

I'm still riding a high from that game, so I can only imagine how Jessa feels. Some of us stay to watch the next matchup and get a taste of what's waiting for us on Sunday. The pace and energy have me buzzing. Not just from the teams on the court, but from our women's team as they take it all in.

I spot Jessa sitting with the others. She looks beautiful—wet hair down her back, fresh face, bright smile. I'm a goner. I mean, I already knew that, but seeing her like this? Anyone could tell. We keep stealing glances across the court, her cheeks turning pink each time. This woman is my future. I've felt it for months. And seeing my family here supporting her? Collins's and Oakes's families too? It makes everything feel complete. Whole. We're surrounded by people who love us.

The next day, the eve of the NCAA Championship game against number one seed University of Palmetto, lasts an eternity. The girls are busy with the team, resting and hydrating, staying locked in for the early afternoon tipoff tomorrow. I knew they'd be occupied, but I didn't expect the hours to crawl like this.

"What's up with you?" questions Corden as I impatiently pace the hotel room. "Let's go do something!"

"Nothing. Just anxious about tomorrow," I say, distracted.

"You're not even the one playing," he points out. "How are you this anxious?"

"I guess it's more about what happens after. Jessa will likely confirm she's declaring for the WNBA."

"That's not exactly breaking news," he says. "We all knew it was coming."

"True," I admit. "But that one decision sets off a chain of decisions I need to make. And I want to make the right ones. For both of us."

"Dude, you act like you're an old married couple." He pauses mid-laugh, eyes going wide. "Wait? Are you going to pop the question?! Is that why you are so anxious?"

When I don't respond right away, he gets in my face. "When?! Who else knows? Did you tell Soren yet?"

I consider continuing to keep this secret and denying everything, but it's too much. I'm a wreck. I sit on the bed of the hotel room and put my face in my hands, "Shit. I wasn't planning on telling anyone. How'd you figure it out?"

"Oh my gosh. Seriously? You have to tell Soren. She's going to flip."

"Whoa, whoa," I say, trying to slow him down. "I don't even know if this is the right time. There's so much going on, and I want it to be a happy moment, not something that overshadows everything else. Maybe it's stupid."

"Grey," he says, suddenly sounding wise, "Jessa will love it whenever you ask her. She loves you. She's clearly all in. Have you two talked about this?"

"I mean we've talked about a future, not about when or how," I say.

"Do you have the ring?" he presses.

I smile despite myself and dig into my bag. I've been carrying this thing around for weeks. It actually feels good to show someone—just not the someone it's meant for yet.

I hand Corden the sleek box. His jaw drops. I had it custom designed because I wanted everything to be exactly right.

"Holy shit, Grey! It's huge and so sparkly." He laughs. "I suppose that means it has the wow factor, huh?"

"You think she'll like it?" I ask. I'm trying to see it through Jessa's eyes. "Yeah, man, she'll love it. It's made for Jessa," he says.

Is that a tear in Corden's eye? He pulls me into a hug before I can comment.

"Seriously," he adds, "you better tell Soren or she's gonna lose it."

I laugh and nod. I call Soren and tell her to come to our room.

"Mom and Dad are pissed that you called me over here and not them," Soren says, entering my hotel room. "They said they are ready to get out of the hotel whenever you are— holy shit!" She stops dead when she sees the open ring box in my hand.

"Soren," I say, trying and failing to hide a grin, "language."

"Does that mean what I think it means? Is that for who I think and hope it's for?" She is practically vibrating off the floor.

"You could just ask the question you want to ask," I say. Corden cracks up beside me.

"Fine," she blurts. "Are you proposing to Jessa? Please say yes. Because I would LOVE to have a sister. Are you doing it this weekend? Is that why we're all here?"

"Yes," I say. "I'm planning to propose. And I wanted you to be one of the first to know. Corden guessed. I wasn't planning to tell anyone, so telling both of you feels fair. I'm still deciding on timing. The plan was for this weekend but I'm a bit stressed about it. I'm going to feel it out. I wanted everyone here to support Jessa because basketball is her world. But yeah, it'd be a bonus if you were here for the proposal."

"Good," Soren says, pulling me into a hug. "Now let me see that rock up close."

The three of us head to our parents' room to kill time. Soren keeps shooting me starry-eyed looks that are going to give away my secret. My parents keep asking what they're missing, and even Corden is being sketchy with his *"don't worry about it"* routine. My family is incredibly frustrating. But I love them.

Part of me wants to spill everything just to get it off my chest, but instead I deflect with talk about interviews and job offers. They tell me how proud they are, how I can't go wrong, but I know better. I need to wait. At least until Jessa knows where she'll land.

The WNBA draft cannot get here fast enough.

35

Jessa

It's NCAA Women's Basketball Championship Game Day in Indianapolis.

I'm flooded with a mix of anticipation and nerves. The day we've been working for is finally here. We've prepared for this moment, envisioned the game, and imagined the atmosphere. And now, we get to compete at the highest level of our college careers. It fills me with wild, electric energy.

We know the pressure is real, especially the pressure we've put on ourselves, but there's no room for doubt or anything beyond our control. We need to start the day with a winning mindset and give this game everything—for our team and for ourselves. This long-awaited championship feels surreal, a dream come true. When it's over, I hope we'll look back on a well-earned victory.

Across the room, Bex has just woken up too. Of course neither of us could sleep in. She pops out of bed and jumps onto mine. "Today's the big day. And our last time playing together," she says, squeezing me from the side.

We both sit and let that sink in. I take a deep breath. "How much time do you think we've spent together over the last four years?" I ask Bex.

"Oh gosh, too much time to track."

"Promise me we'll always find our way back to each other, even when we no longer have basketball," I say, choking up a little bit.

"Nope, not going there. We're not done being roomies yet. Today is about the championship. We can get emotional later." Bex asserts, and I respond in defeat with a forced laugh.

"Let's fuel up with breakfast, and then get ourselves ready for the game," I say.

"Perfect," Bex responds.

Our phones ding with an unknown number in the team text group. We open it and find a video message from Coach Hayes and the men's team expressing how proud they are of us, and they can't wait to see us pull out a victory today. It feels good to have an entire program on your side.

The next text I get is from Greyson.

Greyson: *Hey, just wanted to say how incredibly proud I am of you. Your hard work has led you to this championship game, and your dedication and determination have been evident throughout. Expect to be cheered on with all the possible enthusiasm during every play. Regardless of the outcome, you have already won, and I'm fortunate to have you. Give it your all! You can do this! I love you!* ♥

I respond with a heart, then Bex and I head over to Gainbridge Fieldhouse with the rest of the team to shoot around and start our last pre-game ritual.

The atmosphere in a fieldhouse during an NCAA Championship basketball game is loud, frantic and emotional. It's a key part of what makes college basketball, especially during March Mania, such a special and unique experience.

As we inch towards tipoff, the air crackles with anticipation as fans and our families and friends continue to pour into the arena. Tradition hangs in the air. You can feel the legacy of all who came before us. I'm prepared for this crowd to become incredibly loud as they roar with every successful basket, defensive stop, or pivotal play for or against the teams of their choosing. It's what makes games like this so magical.

Coach Morris calls us in for the huddle and we prepare for tipoff against the University of Palmetto Knights.

Broadcaster One: *The arena is packed, the crowd roaring, and the energy is palpable as the two best teams in the nation, the University of Palmetto Knights and the Hills University Big Horns, face off for the NCAA National Championship title. Both teams have battled their way through a grueling tournament, each player fueled by the desire to cut down the nets and hoist the championship trophy.*

The First Quarter is off to a fast start with a back-and-forth battle.

Broadcaster Two: *The tipoff is controlled by the Knights, and they immediately push the pace. Their star guard drives to the basket and finishes with a smooth layup, igniting the crowd and giving the Knights an early lead.*

Broadcaster One: *The Big Horns respond with star forward number 51 Jessa Blakely, answering with a powerful post-up move and a turnaround jumper, showing her team is ready to compete.*

The first few minutes both teams seem to be trading baskets, with each squad highlighting their offensive firepower.

Broadcaster One: *Knights' sharpshooter hits two quick three-pointers, extending their lead and forcing the Big Horns to call a timeout.*

Broadcaster Two: *The Big Horns come out of the timeout with renewed defensive intensity, forcing a turnover and converting it into a fast break layup by Bexley Collins.*

The quarter ends with the score tight, and both teams leaving it all on the court.

Broadcaster Two: *The Big Horns start the second quarter strong, with their bench players making key contributions and taking their first lead of the game. Number 23 Char Jones checks back into the game and, feeling the pressure, takes over offensively, driving hard to the basket and scoring a tough layup through contact.*

Broadcaster One: *Blakely establishes her dominance in the paint, grabbing offensive rebounds and finishing with multiple second-chance points. She is a beast on the boards.*

The game remains a tug-of-war, with the lead changing hands several times. The halftime buzzer sounds, and we head to the locker room with a narrow lead, thanks to a late three-pointer by Nova.

Broadcaster One: *Coach Hayden Morris of the Hills University Big Horns clearly made defensive adjustments at halftime because her team has come out with a dominant performance, extending their lead with a series of strong drives and accurate perimeter shooting.*

Broadcaster Two: *The point guard tries to spark a comeback for the Knights, hitting another three-pointer, but the Big Horns respond immediately. The Big Horns' suffocating defense is forcing turnovers, leading to easy fast break points.*

The Knights are not giving up and pick up their offensive skills. We're holding a comfortable lead, but the Knights have shown they have fight left in them. Now is not the time to let up.

Broadcaster One: *It seems the Knights are looking to rally, they are out with full force in this final quarter, determined to mount a comeback. They are hitting key shots and putting pressure on the Big Horns' defense.*

Broadcaster Two: *Both teams are making clutch plays in the final minutes, and the court is a war zone. This game is going to come down to the wire, with the score close and every possession critical.*

With just minutes on the clock, we know we must leave it all out here. We push the pace even further and put up a few quick layups. The Knights appear to be in panic mode, throwing up three's that they've been making all game but are now missing and I soar above them to grab the ball and not let anything, or anyone get in my way. *My team is clicking, smooth passes, great looks, and quick and confident movement. I can feel it. We are so close to winning this game.* With seconds left on the clock the Knights miss another shot, and I'm quick to rebound. I'm in possession of the ball. I hold onto the ball. The buzzer sounds, and we erupt in celebration, having secured the NCAA National Championship Title.

Broadcaster One: *The Big Horns celebrate their historic victory, achieving their dream of winning the national championship. While the Knights are disappointed, they fought hard and displayed great talent and should be leaving with their heads held high. This game will be remembered as a thrilling display of women's college basketball, displaying the passion and skill of these incredible athletes.*

Broadcaster Two: *Final Score: Big Horns 87, Knights 75. The Hills University Big Horns are your NCAA National Champions!*

We're celebrating on the court. The media swarms us with post championship interviews and most of the crowd stays in place. We're laughing, crying, cheering—basically experiencing all the emotions flooding us at once. We shake hands with our opponents, spend more time jumping up and down and hugging each other, and then while we're still enjoying the shock of the moment, we're brought together at center court for the presentation of the trophy. Championship t-shirts and hats appear and are distributed.

The trophy in all its beauty is awarded to HU and Coach Morris who holds it proudly over her head as blue and gold confetti erupts onto the court. Coach then hands it to me as team captain. I give it a dramatic smooch on top of the gold and hold it over my head in victory as well. My teammates and the crowd laughs and cheers as we pose with the trophy, have our pictures taken, and pass this heavy display of our win around with so much pride on our faces. Our attention is then turned to the announcement for the Most Outstanding Player of the NCAA Tournament.

"Jessa Blakely!"

Amidst all the whistles and cheers, I stand there, relishing this moment. This moment is what I've worked so hard for. My team is finally being recognized as one the best in Division I basketball, and in an iconic basketball state no less, and now my name has been called as the most outstanding player. This day could not get any better.

36
Greyson

I'm so anxious to get to her. Now that the court has settled down a bit and its mostly close friends and family waiting in the crowd, we are released to see our players on the court. I see her looking for me, but she hasn't spotted me yet. As soon as she does, she leaps into my arms clasping her legs around me and I just hold her. We don't have to say anything because we know this is her moment, one that she deserves, and no one will ever be able to take that away from her.

I give her some time to be congratulated by all her friends and family and hang back, just a bit. I am watching her take all this in. Soren nudges me and gives me a look with her eyebrows raised. Corden follows with a bump of his own. I take that as my sign that the time is right, even amongst all these people because these people are our family.

I reach into my pocket just to make sure the box is still there and make eye contact with Jessa. She suspects nothing as she's still soaking in this moment and beaming. I stand in front of her and take her hands, slowly getting down on one knee. Her eyes go wide.

She looks around, maybe still trying to figure out what is going on. I start talking and the crowd surrounding us hushes, "Jessa Blakely, you are my best friend, my confidant, and the love of my life. I think I've known that since the day you clobbered me at our first pre-season scrimmage. I had no idea who you were, but I knew I needed to know you. You are the most exceptional woman I have ever met, and I want to continue to build a life with you, one filled with love, laughter, and adventure. I know there are a lot of unknowns about the future, but as long as I know you are mine, I will be a happy man. Jessa Blakely, will you marry me?" I finish as I look at Jessa tearing up as she realizes this is really happening.

She begins to cry, pulls me up and wraps her arms around my neck. "Is that a, yes?" I ask, my voice muffled by her shoulder.

She is shaking her head emphatically in a yes motion and finally blurts, "YES!"

I pull away and pull the perfect velvet ring box from my pocket and pop it open, displaying the ring. Her eyes go big again. "Greyson," she says with a gasp, and I smile as I pull the ring from its cushion inside the box and place it on her left ring finger.

I raise her hand in the air with mine and yell, "She said yes!"

All our friends and family cheer.

My parents look a bit surprised but have huge smiles on their faces at seeing their oldest son happy. My siblings are swarming Jessa, letting her know they knew about this as of yesterday.

The only face that seems a bit stunned and isn't reacting is that of Lauren Blakely, whose only daughter, a star basketball player, has made plans for her future without approval from her mother.

37

Jessa

I did not see that coming I think as I admire the huge rock on my left ring finger. I mean I assumed that someday Grey and I would get married, but for him to propose at the end of my college basketball career and right after we won the championship, *holy shit!*

I am so overwhelmed with gratitude and excitement that I'm going to burst but I know there is still one more thing I need to do. I need to talk to Greyson. I roll over and there he is smiling at me. We are all heading back to HU today after lots of celebration last night, so I don't have a lot of time this morning.

"Grey, I have to tell you something," I say, and he sits up in bed to face me. "I'm declaring for the WNBA draft."

"I know," he says, still smiling. I stare at him a bit confused. "What do you mean you know? I've been stressing about this for weeks and truly just made the decision."

"I've known since you first heard it was a possibility that you would declare. You just had to get there yourself. And that spark in your game through the tournament sealed the deal."

"Are you upset?" I ask.

"Why would I be upset? I love you and want this for you, I just knew you had to want it for yourself."

"God, I love you! How did I get so lucky?" I say as I play with my basketball charm from him with the hand that is now sporting a sparkly engagement ring.

"Jessa, I will *always* be here because I know I'm the lucky one. I've been putting plans in motion for our future together and I can't wait to see where the draft pick takes us, so we can officially start our life together."

Acknowledgements

I'm still in awe that this book is a reality. This book is not where I thought my writing journey would start, but I was inspired by The Story Summit Beach Read writing class I took with author, Priscilla Oliveras that really kickstarted my storyline.

Hanna Nuss, your Do School format gave me the structure and accountability to write a full draft in less than six weeks. The writing sprint was just the accountability I needed to make this happen. And your Local. Pub. Co. is just what fellow Iowans need to show anything is possible with the support of those you surround yourself with.

To Holly Althof, my editor, your feedback was inspiring and helped shape the story. This book would not be what it is without you.

A special thanks to the MF Book Club. You are some of the best cheerleaders for spice and romance and lifting up other women.

Finally, to my husband and daughter who challenged and encouraged me to reach for my dream of writing a romance novel and truly believed I could do it. Your support and reminders to get writing were the nudge I needed to put my time and energy into this project, even when there were so many other things we could have been committing our time to.

About the Author

Ashley Lang was born and raised in small-town Iowa, where grit, loyalty, and showing up when it matters are part of everyday life. She is a writer, professor, and leadership coach who gravitates toward high-stakes stories and strong lead characters who refuse to stay on the sidelines of their own lives.

Ashley has a deep passion for strong female leaders and a particular affinity for women in sports—those who compete fiercely, lead boldly, and claim space in arenas that demand both strength and heart. A lifelong and unapologetic romance reader, she believes in love stories that honor ambition, resilience, and hard-won happily-ever-afters.

She lives with her husband—her best friend—their daughter, and their velcro golden doodle, always chasing her passions and the next great story.